SACRAMENTO PUBLIC LIBRARY

828 "I" Street

Sacramento, CA 95814

09/12

D0000041

PRAISE F

"Stein continue   ly
and physically, and An   es could affect mankind. Another
for your must-read pi   *Book Reviews* (4½ stars)

"Anna continues to e   ithout
losing her humanity   il you
come up on her ba   eroine
readers will delight   n some
twist[s] and turns that wo   ntil the
very end, and then you will be hungry for the   llment."
—*Fresh Fiction*

CHOSEN

"With each book in the series, not only have Stein's characters
become stronger but so has her writing . . . hard-hitting urban fantasy with a hard-hitting female lead."   —*Fresh Fiction*

"[I] cannot wait to see where Anna's adventures take her next . . .
Chosen is an excellent book and probably the most enthralling
book in the series thus far."   —*Bitten by Books*

"From the opening chapter of this terrific series, Stein has sent her
gutsy heroine on an uncharted journey filled with danger and bitter betrayal . . . In this pivotal but emotionally brutal book, skillful
Stein reveals some critical answers and delivers some devastating
blows. Like a fine wine, this series is improving with age. Brava!"
—*RT Book Reviews* (4½ stars)

RETRIBUTION

"The fifth book in the exceptional first-person Anna Strong series
is a powerful entry in an amazing saga."
—*RT Book Reviews* (4½ stars, Top Pick)

continued . . .

"Ms. Stein has a true gift in storytelling and continues to add exciting new elements to this well-built world. *Retribution* is an engrossing read with an action-packed story line and secondary characters that are every bit as intriguing as the heroine. This is a must-read for fans of the series!"
—*Darque Reviews*

LEGACY

"Urban fantasy with true depth and flair!"
—*RT Book Reviews* (4½ stars)

"As riveting as the rest . . . one of my favorite urban fantasy series."
—*Darque Reviews*

THE WATCHER

"Action fills every page, making this a novel that flies by . . . Dynamic relationships blend [with] complex mysteries in this thriller."
—*Huntress Book Reviews*

"An exciting, fast-paced novel . . . first-rate plotting."
—*LoveVampires*

"Dazzles readers with action-packed paranormal adventure, love and friendship. With many wonderfully executed twists and turns, this author's suspenseful writing will hold readers spellbound until the very end."
—*Darque Reviews*

"Snappy action and plot twists that will hold readers' interest to the last page."
—*Monsters and Critics*

BLOOD DRIVE

"A terrific tale of supernatural sleuthing . . . provides edge-of-your-seat thrills and a high-octane emotional punch."
—*RT Book Reviews* (4½ stars)

"I loved this book . . . hugely enjoyable . . . an exciting read and everything any vampire-fantasy fan could hope for."
—*LoveVampires*

"Once again Jeanne C. Stein delivers a jam-packed story full of mystery and intrigue that will keep you glued to the edge of your seat! Just like [with] the first book in the Anna Strong series, *The Becoming*, I could not put this book down even for a second. You will find yourself cheering Anna on as she goes after the bad guys. Jeanne C. Stein has given us a wonderful tough-as-nails heroine everyone will love!"
—*Night Owl Reviews*

"Jeanne C. Stein takes on the vampire mythos in her own unique manner that makes for an enthralling vampire thriller. Readers of Laurell K. Hamilton, Tanya Huff and Charlaine Harris will thoroughly enjoy this fast-paced novel filled with several action scenes that come one after the other, making it hard for the readers to catch a breather."
—*Midwest Book Review*

"A really great series. Anna's strengths and weaknesses make for a very compelling character. Stein really puts you in [Anna's] head as she fumbles her way through a new life and the heartbreaking choices she will have to make. [Stein] also introduces new supernatural characters and gives a glimpse into a secret underground organization. This is a pretty cool urban fantasy series that will appeal to fans of Patricia Briggs's Mercy Thompson series."
—*Vampire Genre*

THE BECOMING

"This is a really, really good book. Anna is a great character, Stein's plotting is adventurous and original, and I think most of my readers would have a great time with *The Becoming*."
—Charlaine Harris, #1 *New York Times* bestselling author of the Sookie Stackhouse novels

"A cross between MaryJanice Davidson's Undead series, starring Betsy Taylor, and Laurell K. Hamilton's Anita Blake series. [Anna's] a kick-butt bounty hunter—but vampires are a complete surprise to her. Full of interesting twists and turns that will leave readers guessing. *The Becoming* is a great addition to the TBR pile."
—*Romance Reviews Today*

"A wonderful new vampire book . . . that will keep you on the edge of your seat."
—*Fallen Angel Reviews*

Ace Books by Jeanne C. Stein

HAUNTED

JEANNE C. STEIN

ACE BOOKS, NEW YORK

THE BERKLEY PUBLISHING GROUP
Published by the Penguin Group
Penguin Group (USA) Inc.
375 Hudson Street, New York, New York 10014, USA

Penguin Group (Canada), 90 Eglinton Avenue East, Suite 700, Toronto, Ontario M4P 2Y3, Canada
(a division of Pearson Penguin Canada Inc.) • Penguin Books Ltd., 80 Strand, London WC2R 0RL,
England • Penguin Group Ireland, 25 St. Stephen's Green, Dublin 2, Ireland (a division of Penguin
Books Ltd.) • Penguin Group (Australia), 250 Camberwell Road, Camberwell, Victoria 3124, Australia
(a division of Pearson Australia Group Pty. Ltd.) • Penguin Books India Pvt. Ltd., 11 Community
Centre, Panchsheel Park, New Delhi—110 017, India • Penguin Group (NZ), 67 Apollo Drive,
Rosedale, Auckland 0632, New Zealand (a division of Pearson New Zealand Ltd.) • Penguin Books
(South Africa) (Pty.) Ltd., 24 Sturdee Avenue, Rosebank, Johannesburg 2196, South Africa

Penguin Books Ltd., Registered Offices: 80 Strand, London WC2R 0RL, England

This is a work of fiction. Names, characters, places, and incidents either are the product of the author's
imagination or are used fictitiously, and any resemblance to actual persons, living or dead, business
establishments, events, or locales is entirely coincidental. The publisher does not have any control over
and does not assume any responsibility for author or third-party websites or their content.

HAUNTED

An Ace Book / published by arrangement with the author

PUBLISHING HISTORY
Ace mass-market edition / September 2012

Copyright © 2012 by Jeanne C. Stein.
Cover art by Cliff Nielsen.
Cover design by Judith Lagerman.
Interior text design by Kristin del Rosario.

All rights reserved.
No part of this book may be reproduced, scanned, or distributed in any printed or
electronic form without permission. Please do not participate in or encourage piracy of
copyrighted materials in violation of the author's rights. Purchase only authorized editions.
For information, address: The Berkley Publishing Group,
a division of Penguin Group (USA) Inc.,
375 Hudson Street, New York, New York 10014.

ISBN: 978-1-937007-76-8

ACE
Ace Books are published by The Berkley Publishing Group,
a division of Penguin Group (USA) Inc.,
375 Hudson Street, New York, New York 10014.
ACE and the "A" design are trademarks of Penguin Group (USA) Inc.

PRINTED IN THE UNITED STATES OF AMERICA

10 9 8 7 6 5 4 3 2 1

If you purchased this book without a cover, you should be aware that this book is
stolen property. It was reported as "unsold and destroyed" to the publisher, and neither the
author nor the publisher has received any payment for this "stripped book."

ALWAYS LEARNING   **PEARSON**

To the people of Mexico caught in the cross fire.
I wish there was a real-life hero to save you.

ACKNOWLEDGMENTS

This was a difficult book to write because there is a war going on south of our borders and we seem powerless to do anything about it. But that's the great thing about writing fiction: I can take a problem I'm interested in and "solve" it, if only temporarily and on a small scale, through the efforts of my heroine.

As for the writing process itself, I have the usual suspects to thank. Members of the Pearl Street Critique: Mario Acevedo, Warren Hammond, Tamra Monahan, Aaron Ritchey, Tom and Margie Lawson and Terry Wright.

For correcting my Spanish: Mario Acevedo, Warren Hammond and Mario's friend Armando Provencio.

For being there in this crazy book business: my agent, Scott Miller of Trident Media, and my editor, Jessica Wade at Penguin (and their hardworking staff members).

For support and encouragement: loyal friends and readers who tell me they love Anna as much as I do.

And for everything else: Phil, who is always ready to discuss story with me, and Jeanette, who is becoming known far and wide for turning my books out on store shelves!

Philosophy is perfectly right in saying that life must be understood backward. But then one forgets the other clause—that it must be lived forward.

Søren Kierkegaard
1813–1855

CHAPTER 1

I'M STARING OUT THE BEDROOM SLIDING GLASS door feeling sorry for myself. Stupid, really, since being alone tonight is entirely my own fault. I could be in France with my family. Or at my business partner David's for his annual Christmas Eve bash. Why aren't I? Because both would require that I spend most of the time pretending to eat and drink, pretending to be human. A lot of work. So here I am, all by my lonesome the night before Christmas, feeling churlish, staring at a gray sheet of pounding rain.

Rain. It's all we've had this winter. This is San Diego, for Christ's sake. The land of predictable, even boring, weather. The land of a constant 72 degrees. The land of sun and blue sky.

Not this year.

I can count on one hand the number of nice days we've had. It's beginning to get irritating. What's the use of being a vampire who can go out in sunlight if there is no sunlight to go out in?

Even my reporter boyfriend, Stephen, is not around. He's

with the president visiting the troops overseas. He called me on Skype last night and we were able to exchange greetings. Greetings. What I want to exchange is bodily fluids. But that's not going to happen for another ten days. Since there were about a hundred soldiers gathered around awaiting their turn on the computer, we couldn't even *talk* dirty.

Shit. Shit. Shit.

I need to do something. I need to share the misery. Where would a sulking vampire go to find other discontents as sorry ass as she is?

Luckily, I know just the place.

BESO DE LA MUERTE LOOKS EVEN MORE DESOLATE and run-down than usual, which says a lot since it's basically a ghost town you won't find on any map of northern Mexico. There's only one building in the middle of what could be called Main Street, if the streets had names, that shows any sign of life. A string of blinking red-and-green Christmas lights slumps over the door to Culebra's bar in an attempt, I suppose, to invoke some holiday cheer. Half the bulbs are burned out. The other half sputter unconvincingly.

What was Culebra thinking? Is this his idea of a joke—a fuck-you to the season and its forced joviality? Suddenly, I find myself enjoying those pathetic little lights. They make me smile.

Culebra and I share a warped sense of humor.

There's a single car in front of the bar. A car that looks familiar. It gives me a moment's pause until I recognize whose car it is. Then it takes me another minute to decide if I want to drag an unsuspecting mortal into the black hole of my self-pity.

The car belongs to Max, an ex. Who better to drag into a black hole than an ex? I shrug off any misgivings and walk inside.

Max and Culebra are seated at a table in the middle of the bar. Alone. They have an open bottle of Jack Daniel's

Single Barrel whiskey between them. Half empty. They're puffing away on cigars and blowing smoke rings at each other. If Max didn't look like a well-dressed thug clad all in black, and Culebra like an extra in a spaghetti western, poncho and all, I'd say they belonged in a gentlemen's club.

Max spies me first. "Well, well. Look what the bat flew in."

"Hilarious, Max. I see in the newspapers that you DEA dudes have really done your part to win the drug war. We're practically narco free."

He shakes his head and clucks his tongue. "Ouch."

Go easy on Max, Culebra says, straight from his brain into mine, something he can do because he's a shape-shifter and we share a psychic bond. *He's feeling sorry for himself. Alone at Christmas. You understand.*

The last is said in a kind of "there's a lot of that going around, isn't there?" tone.

I just grunt.

Culebra pushes his chair back and stands up to scoot another chair over from a nearby table. "Sit." He grabs another shot glass from the bar and pours a shot. "Drink."

Loquacious as ever. But I do take the glass and sip. Smooth. Tickles the back of the throat and warms a path all the way down.

Culebra refills his own glass, then Max's. "What brings you here? I figured you'd be at David's shindig."

I take another sip before answering. "Too many people I don't know. Too much work pretending I might want to know them. He travels in a different circle."

Max tilts his glass toward me. "You mean a human circle, don't you?"

He has the knives out. "Who shoved a stake up your ass? I helped you not long ago if I remember correctly. You didn't seem to mind what I was then."

Culebra places the bottle down between Max and me and raises his glass. "Come on now. Truce. It's Christmas Eve. Time for peace on Earth. Good will to . . . creatures, great and small. For some reason, fate has drawn us here together this evening. Let's make the most of it. To friends."

He shoves his glass toward us. And looks around expectantly. I wait to see if Max will move first. He remains stubbornly still, arms crossed over his chest, waiting for me.

Shit. I want another drink. I raise my glass and clink it against Culebra's. Max follows, reluctantly. He avoids my eyes, but does let his glass touch mine.

We drink.

And drink some more. Not much conversation. Culebra isn't even intruding into my head. Each of us seems content to be alone together to wallow in whatever pits of dejection brought us here.

Alcohol, like blood, is absorbed directly into my system. After a half dozen shots, the booze loosens my tongue. There's a question I've wanted to ask these two since I first saw Max and Culebra together a year and a half ago. I had just become vampire and was sent to Beso de la Muerte to hunt down the vamp who made me. Max was working undercover in the DEA and he was here, too, on an assignment. He never gave me a direct answer to what he was doing here then, and it seems the perfect opportunity to get that answer now.

I pour each of them another shot and dive in. "How'd you two come to know each other?"

At first I think Max is going to counter with some bullshit about classified DEA information or fall back on the old "if I tell you, I have to kill you" dodge. But he does neither. He looks over at Culebra and Culebra shrugs.

"She knows everything else."

Max downs his shot. It's the fifth since I've been here and I have no idea how many he had before I arrived. But the alcohol does seem to have smoothed the edge off his animosity. He shrugs back at Culebra. "Do you want to start or should I?"

Culebra looks hard at me, as if gauging how much truth I can take. In fact, that's the very thought that sifts through the haze of alcohol in his head.

"Give it your best shot," I quip cavalierly. What can he possibly say that will shock me? I've seen plenty in the last eighteen months.

He draws a breath. "You ever heard of Felix Gallardo?"

"Can't say that I have. Is he a relative?"

That provokes a snort from Max and a shake of the head from Culebra.

"What? Who is he?"

"The godfather of the Mexican drug cartels," Max says.

"Godfather?"

Culebra nods. "Gallardo was the first to organize the Mexican drug business. Started in the late eighties when he realized he was getting too well known and the narco business was getting too big for him to control by himself. He called together a select group of henchman in Acapulco and designated territories to be run by bosses not yet so well known to the *Federales*. Men who he could trust to report to him."

"It was a smart move," Max says with a tone of grudging admiration.

Must be the booze.

"What does that have to do with you?" I ask Culebra.

"I worked for one of his lieutenants. Boss of the *Cartel de Sinaloa*."

That name I recognize, both for the ruthlessness of its methods and the success it's achieved in getting huge quantities of drugs across the U.S. border. "The Sinaloa Cartel, huh? Were you an undercover agent for the Mexican government? Is that how you met Max? You were working together?"

"Not exactly." Culebra's eyes grow hard. "I was an *asesino*—an assassin."

Culebra an assassin for a narco? I grin. "You're kidding right?"

The steady, serious way he gazes back at me raises the hair on the back of my neck.

The glass I had just raised to my lips bangs down on the table with a thud. I was wrong. I can be shocked. Astonishment knocks the alcohol fog out of my brain. Suddenly I'm sober and shaken. How? Why? Questions tumble over themselves in my head.

Culebra reads them all. He smiles sadly. "The money," he says. "Huge money. I was uneducated, an outcast in my own village because of what I was." He averts his eyes, sarcasm tinges his words with the acid of bitter truth. "Shape-shifters are not considered valuable members of society where I come from. I was an anomaly—a freak. And treated as such."

A pause, as if he's waiting for me to comment. I have no comment. Even my thoughts are conflicted. He finally realizes it and continues.

"I moved to Baja when I was sixteen. Met the boss soon after. Became a runner. Eventually, I got married, had a family. Worked my way up the ladder."

That evokes a comment. "Worked your way up to assassin?"

"I was caught up in the life." He meets my eyes squarely. "I'm not proud of it. I hated it, but I had a family to support. There came a point when there was no turning back."

I can't believe what I'm hearing. Or the dead calm tone of Culebra's voice as he speaks. "You killed people."

He looks hard at me. "And you don't?"

Max makes a snickering noise.

I glare at him before snapping at Culebra, "I kill because I have to, because I'm protecting someone. It's hardly the same thing."

Culebra shrugs. "Semantics. I was protecting someone, too. Myself. My family. I followed orders."

"Your family? Where are they now?"

Culebra waves a hand in a vague sweeping motion. "Dead."

Still, no emotion. Nothing in his head I can penetrate but a dull pulse beat. It's strange. As if his answers come from a separate part of his brain, turning on and off like a recorder at the push of the right button. Programmed answers.

I soften my own tone. "What happened?"

He looks hard at me. "You want the long version or the short one?"

I wave a hand. "I've got nowhere else to be. Do you?"

He pours another shot. Downs it. "Get comfortable. We're going to be here awhile."

CHAPTER 2

CULEBRA TAKES A DEEP BREATH. "I WAS BORN TO A
family of shape-shifters. But I was a throwback. The
first of my generation to manifest the ability. My family
was horrified. They thought the curse had finally been
lifted." He drops his eyes. "The *curse*."

He straightens his shoulders. "My father could never
find steady work so our family always lived in poverty.
What's more, he had no trade or skills that he could pass on
to me, not that he would have. He hated me. I was not allowed to go to school for fear someone would find out what
I was. My own parents set me adrift. Condemned me to a
life of poverty, struggle and isolation. I was sixteen."

He reaches for the bottle. I pass it over, let him refill his
glass and my own. "You're articulate for an uneducated
man."

"We had a Bible," he answers. "The only book we
owned. My mother taught me to read with that Bible. Before she decided I was possessed by the devil."

He drinks, continues. "I moved to Chihuahua, an unemployed drifter. Found a few odd jobs that paid poorly and required long hours of hard labor. I shared the fields and factories with petty criminals who always tried to take advantage of weaker men. I knew I had to defend myself to survive and I quickly learned to use my fists and my wits. I also became skilled at using a knife. It wasn't long before I won respect among the migrants. Word got around and I attracted the attention of local gang members.

"Gangs were always on the lookout for young 'bad-asses' to recruit. There was a constant need for new blood since gang wars continually decimated the ranks. Young, tough, uneducated *vatos* like me who were dissatisfied with their lot made a perfect pool in which to fish."

I am so engrossed in Culebra's tale that when Max pokes me in the arm I jump. "What?"

"Pass the bottle, will you?"

Grudgingly, I do. "Are you done interrupting now?"

Max flutters a hand in a go-ahead gesture and I turn back to Culebra and mimic the action.

"One day as I was walking home from work, a gang-banger pushed me against a wall and demanded my money while other bangers stood around smiling. I was enraged that anyone would steal from a poor *campesino* struggling to earn a living. I pushed my aggressor back and told him to 'go fuck himself.' The banger pulled a knife and came at me. But I quickly grabbed his arm, twisted it behind his back and took the knife away. I spun the banger around and kneed him in the groin for good measure. As I walked away I waved the knife and thanked him for the 'souvenir.'

"The next day members of the local gang again confronted me. But this time, I was invited to have a drink with the boss. He told me that he needed men 'with balls' in his operation and that I handled myself well the other day. I realized that the confrontation had been a test. He offered me a job delivering drugs and collecting payment and offered me a salary about ten times what I was earning as a common laborer. The money was irresistible to a young man with no real future ahead of him. And working for a criminal gang wasn't much different from being an outcast as far as I was concerned. So I accepted the offer as my only opportunity for a better life.

"Like all new hires, I was assigned a mentor to teach me the business. His nickname was Julio the Pick because his preferred method of execution was to shove an ice pick into the back of a man's head. No loud noise, little blood—he liked it that way. Julio was unusual because he was in his forties in a business where most didn't live beyond their late twenties. His longevity was testament to the fact that he was good at his chosen profession and was an asset to the boss.

"Julio had trained many a young 'badass,' but I struck him as someone special. He sensed that I had an innate intelligence and was driven to make my mark in life. All the young 'badasses' liked fancy clothes and pockets full of money to attract the ladies. I was no exception. But Julio and I both knew that I wouldn't be satisfied to just strut around like a peacock. No, I was someone who could rise up through the ranks and become useful to the organization. So Julio took me under his wing and taught me the 'tricks of the trade'—how to disable an opponent in a fight and how to shoot. Shooting straight was especially important since it raised the odds that you would survive the inevitable gun battles that you would face. Julio taught me how to carry my weapon so I could draw it quickly from the holster and where to aim to quickly disable or kill an opponent. But he couldn't teach me, or anyone else, how to think fast on my feet to outwit a rival. That was something you had to be born with. Julio must have felt that I had that quality.

"I was a quick study and practiced long hours to learn my lessons. Julio was proud of me and it wasn't long before I began calling him Tio Julio. I knew that delivering drugs and collecting payment was a dangerous job (after all, why would I be paid so generously if it were not?) and that Julio wouldn't be there when I got my first real assignment. Julio was too valuable to the boss to be sacrificed on a drug run. Besides, this was a way to see who had the right stuff.

Those who survived could move up in the organization. Those who didn't were the cost of doing business.

"Finally, the day came when another recruit and I were ordered to deliver a shipment of drugs to a rival gang and return with payment. We met the rival boss's son and two henchmen at a remote desert location. I knew that doing business with rival gangs would never be easy. So it was no surprise when the son started threatening us. 'Tell your boss that his last batch of drugs was shit. And if he sells me shit, he ain't gonna be paid shit. I know you motherfuckers are schoolboys, so give me the shipment and tell your boss that he'll be paid after we test it. Not before.' I saw the henchmen slide their hands inside their jackets. I sensed that the son was going to take advantage of us newbies and try to impress his father by returning with both the drugs and the money. There would never be any payment. The stomach of my partner was growling so loudly that he was obviously shaking with fear and on the verge of shitting his pants.

"What do I do now? I knew that if we returned without the drugs and the money both my life and my career would be over. I also remembered a lesson taught to me by *Tio* Julio. 'To make it in this business you have to command respect. And to command respect, others have to know that you are willing to kill when necessary.'

"My partner and I looked at each other and I shrugged. The son, with a smirk on his face, directed his men to fetch the drugs from our vehicle. As they started to walk toward us I noticed one drop an empty hand from his jacket. At that instant, I quickly pulled my gun and shot them both through the forehead—first the one still holding his gun and then the second one as he reached for his gun. As their bodies fell, I trained my pistol on the son, whose smirk had been replaced by a look of shock and fear. 'We came here to do business and that is what we'll do,' I told him. I then ordered my partner to put the drugs in the son's car and take the cash. While he shuffled back to our car with the money bag, I frisked and disarmed the boss's son. 'Tell Papa that it's always a pleasure to do business with him.' With that, we drove off, leaving the son standing alone with two corpses."

I find myself staring. "Honor among thieves?"

Culebra raises his shoulders. "Have you heard enough?"

"No. I want to hear it all." I just need another drink. I take the bottle back from Max, who had just refilled his own glass, and top mine off. "Go on."

"News of the drug transaction quickly spread through the organization. The boss realized that he had a talented recruit and complemented Julio, telling him he trained his new student well. He doubled my salary and made me a captain. 'Captain Badass' I called myself."

Max chuckles. I shake my head. Culebra continues.

"Over time, I proved my worth. I came to command the respect that Julio told me was so important in the business. I earned good money. I was able to afford a nice house and car and had found success beyond my father's dreams. I could now afford to support a family and decided it was time to marry. I found a young woman with pleasant looks, but not a great beauty. I prized loyalty and childbearing ability above a pretty face. In time we had two children, a boy and girl and, to my surprise, I became a devoted father. My wife never knew about my shape-shifting ability and I hoped that I didn't pass this trait to my offspring. I wanted them to live normal lives, attend good schools and be socially accepted, not be outcasts as I had been.

"But I wanted more. I wanted to move up the ladder. To become a man of importance, one to be reckoned with, one who would be accepted in social circles I never could have entered before. I read avidly to gain more knowledge about the world. This made me somewhat of a black sheep among my compatriots, but I knew they were losers. I had bigger plans than the next score. I also knew book learning wasn't enough. It took money—big money—and with no formal education or skills beyond drug running, what could I do to earn more and become more?

"I asked Julio what prospects I had. Julio gave me a stern look: 'If you want to make more money, you will have to do what few are capable of and what few can live with—you will have to become an assassin. You will be paid handsomely to kill targets on command from the boss, but you will have to learn to live with the knowledge that you kill others for a living. These targets are not scumbags who threaten your life during a drug deal. You sometimes have to kill scumbags because they threaten to kill you. You justify it as an act of self-defense. But an assassin kills victims that the boss wants eliminated because they interfere with business. You don't know them and they don't know you. This is not killing in self-defense. This is deliberate stalking and murder for money—big money. Don't overestimate your ability to sleep well. You will struggle with your conscience. This is not a profession that you can walk away from if you decide you've had enough. You know too much. Assassins who try to retire don't live too long. As far as a boss is concerned, dead is dead and dead men don't talk.'

"Julio went on, 'I have seen you work. You have the skills and temperament to be a professional killer. But you now have a family and you are a devoted father. Do you really think you could do this? Take my advice. Be satisfied with your present position. You are a captain. You make a good living. Be content with what you have. Don't be like Icarus and reach for the sun.'

"I respected Julio and I considered his advice, but the success I'd achieved made me arrogant. I thought I could handle anything. Money would buy me respect and the social position I craved. So what if I killed a few people? They probably deserved it anyway. If they interfered with the business of a gang boss, they were likely guilty of crimes themselves but were too well connected to be charged with anything. Hell, I was doing society a favor by eliminating them."

"Nice rationalization."

Culebra releases a breath. "You wanted to know."

I nod. "So you started your life as an assassin. How does one do that, exactly?"

"The boss sent me to a school in the Dominican Republic."

I choke on a mouthful of whiskey. "There's a school for assassins?"

Culebra smiles grimly. "A training camp established during the Trujillo regime ostensibly for 'advanced military training.' Bullshit. It was a school for assassins. Dictators and gang bosses need such services. They don't negotiate with the opposition, they eliminate the opposition. Service rendered, problem solved, hands clean." He brushes his hands together as if brushing away dirt.

"I learned to use explosives and poison and kill silently at close range. I learned how to stalk my victims and how to judge the best time to strike. Then it was time to go home and put my education to use.

"At first, my targets were corrupt, politically connected types who tried to extort more money from the boss. One worked for the treasury and ran a money laundry on the side. His fee for service was always rising. If the boss suggested taking his business elsewhere, the finance guy would hint that he had friends in high places and that they would be interested to know what the boss was up to. The fool never realized that his threats made him a target. I remember him because I used Julio's favorite technique to do the job. He lived on a crowded street, so the kill had to be silent. I entered his home when I knew he was alone and snuck up behind him when he was standing at the refrigerator. I grabbed him by the forehead and shoved an ice pick into the back of his skull. He fell to his knees while I rocked it back and forth to mince the brain tissue." Culebra claps his hands and holds them palms up. "*Tio* Julio was right—no muss, no fuss."

Culebra is watching my face. Gauging my reaction. When I don't react, he continues.

"Jobs were not so frequent as they are now so I had more time to spend at home. I found that I enjoyed watching my children grow. I got to know my wife more intimately and even helped her plant a garden. The money was great. I bought a bigger house for my family and a nicer car for myself. We lived in a fancier neighborhood among a better class of people. My children attended a private school and my wife wore finer clothes. Life was good. Little did I realize what a charade this was. Devoted family man by day and killer by night. It couldn't last. And it didn't.

"The end came when the boss's son fell for a pretty, young woman from a notable family. She refused his advances and bruised his ego. The son became depressed when he learned that she had accepted a marriage proposal from another young man, a judge's son. The boss was angry that his son 'wasn't good enough for this bitch.' So he decided to show what happens when people disrespect him or his family. He gave me the job to ensure that the young woman would never reach the altar on her wedding day. She had to die on her way to the church.

"When I got the order I felt as if I had been punched in the stomach. There was no way I could kill an innocent young woman on her wedding day. I would spend the rest of my life seeing her face in my daughter's eyes. The boss wanted me to plant a bomb under the car her family would use to drive to the ceremony and detonate it by remote control when they approached the church. But I couldn't go through with it and didn't. The marriage ceremony went off without a hitch. I knew the boss would come after me for failing to carry out an order, but I would deal with that. Strangely, I never thought that my family would be involved. After all, this was a business matter and they were civilians. How wrong I was."

CHAPTER 3

CULEBRA'S EXPRESSION GROWS DARK, AS IF HE'S now speaking of things that fill him with more than pain and guilt. Remorse is there, too.

My own emotions are conflicted. His story is not a new one. It's the story of every gangster who thinks himself above the law. But this is Culebra. My friend. Reconciling the man I know now with the man he describes has my head spinning.

I feel his eyes on me.

"Do you want me to stop?"

"I want you to tell me what happened to your family," I reply softly. "How you could have thought for a moment that your family would be spared and only you would have suffered the consequences of disobeying your boss? Your *job* was getting rid of those who did just that. How could you not have known better?"

"I was arrogant," he snaps back, not defensively, but with anger obviously turned back on himself. "Stupid. I believed I was so goddamned important that the boss would see how valuable an asset I was. I'd hide out. Buy time to let him cool off. So I dropped out of sight and made no effort to contact my wife or go near the house. After a few days, I snuck into the house after midnight, making sure I hadn't been followed. I planned to gather up my wife and kids and take them to a safe place until I could arrange to make things right with the boss. How I would explain all of this to my family never entered my mind. My first thought was to get us to safety. But when I passed through the front door, the smell of blood filled my nostrils. There was blood on the carpet in the children's room and on the walls of my bedroom. There were no bodies. But I knew what had happened. The scene in that house has never left my mind."

Culebra's breath catches again. He composes himself quickly. "I was filled with an intense rage that I had never felt before. I didn't care what happened to me. If that motherfucker could kill my family for disobeying one order after all the years I was faithful to him, I was going to exact vengeance on him, his worthless son, and anyone else who got in my way. I was going to descend on his house like the angel of death. My first order of business was to drive out to a hideaway in a remote part of the desert where I stored my cache of guns, explosives and equipment. I would be armed to the teeth when I paid the boss a visit.

"I drove out to my desert ordnance dump. But I was angry—and careless. I didn't notice the black Escalade in my rearview mirror until it was too late. I recognized the boss's men almost immediately. They may have been waiting for me somewhere near my house. Letting me go inside and see what they had done. To realize what my disobedience had cost. Now it was my turn to experience the boss's revenge. I stepped on the gas to speed away, but just then the gunfire started. It ripped through my rear window and knocked out my front windshield. One of the bullets grazed my head." His hand goes to his forehead and he rubs at his temples reflexively. "There was so much blood.

"I lost control of my car and it tumbled into a ravine. I was thrown from the vehicle and landed in a gully while the car continued to tumble on over a patch of rocks. The rocks punctured the fuel tank and created sparks and the vehicle exploded into a fireball. I heard the Escalade stop on the road above. The men got out to watch the fireworks. My body must have been hidden from view in the gully because they didn't come searching for me. They assumed that I died in the explosion and after a few minutes, they returned to the Escalade, turned around and drove off.

"When I felt it was clear, I crawled out of the gully and onto the roadbed. I stood up and staggered, light-headed from the loss of blood. Besides the head wound, I had been shot in each arm, bruised and cut from being thrown around in the car. I was probably about twenty miles from Ciudad Juárez, in the middle of the desert, with no car and no water. The only thing I could do was start walking north toward the border. I took off my undershirt, tore it into strips to make bandages. I wrapped one strip around my head to try and stop or at least slow the bleeding and others to fashion tourniquets for my arms. I started walking. After some time, I don't know how long, I passed out. The next thing I knew I was lying in a bed in an El Paso hospital surrounded by DEA agents."

He looks up at Max.

Max had just raised his glass to his lips. Whatever he sees in Culebra's eyes makes him lower the glass. He takes up the story.

"We were on a routine border patrol when we found Culebra. We thought he was an illegal who had been attacked by coyotes. He'd almost made it to the border. It was a miracle he made it at all. The gunshot wasn't serious, but he was dehydrated and exhausted. He'd lost a lot of blood."

Max watches Culebra as he tells the story. Culebra, for his part, keeps his head down, his eyes on the glass clasped between his hands.

"He was near death for three weeks. We found papers on him—Mexican and American passports in different names. One we recognized. The name connecting him to the Sinaloa Cartel. As soon as he was well enough, we moved him to a safe house for questioning." A cold smile. "He was a tough nut to crack. Wouldn't tell us what happened. Wouldn't name his shooter."

"So how did you convince him to talk?"

"We found the bodies of his family. Buried in a shallow grave not far from where we found him. It was a fluke. We'd gotten a tip about the location of a cartel body dump. His family happened to be among the dead we were able to identify. Ballistics matched the bullet that we took from him to the ones that killed his family. Seeing their bodies, knowing they were killed by his own people reminded him of what he wanted most. Revenge.

"Culebra has been of great help to us. We captured Gallardo with information he supplied. We've taken a lot of drugs off the street and closed some major supply routes. He's more than made up for what he was."

"But the drugs keep flowing and the gangs get stronger." I don't realize how angry and disappointed I'd become until that anger turns my blood to fire. I round on Culebra. "Do you really think you can ever make up for what you were? A killer. An assassin for a drug dealer. Do you know how many deaths you are responsible for? Thousands. On both sides of the border. Your family—" The words spill out, forced from a roiling gut. "I don't understand how you could have allowed yourself to be involved in such a thing. You risked your life not long ago to save a young girl—a stranger—from Belinda Burke. That's the Culebra I know. The one you are describing now is someone I don't recognize."

Culebra makes no attempt to explain or excuse. Anger overcomes disappointment. Bile burns the back of my throat. His silence lights the fuse and trips an explosion of invective.

"Of all the people I've come to depend on in my life, I thought you were the purest of heart. You came here and offered refuge to worldly and otherworldly creatures seeking . . . How could I have . . . . "

Max breaks in. "This place was Culebra's idea. You know the good he does. He still helps us when he can, but basically he is left alone to help whoever—or *whatever*—he chooses."

The last is said with an inflection as sharp as a pointed stake. He's not looking at me. Learning I was vampire was what broke us up. I thought we had gotten past that. Especially since he came to me not long ago for help with a rogue vampire. A rogue I took care of. Maybe the booze is stirring up feelings of betrayal in him the way Culebra's story is stirring up feelings of betrayal in me. Irrational maybe, but real just the same.

In a muddle of alcohol-fueled emotion, I'd not shielded my thoughts. Culebra's intrusion into my head is as soft as a whisper. *I can't undo what I was, what I did.*

The weight of his sadness and regret is heavy. I know the toll past mistakes can exact. I've also seen firsthand the misery narcos inflict. Max and I have both been victims.

I push the chair away. It's better I go before I say or think something that might irreparably harm my relationship with Culebra. Neither man says anything when I stand up.

As I leave, I see the shadow of shame in Culebra's eyes. It's not enough.

CHAPTER 4

THE SUN COMING THROUGH THE GLASS DOOR AND right into my eyes is a painful wake-up call. I have to force myself to sit up, blocking the sun with a hand. It's Christmas Day. My pounding head reminds me of last night. Bits of Culebra's story insinuate themselves into my consciousness, stinging like wasp bites. Then there's the aftertaste of all that whiskey. My throat burns. My tongue feels like I've been licking the insides of those oak barrels the stuff was aged in. I roll my head in my hands and groan.

From a galaxy far, far away, I hear the ring of a doorbell.

I sit up straighter.

My doorbell.

Shit.

I'll ignore it. Even Santa wouldn't have the bad judgment to ring *my* doorbell this early.

The doorbell rings again. This time, one long sustained clash of bells, like someone is leaning an elbow on the fucking thing.

Persistent bugger.

Foolhardy.

Slowly, I haul my ass out of bed, pull on a pair of sweats, shrug into a tee and start downstairs, dragging fingers through my hair as I go. Hand on the doorknob, I grind my teeth in anticipation of kicking the ass of whoever is standing behind the door. The scowl on my face should give even Santa pause. I yank open the door.

"Surprise!!"

Is it! Three pairs of laughing, wonderfully familiar, totally unexpected eyes gleam at me for a second before I'm completely wrapped in three pairs of arms all hugging me and clapping me on the back and kissing my cheeks in one fell swoop of exuberance.

My family has come to visit.

The scowl gusts away like a candle blown by a breeze. I'm laughing and hugging back and overwhelmed by how happy their unexpected presence makes me.

I herd the trio into the living room and get them seated on the couch. I take the chair opposite so I can look at them. It hasn't been that long since I've seen them, three months or so, but each time I do, I take mental inventory. When they're gone, the memory is all I have to cling to.

Mom looks as healthy and happy as ever. She's gained a few pounds in the year she's been away, but she wears it well. Her hair is no grayer than it was, but the hairstyle is different. Cut in a stylish bob that makes her look much younger than her sixty-plus years. Dad hasn't changed a bit. Still carries himself like the successful businessman he was—or is. He's gone from retired investment banker to running a winery. The change agrees with him. Tan, broad-shouldered, he reminds me more than ever of a Roman nobleman with his close-cropped hair of gray curls.

But Trish. My niece looks different every time I see her. She's grown from an awkward thirteen-year-old into a graceful, self-confident soon-to-be fifteen-year-old. Her hair is drawn back from her smooth, even-featured face with a barrette and cascades down her back to just below shoulder length. She's wearing jeans and a designer T-shirt with a logo I don't recognize—something French.

They've been chattering like excited squirrels. "You all look so *happy*," I find myself interjecting. "So wonderful!"

Mom beams at me. "Oh, Anna. We love France. Trish is doing well in school. Speaks French like a native."

"Merci beaucoup, grand-mère," Trish says with a grin.

Mom laughs. "Your dad has become quite the vintner and business is growing. Just a year and our wines have begun taking prizes in local fests."

"Of course most of the credit has to go the great staff we inherited with the winery," Dad says with a modest smile. "But we've experimented with some new grape blends that are getting noticed."

"And wonder of wonders," Mom adds, "Your dad is beginning to appreciate French food."

She reaches over to take his hand. They're like a couple of kids again. Dad beams. "I like your *mother's* French cooking," he says, eyes twinkling. "It's a start."

Trish has been looking around. "No Christmas tree, Aunt Anna?"

I shake my head. "Too busy. But David and I have one at the office."

Yikes. A thought strikes me with the force of a sledgehammer. I should be offering them breakfast and I have no food in the house. Not a scrap. Comes with the territory, being a vamp and all.

How do I explain that to my family? "I wish you'd told me you were coming. I don't have anything to offer you."

"I know we've surprised you, Anna," my mom is saying. "How about we take you to breakfast? If I remember correctly, you were never much of a cook."

Thank you, Mom. "Where would you like to go? How about the Mission Café? It's right down the street. I think it's open for breakfast today."

"Got something better in mind. Let's go to the house."

"Your house? In La Mesa?"

"It's the reason we're here," Dad says. "We've made a decision."

Before I can react, Trish says, "We got in late last night. So we went right there and opened it up. We went shopping and everything."

"And we have a lot of things to do," Mom says. "Things that affect you. Trish has a break from school so we thought this the perfect time."

Wow. Mom is standing up and the others do, too. My cue to do the same. "Did you drive here?" It's the only thing I can think to ask.

Mom touches my cheek. "We've probably overwhelmed you. Let's get to the house and we can sort it all out."

Dad rattles car keys. "The rental is right out front."

Trish links her arm through mine, steers me toward the door. "What's with the new boyfriend? We've been watching him on the news. He's totally hot, Aunt Anna."

"I'll tell Stephen you said that," I say, thinking this is the best Christmas present. Ever.

CHAPTER 5

I T'S BEEN ALMOST A YEAR SINCE I'VE BEEN IN MY PARents' house. It was last Christmas, in fact. Just before they left for a new life in France. A life that didn't, that couldn't, include me.

In spite of open windows, there is still an air of mustiness, of emptiness. A house devoid of life. Until Trish's laugh chases away the gloom. We've finished breakfast (another marvel of sleight of hand as I pretend to consume eggs and toast when in reality, the food becomes a lump in my napkin) and are sitting cross-legged on the living room floor, surrounded by boxes and memories. The announcement came during the meal.

My folks have decided to sell the house.

I'm still in shock, though I know it's the right thing to do. This place represents the past. France is their future.

I look around at the three people I love most in the world. They're here to pack up what they want to take back with them. In the process, Trish gets a peek into the history of her family.

She never knew my brother, the man she thinks is her father. He died before she was born. It's only her presence that makes what would be an unbearably sad task, going through his things, tolerable. She's eager to learn everything she can about him and for the first time, Mom and Dad can share their memories without the gray specter of grief casting a pall. They can laugh and remember the good things.

I join in with memories of growing up in the shadow of a brother who always made straight As, who excelled at any sport he took a fancy to, who never caused my folks the slightest bit of anxiety—in other words, the direct opposite of me.

Predictably, my folks deny that I was a problem child. They have to, don't they? But Trish enjoys the banter and reads between the lines. We loved each other unconditionally, without reservation. She knows this and I see the conflict in her eyes. Sadness because she was denied knowing that kind of happiness in the miserable home she grew up in with her mother, and gratitude that she is at last safe and loved.

I reach over and give her arm a squeeze. If I ever second-guess myself that bringing Trish into our family was a mistake, I'll remember this moment. The glow on my parents' faces, the love in Trish's eyes. She may not be related by blood, but she is related by heart. Nothing else matters.

IT TAKES THREE DAYS TO SORT, PACK, LABEL AND SHIP almost forty years of memories. I take a few mementos that belonged to my grandparents—the original owners of the property where I now live.

They left the cottage to me and when a spiteful vampire burned it down not long after I was turned, every picture, every keepsake I had was destroyed. It would be nice to replace a few of those items. To restore their presence in real, tangible ways.

Too soon it's time for my family to leave. Trish's school

holiday is almost over. Mom calls for a donation truck to empty the house. A Realtor is contracted to handle the listing. There are a few items of furniture that Trish may want sometime in the future and they are stored in a rental unit not far from me.

Hand in hand, the four of us walk through the house for the final time. But it's not with heavy hearts. It's with eager anticipation for the future. One door closed. Another opened.

Even the rain grants a reprieve that last day. The sun feels hot and bright on my face as I shepherd my family into my car for the drive to the airport.

I should feel sad. Instead, I feel peace. We part with promises to visit again soon. I give Trish an extra hug before watching them disappear into the terminal. She will make the transition so much easier for my parents.

The transition that will come when they must go again from having two children, to having just one.

The knowledge is bittersweet. I've given them a niece to take the place of the vampire. My future with my family is now her future.

I wish my heart could accept it as easily as my brain.

CHAPTER 6

JANUARY 1. NEW YEAR'S DAY. WHAT A ROLLER coaster of a holiday season I've had. One good thing that came from my family's surprise visit was that I didn't have time to think about Culebra. Now that they're gone, his story keeps intruding into my head.

An assassin. How could that be?

I'm in the office, taking down the lights we'd strung on the deck. Tracey and David are still on vacation. It's the first break we've taken since Tracey came on board. I'm enjoying it. I trust they are, too. And with Stephen due to come home in a few days, I'll be able to take advantage of the fact that I've been pulling office duty and let my partners take over. Stephen and I can spend some quality time together. Some quality bed time.

I get that tickly, tingling feeling that comes when I think about sex with Stephen. He's human, but I don't have to hold back with him. He allows me to love him completely, which means I can feed from him if I need or want to. He doesn't impose limits. Quite a difference from the other human lover I had—Max. I thought he had gotten over our breakup, had gotten past the bitterness. Seeing him at Culebra's made me realize he hadn't let go of any of it. He blames me for being what I am.

As if I had a choice.

As if I'd voluntarily choose to give up my family or the possibility of children or the million other simple pleasures I no longer enjoy because I'm vampire.

As if I'd take on the burden of being the Chosen One, always looking over my shoulder, always aware of my role as protector if there were any way to avoid it.

I realize I'm working myself into a fit of righteous anger when the string of lights I'm tugging on breaks with a snap.

Shit.

I stare at the broken strands.

Max can still push my buttons.

I toss the lights into the trash.

At least he took my mind off Culebra.

THE OFFICE LOOKS PRETTY GOOD. LAST HOUR I STORED the decorations, did some filing that had piled up, straightened the desk, even swept the floor. A little physical activity is always a good way to clear the mental decks.

It's late afternoon. The sun is low on the horizon, and I step outside. Clouds are boiling up from the south, which means more rain. The air is heavy with it. Time to get home and settle in with a nice glass of Merlot.

You know the feeling you get when someone is watching you? The itch just out of reach under your skin? I have that feeling now and it stops me cold. My senses spring into hyperdrive. I tilt my face up to sniff the air.

And I catch it.

At first I think I must be imagining it. The scent of fresh washed hair and sunshine. I know who it is before I see that the office door is open and spy the two figures standing there.

For the second time in a week, I get a surprise.

CHAPTER 7

A FOUR-YEAR-OLD DARK-HAIRED DERVISH WHIRLS into the room with a whoop and runs into my arms. I scoop him up, twirl him around and hug him until he squeals. His father watches, grinning from the doorway.

"Frey! What are you two doing here?"

John-John, his son, answers before he can. "We're visiting. I'm going to see Daddy's home. And we want you to come with us. You will, won't you?"

I set him down and crouch so we're eye level. "When did you get here?"

"Just now." John-John is dancing with excitement. "We came right from the airport. Daddy saw your car so we knew you were here."

Frey brushes a shock of hair off his son's forehead. "Easy, *Shiye*. Give Anna a chance to catch her breath."

I don't need to catch my breath. Or at least I wouldn't need to catch my breath even if I had breath to catch. I'm so happy to see Frey and his son, I jump up, snatch my keys and bag and look past them to the open door. "Do you have a car?"

"We came in a cab," John-John says. "A yellow one. The driver didn't look so happy when we made him stop here."

I nod. The office is only about a five-minute drive from the airport on Pacific Highway. "I'll bet. Well, I'm glad you stopped. Have you seen the ocean yet?"

He shakes his head. "Only through the plane window. Not close up. Will you show me?"

"I will. We'll take a ride up the coast before we go home if it's all right with your dad."

"Azhé'é?" John-John turns those expressive dark eyes to his father, using his native Navajo.

Frey nods. "Let's go."

He holds out his arms to John-John and me and we each take a hand. It's amazing how natural it feels, the three of us together like this.

Frey's luggage is piled by the door, a car seat balanced on top. He and John-John grab their suitcases and I take the car seat. We jabber all the way to the parking lot, then John-John and I watch as Frey fumbles the car seat into the back. Finally, we get John-John safely buckled in, Frey takes the passenger seat beside me and we're off.

I follow Pacific Coast Highway up through the beach communities until it becomes too dark for John-John to see the ocean, and then I turn back toward San Diego, promising more trips during the daytime when we can play near the water. I remember the toys in John-John's bedroom on the reservation and promise a trip to Legoland, too. John-John fills me in on all he's done in the last months since I left him and Frey at their home on the reservation in Monument Valley. School, riding with Kayani, hiking with his father.

He seems well-adjusted, happy even though I detect an undercurrent of sadness under the exuberance. He lost his mother while I was there. It was a traumatic time, and it was my fault. I can't believe they've both forgiven me.

While John-John and I chatter all the way to Frey's condo, Frey is strangely quiet.

Maybe I've overestimated Frey's ability to forgive.

Once at the condo, we get John-John settled in. Frey and I make up a bed for him in the guest room while John-John explores the library. This is Frey's legacy as a Keeper. John-John will someday inherit his father's vast treasure trove of books that explore every aspect of the supernatural world. He inherited his father's ability as a shape-shifter, too, though that won't manifest itself physically until he's in puberty.

At least that's what Frey hopes. John-John already possesses the ability to link psychically with vampires and other shape-shifters. He is years ahead of Frey in developing his abilities, a sense of both pride and concern for Frey.

Frey orders groceries from a nearby store and while we wait for them to be delivered, John-John appears from the bedroom with a small wrapped box. He's squirming with excitement as he presents it to me.

"Open it, Anna," he says.

I tear open the paper to find a ring box. I glance at Frey, an eyebrow raised.

A ring?

John-John plops himself down beside me. "Go on. Go on. Open the box."

I link an arm around his shoulders and hug him close as I flip open the top.

It is a ring. A beautiful ring.

A band about a half-inch wide of carved turquoise and silver.

John-John takes it out of the box and slips it on my left ring finger.

"This is for protection," he says. "Turquoise is sacred to the *Dine'é*. It will keep you safe from curse magic."

My throat is suddenly dry and tight with emotion. I have to clear it to be able to say, "Did you pick it out?"

He shakes his head. "It's a gift from another friend."

"Another friend?" Besides the people in this room, the

only other person I know on the reservation is Kayani, an officer in the Navajo Police and a close friend of John-John's deceased mother. I hardly think he'd be sending me a gift. "Who is this friend?"

"Sani. He told me to bring it to you. To help you remember."

My eyes snap to Frey at the mention of Sani, the Navajo shaman. I hadn't mentioned what happened last summer between Sani and me to either of them. Frey meets my startled gaze with a smile of mild amusement and nods toward his son.

John-John catches the question in my head. "Oh, we are friends, Sani and me. Since I was little."

Little? He's four. The answer makes me smile.

Frey's looking at me with more exasperation, though, then amusement. "I guess you forgot to tell me that you met the shaman, right?" he asks. "Because I know you would have wanted to tell me something as important as that."

CHAPTER 8

JOHN-JOHN IS ASLEEP. FREY AND I ARE SITTING ON opposite ends of his couch, glasses of wine in our hands, faces toward the flames of a flickering fire. Outside, the rain has finally blown in, gusting against the windows, making the crystal wind chimes on his deck twirl and dance.

I glance at my watch. It's almost midnight. I should leave.

I don't want to.

I take a sip of the wine. From the corner of my eye, I catch Frey watching me. I turn my body slightly, toward him. "John-John seems good."

He doesn't need elaboration. "He is a remarkable kid. He has bad days, sure, but he takes care of me more than I take care of him."

Frey lets a long minute stretch between us before he adds, "He really was excited about bringing you that gift from Sani."

I look down at the ring on my hand. In the firelight, the

silver catches and reflects light like tiny rays of sunshine in a mirror. "It's a beautiful ring."

"Do you want to tell me how you met Sani? What he said to you?"

"First, let me ask you. Have *you* met Sani?"

He shakes his head.

"Then how does John-John know of him? When do they meet?"

Frey releases a breath. "My son is remarkable in many ways. He and Sani have forged a friendship and I can't even tell you how. There are some older boys on the reservation that he rides with. Three times he's come back from those rides with stories about the shaman. I thought he was recounting tales learned from his friends, but when he came back with that ring, I started to suspect something more. The older boys won't say much about it—just that Sani appears sometimes and talks to them."

A feeling of warmth spreads over me. John-John couldn't have a better teacher or protector than Sani. He is watching over him just as he promised.

Frey quirks an eyebrow. "Now it's your turn. How did you meet him? *When* did you meet him?"

I settle my head on the back of the couch and stretch my legs. In my head I relive my meetings with the most holy of the Navajo shamans: Sani, who has the power to restore life to the dead. It's the reason Frey and I traveled to Monument Valley. I wanted to see if he could restore my mortality.

Carefully, I compose my thoughts.

"Sani," I tell Frey, "helped me see the truth. I am destined to be a protector and my power lies in the melding of two natures—that of human for morality and integrity and that of vampire for strength and cunning. Even when I asked that John-John's mother be brought back and was willing to trade my life for hers, he refused. Sani told me that I am a warrior, a leader, and my path is set, just as John-John's mother's was set. It was her time. It wasn't mine. Not yet." I glance self-consciously at Frey. I realize what I said sounded melodramatic and egotistical. "Sani's words. Not mine."

A wry smile tips the corners of his mouth. "I do believe Culebra and I have been telling you the same thing for a year and a half. You accept a stranger's word but not ours. I should be hurt."

"You're right. I should have listened to you. I admit it."

"You say that now," he says. "But will you remember the next time I give you advice?"

"Probably not."

Frey laughs. "At least you're being honest." Then he sobers. "Thank you for what you tried to do—bring John-John's mother back."

We lapse into a comfortable silence. The crackling of the fire, the heartbeat of rain on the windows, the tinkling of the wind chimes, all lull me into a cozy warm cocoon, and before I realize it, my eyes have closed. I feel Frey lean over, take the glass from my hand. His lips brush my forehead and as if from far away, a whisper.

"I've missed you, Anna."

From the warm, soft bubble of twilight sleep, I feel my lips curl into a smile. "I missed you, too, Frey."

Then I let go and fall into full night.

SOMETHING CUDDLY AS A PUPPY HAS CRAWLED UP ON the couch and is snuggling down beside me. When I open my eyes, the top of John-John's head rests just under my chin. I don't let him know I'm awake. I wait. Then, I pounce, tickling his tummy until he's laughing so hard, we both tumble off the couch in a tangle of waving arms and legs.

When I look up, Frey is standing over us, hands on hips. "What's going on?"

He's dressed and when I glance at the clock on the mantel, I'm shocked to see it's already eight.

I hoist John-John and slide back onto the couch. In unison, John-John and I say, "Nothing."

He shakes his head. "Ready for some coffee?"

"Me, too?" From John-John.

"No," Frey answers in a parental tone. "It's milk for you."

John-John and I follow Frey into the kitchen where the table has already been set for breakfast. I can tell which is my place. There's only a mug on the placemat. But for once, I'm not self-conscious. John-John knows and accepts what I am. Something his mother certainly didn't.

That thought brings a wave of shame. How can I fault her when I'm the reason she's dead.

You're not, you know. A small, childish voice penetrates my thoughts. *Sani explained it all to me.*

John-John's voice in my head surprises me. I can't believe I'd forgotten. Frey and I have no psychic link. I broke it through a stupid act of impulsiveness. But John-John can hone in on my thoughts. And he has. Color floods my face, hot with humiliation.

Frey, who caught his son's message to me, comes to stand beside my chair. "John-John is right. What happened to Sarah was tragic. But it was not your fault."

He's holding a bowl of oatmeal and a pitcher of milk. He sets the bowl in front of John-John, passing a hand gently over the top of his son's head. "We know she's at peace. John-John is safe."

With the resiliency of childhood, John-John's thoughts brighten and he starts to work on the oatmeal. Frey brings a coffeepot to the table and pours us each a cup.

"I've been thinking," he says after a moment. "How about the three of us take that trip to Legoland today?"

John-John's high-spirited whoop is matched decibel for decibel by my own.

CHAPTER 9

FREY AND I CHASE JOHN-JOHN ALL OVER LEGOLAND.
I grew up with Disneyland being the theme park of
choice so this is a new adventure for me, too. It's amazing
how much energy a four-year-old has. Even with a vampire's constitution, it's work to keep up.

But it's fun. Especially the Raptor Splash where John-
John and I take on Frey—pelting him with water balloons
from our battle station launcher. We come off that ride
soaked to the skin and laughing our heads off.

Of course that necessitates a shopping trip for dry
clothes, it being January and all. Great marketing ploy, that.
When the three of us exit the Brick Brothers Trading Company we look like true California surfer dudes: John-John
and Frey in their Quiksilver Diplo pants and tees and me in
my Roxy hoodie and jeans.

Then, after still more rides, it's a trip to the Big Shop.
John-John picks out a Dino-themed Lego set to take back
home with him. And at last the kid shows signs of tiring. His
squeal on the rides is a little less piercing, his gait a little

less frenetic. Like a spinning top winding down, he finally looks up at Frey and holds out his arms. Frey hoists him onto his shoulders and, armed with packages and souvenirs, we wearily and thankfully make our way back to the car.

As soon as we get to the condo, John-John crawls onto the couch and falls fast asleep. Frey lifts him up and carries him to the bedroom while I pour us each a glass of wine.

One glass, I tell myself. One glass and then I'm going home.

When Frey returns, I hand one of the glasses to him, echoing out loud what I'd been thinking a moment before. "One glass. Then I have to leave."

"Why? It's early."

I point to the couch. "Any more than one and I'll end up falling asleep again."

"So? You looked pretty comfortable on that couch."

"No. If I stay, you'll tempt me with a trip to SeaWorld tomorrow and then I'll miss another day of work. I have to at least check in. And Stephen is coming home in a few days and I—"

Something dims in Frey's eyes. He turns away and sinks down onto the couch.

"What?"

Frey takes a long pull of his wine and avoids looking at me. After a moment, his shoulders seem to relax and his expression softens. "How is Stephen?"

"He's fine."

"And the two of you . . . ?"

"Are we making it work? I think so. There's something about a life-and-death battle against a godlike demon that tends to bring people together."

My attempt at humor is obviously lost on Frey. No smile. Under his breath, I hear him say, "You and I have fought a few demons together, too."

"What?"

No response except, "So it's over with the tribunal?"

"How did you know—?" I stop. "Of course. You've been talking to Culebra."

"We've kept in touch."

"Yes. Belinda Burke and the tribunal are finally behind us." I mentally cross my fingers. Belinda Burke? That bitch is undisputedly dead. But the tribunal? I can only hope.

Frey lets another long moment pass. "John-John had fun today, didn't he?"

"He's such a great kid."

"I've been giving a lot of thought to my decision to stay on the reservation. It's one of the reasons I brought him here."

"You're thinking of moving back?"

"Not full time. I would never cut John-John off from his grandparents or force him to leave the only home he's ever known. But maybe we could split our time. Stay here for the school year and spend winter and summer breaks on the reservation."

"That would be so great."

"Kayani is willing to take care of the horses and the house while we're here. I've spoken to him about it already. He thinks it would be good for John-John to broaden his horizons."

"And John-John? What does he think?"

"I haven't talked to him yet. I wanted to give him a chance to experience life in the big city for a week or so. It's quite a change from what he's used to. He may not like it. And it's as much his decision as mine."

I nod. Then, "What's the other reason?"

"What?"

"You said rethinking your decision to stay on the reservation was one of the reasons you're here. What's the other?"

He stares into the fire, and something in the set of his jaw gives it away. Still, I won't say it first. I can't.

Frey lets another long moment pass. "You," he says at last. "I came back for you."

His words hang in the air. They may as well be in blazing neon over the fireplace.

I don't know what to say. So, for once, I exercise restraint and say nothing.

Frey looks up at me from his seat on the couch. "I shouldn't have said that."

Still, no intelligible response springs to mind.

Frey smiles. "I've rendered you speechless."

I drop down beside him. "You have."

He releases a deep breath. "I realize you and Stephen have gotten close. But he's human. Do you really think you can make it work for the long term?"

"Can anyone make anything work long term? My parents are the only couple their age I know that have been together as long as they have. And that wasn't easy. I remember how hard it was after my brother died. And there were other times. Things my parents didn't know I knew. My father had an affair once. I thought he'd broken my mother's heart into so many pieces, she'd never be able to put it back together. But they survived. They got stronger."

"Because they loved each other." Frey's soft voice is like a caress. "No one exasperates me the way you do. Or tests me the way you do. Or completes me the way you do. You have the most generous heart of anyone I know. I want John-John to learn from you. I can't think of a better role model. It took being away from you to make me realize how much I need you to be part of our lives."

His words slow, then stop abruptly. He's facing away from me as if afraid to see how I'm reacting. He shouldn't worry. I've never been so touched. I turn his chin gently so I can read his eyes.

"I will always be a part of John-John's life. As long as you let me. I love that little boy." I let my hand drop and the motion makes light reflect off Sani's ring, a spark that seems to penetrate the haze of confusion whirling in my head.

"You and I have been close for a long time. We've been through a lot together. You are the one I go to when I'm in trouble and you've never turned me away. Maybe you think you're in love with me. But you're emotional now because of John-John and the huge responsibility you've taken on."

Frey stirs, ready to respond, but I have to get this out.

I place a finger over his lips. "It would be easy after a day like today to jump into a relationship with you. You and John-John are the family I can never have. But I want more. I want a partner who loves me the way my father loves my mother. Is it Stephen? I don't know yet. It's still too new. But I don't think it's you. Not now. Not yet."

The corners of Frey's mouth turn up in a wry smile. He kisses the tip of my finger. "Should I have started off with 'I love you'?"

"It would have helped."

He puts his arm around my shoulders and pulls me close. I don't resist but let my head rest against his chest. "Does that mean you'll still go on play dates this week with John-John and me?"

I close my eyes, breathing in his smell, listening to his heart, nestling closer. Feeling safe. "Try and stop me."

REMARKABLY, WE MANAGE TO GET THROUGH THE NEXT few days of Frey's visit without another bombshell being dropped. I handle my office thing in the mornings (even fugitives lay low during the holidays), and the afternoons are spent showing John-John around San Diego. He loves the ocean, is spellbound by it. The weather cooperates by giving us two afternoons of bright sun so we can gather seashells and make sand castles. By the end of each day, his little fists are full of treasures that he can take home with him. Tiny shells, glass polished by the sea, a perfect starfish. In my mind's eye, I picture these prizes on the bookcase in his living room, next to the pictures of his mother, and bits of rocks and feathers he'd gathered on his daily rides. It makes me happy to know this visit will become part of his memories, too.

But then I am alone, sitting in my car, staring at the ring on my hand. I've just dropped Frey and John-John off at the airport. We parted with hugs and kisses and, like another family departure just a while ago, promises of visits to come.

Another family.

I like the sound of that.

The airport security guard is approaching, waving and telling me to move on. It snaps me back and I put the car in gear. Time to get back to another reality.

Stephen will be home tomorrow.

CHAPTER 10

THE COTTAGE IS SPIT-SHINED. CLEAN SHEETS ON the bed, fresh towels in the bathroom, some cheese and bread in the refrigerator in case Stephen is hungry, a new exotic preparation guaranteed to make that big moment even bigger sitting on the nightstand.

I'm looking at that now, shaking my head. This may be overkill. We've never needed any outside stimulant to make that big moment bigger. I'm not sure we could take it if it did.

I slide it into a nightstand drawer, feeling foolish for having spent money on such nonsense.

Besides, I'm more than ready for Stephen. We've been apart for two weeks.

For the tenth time in as many minutes, I glance at my watch. I'm picking him up at the airport at two. It's one. I'm nervous—no, it's more like *anxious*, and I have no idea why. Since we met, we've been inseparable. Only when he's sent on assignment, like this one with the president, have we slept apart. When he's in town, we're either at my place or his. Every night.

I suppose we're in that first flush, "can't get enough of each other" phase. We met under very unusual circumstances. Stephen had been kidnapped by the tribunal—still not exactly sure what that bunch is all about—to ensure my presence at a trial where I had to defend myself against a charge of murder. The victim? The black witch Belinda Burke. It didn't exactly turn out the way my "prosecutor" intended. In fact, when all the facts were known, he was in as much trouble as I was. But as is so often the case with otherworldly beings, it didn't end with a verdict of not guilty. That same prosecutor attacked Stephen and me when we returned to Earth. We killed him together.

That's what I meant when I told Frey a life-and-death battle against a godlike demon tends to forge bonds. During the entire time we were together on that "adventure," Stephen didn't flinch or turn away from what I was. And when we were safe, back on Earth, he stayed with me.

Is that love?

Yes.

I think so . . .

I don't know.

Damn it, Frey.

I give myself a mental thump. Bringing John-John here, giving me a glimpse of what the three of us could share, has burrowed into my subconscious like a tick. Frey is smart. He knew exactly what he was doing. After that one conversation, he never again mentioned love or sharing a life with him. He didn't need to. The time he and John-John and I spent together was magical. It implanted the notion that it was possible for me to have a family, a family that included a child. A notion I'd given up on.

Cunning.

From downstairs, the trill of my cell phone.

I jump up and run to get it.

"Hey, you," a familiar voice says. "Where are you? I thought you were coming to pick me up?"

I shoot a startled glance toward the mantel clock. It's after two. Shit.

"Oh my god, Stephen. I'm sorry. My watch must have stopped." A lie. I was lost in my daydream.

"Well, get over here, girl. I can't wait to see you." A pause. "No. I have a better idea. I'll take a cab. It'll be faster."

"Are you sure?"

"Just make sure you're naked and ready when I get there."

"I'm ready now. I've missed you."

"Me, too. See you in a few minutes."

Perfect timing, Stephen. You're just the antidote I need to chase Frey's fantasies right out of my head.

I ROLL OVER AND SMILE DOWN AT STEPHEN. HIS EYES are closed but I know he's not sleeping. His lips are curled in a little smile. Satisfied. Spent.

His head rests on the pillow, his right arm curled up behind it. He doesn't look any worse for the two weeks he's been gone—a little thinner maybe, but that only accentuates the square cut of his jaw, the razor-sharp cheekbones that look so good on camera. His hair is mussed, longer than I've seen it, golden blond touched on the temples with silver. It gives him an air of quiet confidence, of maturity that in spite of his young thirty-some years, attracts viewers and makes his evening news show one of the most watched in Southern California.

I brush a lock of that hair gently off his forehead. "Are you thirsty? Hungry? God, you must be. We've been at it for hours."

He opens his eyes and grins up at me. "Have we? You make me lose track of time." He glances toward the slider. "When did it get dark?"

I laugh and sit up. "I have some bread and cheese downstairs. Not much. But I figured you'd want to go to dinner at some point."

He pulls me back down against his chest. "Not yet." His voice is gruff. "We have two weeks to make up for."

I slide my hand down between his legs. "You're hard."

His hand travels down my stomach, fingers stroke, probe. "You're wet." He brushes his lips against mine. "Can you go again?"

"Chosen One, remember? Stamina woman."

He lifts his chin. "What about you? Are you thirsty?"

An offering. I realize I am. I nuzzle close, touch the spot with the tip of my tongue. I listen for his heartbeat, for the pulse of his blood. His excitement builds. I feel it, not only in the hardness of his erection, but in the quickening of his blood.

I straddle him, pin his shoulders to the bed with my hands, his hips with my knees. I lower my own hips, advancing, retreating, until I have him completely inside me and he's groaning with impatience. He wants to thrust up, but I don't let him.

Until the moment I break the skin. His back arches, he gasps and moans. But he doesn't fight. He surrenders. To the pleasure, to the rhythm, to the vampire.

His blood tastes of cold desert air and snow. Simple food. A bit of fear. Longing. I'm there in his sleepless nights.

The realization that I've become a part of him fills me with sudden alarm. Then, confusion. Isn't this what I've wanted?

He's nearing climax. His body tenses, his hands grip my hips and he forces me down, deep. I'm swept up, too. I stop drinking and meet his movements with my own—frenzied, turbulent, using the overpowering physical sensation of a mind-numbing climax to shatter the uncertainty.

CHAPTER 11

STEPHEN AND I FINALLY COME UP FOR AIR. WE'RE downstairs at the kitchen table. Stephen wolfs down a cheese sandwich like it's the best thing he's ever eaten. Makes me wish I could share that simple pleasure with him.

Nothing different here. Frey eats, too, you know.

The voice unwanted, unbidden whispers in my ear.

So what now? I'm comparing Stephen with Frey?

"Something wrong?" Stephen's eyes are on me. "You look upset."

I shake away the specter with a shake of my head. "No. Just wishing I could share that sandwich. It looks good."

"It is. Got to rebuild my strength. You took a lot out of me, you know."

He leans toward me and I meet him. Our lips brush. He whispers, "I can't believe how amazing sex is with you. Like nothing I've ever experienced. I think you may be ruining me for anyone else."

Anyone else? I pull back a little.

He catches it. Takes my hand. "That may not have come out right."

"Is there something I should know?"

"God, no. In fact, I have something to ask you. I'm hoping it's something you'll like."

Excitement shines from his eyes. I hope panic isn't shining from mine. "What is it?"

He pushes his chair back and takes my hand to pull me up with him as he stands. At least he isn't getting down on one knee.

"I've had a job offer. A great job offer."

"What kind of job?" An automatic response to hide the confusion rattling around in my head. I don't know whether to feel relief or disappointment. What was I expecting? One moment I'm insulted because I perceived him to be comparing me with someone else in his life, the next I'm aggravated because it's a job offer he's excited about and not me.

What is wrong with me?

Thank god he can't read my thoughts. He'd be suffering whiplash. He's still talking, hands windmilling the air.

"The network recommended me for the post of White House liaison. This junket was to see how I got along with the Press Corps, with the president. He's given the thumbs-up. The job is mine if I want it."

He's running out of air. He breathes in, exhales a forceful breath. "What do you think, Anna?"

"It sounds great. But that would be quite a commute wouldn't it?"

He laughs. "Yeah, it certainly would. But I won't be commuting. If I take the job, it's full time. I'd have to quit the local affiliate. I'd be stationed with the network bureau in Washington."

He doesn't give me time to process what he's said before adding, "I want the job, Anna. And I want you to come with me. I want us to live together in DC. Think of it. For a reporter, there couldn't be a better or a more exciting assignment. A front-row seat to history in the making. And we'd be right there in the middle of the action."

I turn my face away. I have to. It's an impossible situation. I couldn't leave San Diego. How could I? Everything I know is here. Stephen is looking at this as if I'm human. He sees the simple obstacles of moving—selling or renting my home, giving up my business. Things easily overcome. But there are other things, things much more complicated. I'd have to find a place in Washington to feed, introduce myself to a new supernatural community, not to mention a new mortal one.

He picks up on my reticence. "I shouldn't have sprung this on you. I know it's a lot to process. But you have no family tying you to San Diego now. And it's a much shorter flight to Europe from the East Coast than the West."

"Stephen, there's more—"

"Your business. I understand it wouldn't be easy to give that up. You and David are friends as well as partners. But you could find something to do in Washington. Maybe not as exciting as what you do now. Police work, or working for a private detective agency. Plenty of sleuthing to do in the land of political intrigue."

He's not letting me get a word in. Maybe in his excitement he's forgotten that we don't have a normal girlfriend/boyfriend situation. Maybe he's so excited about the big boost to his career, so flattered to have the opportunity that he's blind to everything else. Should I burst his bubble now? Or should I let him go on thinking that there might be a chance I'd actually be able to make a move like that with him?

Like with Frey a few nights ago, I'm dumbstruck. Why is this happening now?

"Hey. Is that a new ring? It's beautiful. A Christmas present?"

I don't realize I've been twisting Sani's ring around my finger until Stephen mentions it. He takes my hand and holds it up for a closer look. "Silver and turquoise? Really nice craftsmanship. Native American?"

It's such an abrupt change of subject, I bark a little laugh. It comes out forced and self-conscious to my ear but evidently not to Stephen's. His gaze remains curious. "Navajo. I didn't realize you knew anything about Native American jewelry."

"It's Susan's passion. I guess I've picked up a few things along the way."

Susan is his sister. A witch with the Watcher organization and one of the reasons we met. She and her sister witches made it possible for me to penetrate the astral plain and dispose of Belinda Burke. Because of that connection, Stephen was kidnapped and held to assure my presence at the "trial."

"Does Susan know of your job offer?"

He shakes his head. "I plan to talk to her tomorrow." He pulls me close to him. "Tonight is for us."

Then we're kissing and one thing leads to another. We don't make it upstairs to the bed this time, the couch in the living room is convenient and comfortable.

He is right about one thing. The sex Stephen and I have is certainly remarkable. Maybe the best sex ever.

You haven't given Frey a chance. That damnable voice is back. *It's been too long. You thought sex with him was pretty damn good, too.*

I almost say shut the fuck up, out loud, until I catch myself.

And then Stephen is busy with fingers and tongue and I don't have to.

CHAPTER 12

STEPHEN HAS JUST LEFT TO SEE HIS SISTER AND I'M suffering from sensory overload. His smell fills my nostrils, the warmth of lovemaking and feeding sends heat to my skin.

Still, I didn't get up to see him out. I couldn't. Very little sleep and a body numb from a lot of sex leaves me inert, snuggled under the covers while Stephen jumps out of bed, showers, and takes off with the promise to be back before dark.

Where is he getting the energy? A day in transit to get home, a night of energetic lovemaking, very little food, no coffee even, and he's bright and chipper and whistling his way out the door.

Probably from his excitement about this new job offer, my little voice replies.

And I think it's right. While Stephen didn't push for a commitment from me, he did manage to work into every conversation how great it could be for us in Washington. If he sensed my lack of enthusiasm, he didn't mention that, either.

It might have been better if he had. It might have been better to make me put into words just what it is that has me so ambivalent about something he wants so much.

What would I have said? How could I have made him understand how impossible it would for me to hide my true nature in such a media-saturated city? Especially as the consort of a high-profile reporter?

I couldn't.

I pull a pillow over my head and stifle a groan.

The telephone on the bedside table rings. I toss the pillow aside and reach for the receiver. "Hello."

"Anna, it's Max."

Great. "What's up?"

"Have you talked to Culebra?"

"Not since Christmas Eve."

"You hurt his feelings, you know."

"I hurt his feelings? How? By being shocked to find out about his past?"

Max answers with a hiss into the receiver so pregnant with recrimination, it's like a slap.

Maybe because I'm tired, maybe because my head swims with too many uncertainties about my own life, maybe because I'm looking for an excuse to vent, the words spew out. "So, Max, tell me. What should I have done? Pat him on the shoulder and say it's all right that he was an assassin? That it's all right that he killed indiscriminately on the orders of a drug lord? That it's all right that it led to the massacre of his own family? Just tell me. What is the proper reaction?"

"So you're going to write him off?" Max's heated reply comes just as quickly. "Just like that. You can be such a bitch, you know that, Anna? He's done a lot for you. Made it possible for you to pretend to be human as long as you have. Kept you from turning into a predator. Without Culebra in your life, where do you think you'd be now? Probably dead—oh, excuse me, *really* dead because you'd have had the Revengers after you the first time you left a corpse. Yeah, there are vampire hunters out there, remember? And

I swear to god, right now I have half a mind to turn you over to them myself."

"Jesus, Max—"

He cuts me off in midsentence. "Save it."

And disconnects.

Whoa.

I stare at the receiver in my hand.

Since when has Max become Culebra's champion? I'm tempted to call him back, remind him that he has a strange attitude for someone who works for an agency whose main purpose is to put narcos out of business. Culebra helped him do that job once, okay, but that doesn't balance the scales. How could Max think that it did?

And what in the hell does he want me to do? If Culebra is suffering a crisis of conscience, good. He should be.

And killing doesn't bother you? The annoying voice in the back of my head chirps up once again. *How many people are dead because of you? How many supernatural creatures, your own kind, have you eliminated? How many humans? You had reasons. But you killed nonetheless. So exactly how different are you from Culebra?*

It's not the same thing. It wasn't indiscriminate. It was never indiscriminate.

Was it?

You worked for Warren Williams and his Watcher organization once. He used you like a loaded gun, pointed you at the target and pulled the trigger. Wasn't that indiscriminate?

Am I really arguing with myself?

I thrust away the covers and get out of bed. May as well. I doubt I'll be getting any sleep. I'm sore and sticky and pissed. I head to the shower and crank on the hot water. When the room is filled with steam, I step under the spray and let the heat scald my skin red. I soap up and scrub. Still, thoughts keep spinning themselves around inside my brain like a dog chasing its tail.

Why do things have to change? A few days before Christmas, I was simply looking forward to Stephen coming home. Since then I've had a confrontation with Culebra, found out my parents are selling their house, been presented with an out-of-the-blue proposal from Frey and blindsided with Stephen's announcement that he wanted me to move with him to the other side of the fucking country.

And even before all that happened, I wasn't happy. I felt sorry for myself because I was alone on Christmas Eve. My family's visit was nice, but over too soon.

Shit.

Max is right. I am a bitch.

I DON'T KNOW WHEN THE THOUGHT TO GO SEE CULebra wiggles its way into my consciousness. One moment I'm being self-righteous and indignant and the next I'm in the car headed south.

Why? Couldn't put it into words. Maybe Max has a point. Eighteen months of friendship deserves more than a brush-off.

I left a message for Stephen after ringing his cell phone and having it go straight to voice mail. He may have turned it off while visiting with his sister. No matter. I'll be back at the cottage before him, I'm sure.

Lines at the border are long. Security is heightened during the holidays. And the increasing drug violence along the Texas and Arizona borders is spilling over to tighter security along ours.

Hear that, Culebra?

When it's my turn, I flash my passport and get waved through.

I'm about fifteen minutes outside Beso de la Muerte when I see a man. A lone figure a quarter of a mile from the road, weaving around cactus, stumbling over rocks and brush. I pull over, wondering if he's an illegal. Or a victim of one of the unscrupulous coyotes working the area. In either case, he's lost his bearings. He's not heading toward the border, he's moving parallel to it. And this is the middle of the day. Even if he makes the border, he'll run right smack into a patrol.

I climb out of the car at the same instant he takes a header into a ravine. When I don't see him get right back up, I'm racing over the desert toward him.

I reach him just as he attempts to sit up. He's holding his head in both hands, a jagged gash at his hairline spilling blood into his eyes. The scent of his blood gives me pause. It's full of fear. The raw smell of panic increases when he spies me. He jumps to his feet, backing away, spewing Spanish too fast for me to understand.

I hold up my hands, try to remember how to say something reassuring in a language in which I haven't had much practice.

"Estás lastimado. Puedo ayudarle."

He doesn't look reassured. Maybe I got it wrong. I try English this time. I point to his wound. "You are hurt. I can help."

He looks at the blood on his hands as if seeing it for the first time. "You are not *policia*?"

His English is halting but good.

"No. Where were you going?"

He sinks down on the edge of the berm. "I'm looking for a friend."

As far as I know, there's nothing out here, or even close, except Culebra's. And this guy is a human, a stranger to me, so it's doubtful he'd be heading there. Unless . . .

"Are you looking for Culebra?"

"Culebra?" He looks around, startled. "A snake? Why would I be looking for a snake?"

Okay. That answers that question. He doesn't know Culebra. However, it would be much quicker to get that head wound taken care of in Beso de la Muerte instead of trekking all the way back to the border—a border where we'd both be detained.

I take a step toward him, hold out a hand. *"Ven conmigo.* I can get you help. For your wound." When he shies away, I add, *"Para su herida."*

"No policia?"

I shake my head. *"No policia."*

He looks as if he wants to refuse, but when he tries to stand up and his legs buckle, I'm there to steady him. He gives in with a shrug and lets me help him back to the car. I give him a rag from the trunk to hold against the bleeding wound and a bottle of water. He drinks it down in one long pull and rests his head wearily against the back of the seat.

He falls asleep as soon as we get on the road. It gives me a chance to check him out. He's dark skinned, has dark hair, probably a nice-looking face under all that blood. He's not young, not old—late forties maybe. His clothes are dirty but not ragged. Good quality jeans, a long-sleeved cotton shirt buttoned all the way to the neck. He has sports shoes with a sole hardly worn so he hadn't been trekking far. Maybe he drove part of the way and his car broke down so he had to abandon it.

But drove from where?

I didn't pass a car. If he came from the opposite direction, from Tijuana for instance, how did he end up out here?

Questions I won't be able to answer until we get to Culebra's.

There's a lot more going on in Beso de la Muerte today. At least a dozen cars line the road in front of the bar. Should I take the guy inside? He's still asleep, but it would be no problem to carry him.

Until he wakes up and wonders how I'm able to do such a thing. Or sees the unusual mix of worldly and otherworldly customers that frequent Culebra's bar.

No. Instead, I send a telepathic message to Culebra. *I'm outside. I have someone with me. A stranger. He's hurt. Not sure I should bring him inside.*

In less than a heartbeat, Culebra is standing by the car. He leans in and when he sees the man, a flash of recognition flares in his eyes before he looks quickly away. He slams the door on his thoughts, too, closing his mind with an almost audible click.

He opens the rear door and climbs in. Not surprisingly, he says, "Take him to the cave."

I put the Jag in gear and pull around back. I know this area as well as I know the bar. This is where Culebra's "guests" stay, where he lives, where an unlicensed doctor has his "practice."

Culebra jumps out before I can and reaches inside for the man. He lifts him as gently as he would a child.

The man stirs then, and his eyes open, focus on Culebra.

"Tomás," he says. "I found you."

CHAPTER 13

CULEBRA DOESN'T RESPOND BUT HURRIES STRAIGHT back into the mouth of the cave.

Tomás? Who's Tomás?

I follow close behind. He brings the guy to an area set up like a MASH unit and lays him on the gurney. All the while, the guy is muttering to him in Spanish. His voice is barely above a whisper and Culebra is letting nothing of what he hears infiltrate his thoughts so I have no clue what's being said.

It's deliberate on Culebra's part, a mental barrier as impenetrable as the rock walls surrounding us. There's only one thing coming through loud and clear.

His concern for the injured man.

Culebra calls out for help.

A familiar figure appears at the door. Thin, slump-shouldered, mid-forties, human. His pale face and sallow complexion make him look like he spends very little time out of the confines of the cave. He's dressed in clean jeans and a polo shirt. He nods his head in my direction, an acknowledgment and greeting.

I've met him twice before. He took care of David once and then kept Frey and Culebra alive while I battled the witch holding them in a spell. He is a doctor who lost his license in the states most likely because of the drug habit his slightly trembling hands signify he has not yet shaken. But clean or not, he knows his stuff and he wastes no time getting to work.

He has Culebra pour hot water into a basin. He grabs sterile cloths and bottles of some sharp-smelling liquid. He soaks the cloths in the water and gently washes away the blood and dirt, exposing the wound. He disinfects it, uses his fingers to examine the cut, poking and pulling at the skin until he seems satisfied. Then he covers the wound with a butterfly bandage.

During all this, his patient moans softly but doesn't try to pull away. Culebra lays a reassuring hand on his arm. "*Fácil*, Ramon."

I look hard at Culebra. Ramon, huh?

The doctor spends a moment longer probing the guy's scalp, feeling, I suppose, for any swelling that might indicate a contusion. Next he shines a bright, pinpoint of LED light from what looks like a small flashlight into his patient's eyes, first one, then the other.

Finally, he pats the guy on the shoulder and looks at Culebra. "He should be fine. The cut looked worse than it is because of the blood. He doesn't need stitches. He has a knot on his head but there are no obvious signs of concussion. His eyes react correctly to light and are focusing. How long was he wandering around?"

He looks to Culebra, who looks to me for the answer to that question, but I can only shrug. "I don't know. I found him about half an hour ago."

Culebra addresses the question to the wounded man. He replies in Spanish, which Culebra translates for us. "Maybe four hours. He's not sure. His car broke down and his cell phone went dead. He thought he was headed toward Tijuana. When he fell, he hit his head and had trouble getting up. That's when Anna found him."

"Lucky thing she did. And lucky this is winter and not summer. Dehydration isn't indicated, but it won't hurt to get some water into him. Keep him awake. Can't rule out concussion yet. If he starts vomiting or acting strange, let me know right away."

Culebra thanks him and the doctor disappears back into the cave. I realize I have yet to learn his name. He's like a genie, here when you summon him, retreating back into his bottle, or most likely needle or pipe, when you don't.

Culebra is helping the man, Ramon, off the gurney. He seems suddenly to remember that I'm in the room, too. "Thank you for bringing my friend here." He says it like he's dismissing me. His eyes are distant.

I'm not one who is easily dismissed, especially when it comes to a stranger who called Culebra a name I'd never heard before. "Why did he call you Tomás?"

"Anna, please. You should go."

Probably should. But I'm not. Whoever this Ramon is, he doesn't know the name Culebra. Why? And I found him wandering in the desert a few miles from Beso de la Muerte. Not Tijuana.

"You recognized him. I saw it. Who is he?"

Ramon is on his feet, looking better now that most of the blood has been wiped from his face. He squares off, standing on his own, stepping away from Culebra's supporting arm. Looking my way, then back to Culebra, he says something so quietly, I only catch a word or two.

But it's enough. I recognize one of the words. *Hermano.* And another. *Peligro.*

"*Hermano?* Culebra, he's your brother? Is he in danger?"

Each time I use the name Culebra, the injured man seems puzzled. It's obvious to whom I'm speaking, but it's just as obvious that this man has no idea why I keep referring to him as a snake—the translation.

I ask the question again. "Is this your brother?"

Culebra takes my arm and steers me none too gently toward the door that leads to the path outside. Tension radiates from his body, vibrates through his grip. *Yes. I will explain later. Right now I need time with him.*

Is he in trouble? Can I help?

For a moment, a spark of the old Culebra, of my friend, softens the lines of strain on his face. He releases my arm. "I'm sorry. I don't know why Ramon is here. But he won't talk in front of a stranger. Please, you need to go. I'll call you when I can."

There is a tone in his voice, a shadow in his eyes that I've never seen before. I don't recognize what it is, but I do recognize that he is *asking* me to leave.

Reluctantly, I agree. But as I leave him and start back to the car, I'm digging my cell phone from my purse. My gut is screaming and I've learned never to ignore the sign.

I scroll to a name and hit Send.

"Max?"

"Anna?" He sounds as surprised to hear my voice, as I am to have called him.

"I need to talk to you. I think Culebra may be in trouble."

MAX HAS AN APARTMENT IN SOUTH BAY, AN AREA OF Chula Vista. I'd spent time here a lifetime ago. A lot of time.

Nothing has changed. When he ushers me in, I recognize the same furniture, functional, plain, arranged in the same way. Couch on one wall, two chairs on another, a TV stand with components against the third. Nothing personal adorns the walls or the end table or coffee table. There are empty pizza boxes stacked in a corner near the door and a green recycle bin filled with empty beer bottles poised next to it. I find myself shaking my head.

No signs of a real human life. This is just a stopping place between undercover assignments. I imagine nothing has changed in the bedroom, either. Something I have no desire or interest to find out.

Max wastes no time peppering me with questions as soon as I'm inside.

The only problem is, I can't answer any of them. I don't know anything except a few sketchy details. So I tell him what happened. How I found the guy. That Culebra called him Ramon.

Max reacts to the name. "Ramon? Are you sure?"

I nod. "Did you know Culebra had a brother?"

"He doesn't."

"He must. Ramon used the word '*hermano*' and Culebra called Ramon his brother. I couldn't follow their entire conversation, but one of them is in danger. I understood that much."

Max is shaking his head. "Ramon is not his brother. At least not in the way you're thinking. But you're right about one of them being in danger. Ramon was a member of the cartel Culebra worked for. If he's here, it may mean someone has tracked Culebra down. Either Ramon came to warn him or he came to kill him."

CHAPTER 14

IT'S AMAZING HOW PERSPECTIVE CHANGES WITH CIR-
cumstance. A week ago, when I heard Culebra's story for
the first time, a threat from his past might have evoked a
reaction of ambivalence. After all, you lay down with cartel
dogs, you get up with cartel fleas.

Now, all I see is the look in Culebra's eyes when he
asked me to leave. I recognize what it was now. He wanted
me out of harm's way. He knew if he became combative or
ordered me to leave, I'd dig in my heels and refuse to go.
He chose the one way that guaranteed my cooperation.

He asked nicely.

Shit. I'm on my feet. "We need to get back to Culebra.
Now."

Max doesn't argue. "Let me get my gun."

He disappears into the bedroom and returns a moment
later with a jacket and his weapon. The Glock is in a com-
pact Blackhawk! slide holster with a pouch for an extra
mag. A lot of firepower. Makes me realize he takes the situation seriously.

"Do you need a gun?" he asks me, clipping the Glock to his belt. He grabs a duffel bag from the corner as he talks.

I shake my head. The last time he provided me with a weapon it was a big 45 that I ended up getting shot with. No. Vampires come armed. Naturally.

"Let me drive," he says, steering me toward the alley in back. "Ramon will know your car. He hasn't seen mine."

His vehicle is a big Ford Explorer, a couple of years and a lot of miles old. It's covered with dirt on the outside, littered with fast-food containers and empty coffee cups on the inside. There's a tarp pulled over the cargo section in back and even that's littered with papers and old newspapers.

I scoop an armful of *stuff* out of the passenger seat and toss it into the back. I don't have to say a word. My obvious disgust is evident in body language as I rub an old napkin over the seat and gingerly lower myself onto what I hope is not a sticky surface.

"Sorry," Max mumbles, tossing the duffel into the back on top of the debris. "Been on surveillance most of the last two weeks. Wasn't expecting company."

"Obviously."

He cranks the engine over and lead foots it into the street. He flips a switch and above the visor, red and blue LED lights start pulsing.

"Pretty slick. Didn't even see them."

He shoots me one of those disdainful looks that states the obvious. *You aren't supposed to.*

We blaze our way toward the freeway. Max concentrates on the driving. I concentrate on what I can do to this Ramon to make him talk. Vampire stirs in anticipation.

Once we're clear of city streets and on our way to the border, I ask Max about Ramon. Had Max come in contact with him in an official capacity?

Max keeps both hands on the wheel and his eyes on the road when he answers. "No. My focus has been primarily on the area here, near Tijuana. Ramon and Culebra operated out of the golden triangle—Chihuahua, Durango and Sinaloa."

"But you recognized the name."

"Culebra mentioned a Ramon as someone he grew up with, someone who came up with him through the ranks." He shakes his head. "It's a common enough name but from the way you describe Culebra's reaction when he saw him, I'll bet it's his old cartel buddy."

"How did he find Culebra? What's he doing here after all these years?" The questions are more to give voice to thoughts twirling around my head than directed at Max.

Still, he answers. "There's a lot of infighting going on between the cartels. Who knows what old vendettas are being stirred up? Culebra left a lot of enemies behind. Maybe not everyone believed he died in the car wreck. Culebra goes into Tijuana occasionally. Maybe someday recognized him. The guys he crossed don't give up easily. They may have been trying to track him down for years."

His tone suggests he knows more about Culebra's past than what I learned on Christmas Eve. "There's more? Tell me."

"I don't know all of it." His eyes slide toward me. "I think it's best if you ask Culebra."

He shuts down. The set of his jaw tells me I'm not going to get anything more. I turn back in my seat and face the road. We're approaching the border. I fish my passport out of the pocket of my jeans in preparation but Max pulls around the tourist lanes and into the law enforcement turnout lane. He exchanges a few words with an officer on duty, flashes his badge, and we're once more on our way.

I slide my passport into the glove compartment with my wallet. No sense taking a chance of losing them.

This time when we head into Beso de la Muerte, the street is deserted. I get the gut-churning feeling that we may be too late, that something bad has already happened. Max slips his gun into his hand and we approach the bar's swinging doors, noiselessly, both of us on alert.

I touch Max's arm and he stops. I lift my face, sniffing

for a scent of human, listening for a heartbeat, probing to pick up the stray thought of a vamp or shape-shifter inside.

Nothing. A shake of my head and Max and I push open the doors.

The bar is empty. The quiet presses in, an unnatural quiet. The tables are still littered with bottles and glasses, some half full.

Culebra sent everyone away.

The gut churning gets more intense. I'd found the bar abandoned like this once before. It was not a good omen then. Odds are, it's not a good omen now.

CHAPTER 15

MAX PICKS UP A BEER BOTTLE FROM ONE OF THE tables, swirls the contents. "Still cold."

"Let's try the cave."

We get into the car and drive around to the mouth of the cave. I know before we get out, though, what we'll find. When I call out for the doctor, I get an empty echo in reply. We make a cursory sweep, but just like the bar, the cave has been abandoned.

A light is on in one of the living areas, a cup of coffee, still hot, sits on a table in another.

"Can you pick up a trail?" Max asks me. "You know Culebra's scent. Is there anything you can follow?"

Only the obvious. I lead Max out to a space near the back door of the bar. Where the scent ends. I point to tire tracks. "They took his truck."

"That's a start," Max says. "You can track a truck, can't you?"

"I can't. Vampire can. You'll never be able to keep up."

He frowns in irritation. "So, what are you telling me? You're going off on your own?"

"I have to. Listen, stay here. I'll call you when I figure out what direction they're going. You can follow and we'll connect up as soon as we can. They don't have much of a head start. It shouldn't take long."

Max has enough knowledge of vampires to know it's the only logical course of action. Doesn't mean he likes it. His frown intensifies. "You will call me."

"Yes. I will—"

As if channeling the telephone, mine rings. When I see who is calling, and realize that I've been gone much longer than the couple of hours I intended to be, I grit my teeth and open the call.

"Stephen. God, I am so sorry."

"Where are you?"

He doesn't sound angry, just puzzled. And he doesn't wait for me to respond. "I got back early. I've been waiting at the cottage since two. It's almost five. Are you on your way home? Susan wants us to come for dinner tonight."

Inwardly, I groan. "I can't. Something came up. You go. Give Susan my love."

"Are you sure? Are you on a job?"

"Yes." Sort of. "I don't know when I'll be home. Why don't I meet you at your place when I'm done?"

"Will it be late?"

Most likely. "It may be."

He makes a clucking noise in the receiver. "I'm only home one night and you run out on me. Good thing I'm an understanding kind of guy. Say hello to David and Tracey for me. And Anna?"

"Yes?"

"Be careful."

He ends the call.

At least I didn't have to explain that I'm not with David and Tracey. He doesn't know Max or *about* Max. Wonder if he'd be so understanding if he knew I was with an old boyfriend? Or that I was on my way to track another old friend into Mexican drug territory?

God. There was no aggravation in his voice, no sarcasm. He trusts me completely. I get the sinking feeling that maybe he shouldn't.

Max is watching me, having no doubt read between the lines of the conversation. "You've been with this guy, what? Five minutes? And you're lying to him already?"

I feel the hair stir on the back of my neck. "I didn't lie to him."

He snorts. "Only by omission. You know fucking well there's a good chance you're not going to be meeting him tonight. Maybe not tomorrow night, either. Does he know about this place? About Culebra?"

I turn away, snapping my phone shut and slipping it into my jacket. The truth is, Stephen doesn't know about Beso de la Muerte or Culebra. Not yet. When he's in town, he lets me feed from him. When he's gone and I need to feed, I come here. We haven't been together that long. There's been no reason to tell him.

When I don't respond, Max throws up his hands. "Another stupid mortal under the thrall of a vampire. Yeah, I heard you tell Culebra he knows that you're a vampire. At least that's something."

There's that flash of bitterness again. He thinks I cast a spell to get Stephen? Does he think I cast a spell over him when we were involved?

I swallow back the anger. I'm not about to get into a pissing contest neither of us can win. This isn't the time. I ignore Max and start to examine the tire tracks. They lead off to the south, away from the border and into the desert.

"I'll call you" is all I say before trotting off, summoning the vampire to the surface. Both of us are happy to leave the confines of a mortal existence and the dark antagonism of the man I feel staring after me.

Freedom is in the rush of wind on my face as I pick up speed. Darkness is close, which makes tracking easier. Just as animals distinguish the tracks of predator and prey, I distinguish the marks of Culebra's vehicle in the dirt. The right front tire has a nick in the outer rim. I pick up the smell of oil and exhaust.

I welcome full darkness when it falls. There is no moon, which makes senses more acute, vision sharper. The truck I follow goes deeper into the desert, shuns the lights of Tijuana and the scattered shantytowns on its outskirts. There are many smells here—animal and human. Cooking meat. Frying lard. Offal. Nothing tempts the vampire. I am well fed.

There are roads here, too, but the truck travels on none of them. It continues on dirt and hardscrabble going east. It will make the going harder and slower for the vehicle, faster and easier for the vampire.

It only takes thirty minutes to spot it. In the distance, a plume of dust. I run to catch up, careful to stay out of sight and when I see the silhouettes of two men inside, catch Culebra's scent from the open window, only then do I stop to let the human Anna return.

I pull out my phone, call up Max's number and hit send. He picks up on the first ring.

"Where are you?"

I look around. "I'm not really sure. About forty-five minutes east of Tijuana. The truck is a mile or so ahead of me."

"Any road markers?"

"No road. Staying to the desert."

There's a pause. "That doesn't make sense. The terrain is going to get too rough for Culebra's old truck. They must be afraid someone's watching the main roads." Another pause while I assume he's checking the map. "What are your GPS coordinates?"

I touch the "maps" app on the face of my phone, find the GPS coordinates and read what pops up on the screen. Max sends me his location and I scroll to it on the map.

"Look," Max says finally, "this may be a long shot. But I think they might be headed for Tecate. There are a couple of private airstrips there."

"What kind of private airstrips?"

"The 'no questions asked' kind of private airstrips. The kind you'd use if you want to reach the interior quickly and quietly. Do you know Tecate?"

"Not really. David and I tracked a skip to the border crossing at Tecate once, but we caught up with him before he made it across."

"It's not that big. Keep following them. If I'm right, they'll be stopping soon. Call as soon as they do so I know where to meet you. If I'm wrong and they head in another direction, let me know that, too. I'm starting out now. Sticking to the main roads will make the trip much shorter. I can be there in forty minutes tops."

The last thing I hear before he disconnects is the rumble of the Ford's engine as he cranks it over.

Culebra's truck is still moving. But I begin to realize Max may be right when the lights of a city I can only guess is Tecate blink in the distance. He'd better make it fast. I can track anything across the ground, but if Culebra and Ramon take off in a plane, for us, the trail comes to a screeching halt.

CHAPTER 16

To a vampire's acute senses, Tecate is a town caught between ocean and desert. Close enough to catch the sea breeze, smelling of sand and brine, far enough away to have a desert landscape of cactus and sand. The perfume of the ocean is often swept away by the smell of hot dust and decay. A dichotomy that tickles my nose.

The way is rough, but rougher still for the truck. It bounces and lurches, slow going.

Not for me. It gives me a chance to catch up, to get so close I see Ramon smoking in the passenger seat and smell the smoke drifting out through the open window.

So close I could speed up and ride the rest of the way, hunkering down on the rear bumper of the pickup.

But I don't.

There's too much about this scenario I don't understand. I don't trust.

Finally, with the city in sight, Culebra steers onto a dirt road that appears abruptly out of the hardscrabble and curves away from Tecate. He picks up speed and we begin to pass an area of industrial buildings—warehouses, if I had to guess. The parking lots are nearly empty, only one or two cars scattered in front of the few buildings with lights still burning.

I look around out of a human's eye now, trying to pinpoint something to let Max know where we are.

I get my chance when the truck veers again, this time onto a paved road. A sign says CUCHUMA. He keeps going. I stop and call Max.

"We're on a road called Cuchuma," I say when he picks up. "Here are the coordinates."

Max waits to reply until he sees what I've sent. "Good. I know where you're headed. I should be there in fifteen minutes. Cuchuma connects with a road called Del Carmen. They'll take Del Carmen south and turn onto an unmarked road. Keep following. You're almost to the airstrip. There's an abandoned outbuilding about a half mile from the airstrip. Meet me there."

I snap the phone shut and let the vampire surface again. Now that I know where we're going, I can enjoy the freedom of the run. I let my animal senses pick up the smells of rock and desert, vermin and predator. Fox is here and snake and rabbit and coyote. Coyote spies me and lowers its head, growling. Its rumble attracts its brothers, hiding in the brush. It's the way coyote hunts—one to lure an unsuspecting victim, then the others to attack as a pack. They smell human but something else, too. Animal.

My growl convinces them to go on to easier prey. They back off, deep-throated rumbling changing from challenge to irritated submission.

Vampire bares her teeth in a smile.

The truck is at the junction to Del Carmen. It turns as Max predicted. Vampire relinquishes control to the human Anna. Pace slows, thought processes center now on what to do when Culebra gets to the airstrip. Should I try to stop them if they have a plane waiting to take off? How far behind is Max?

The airstrip is ahead. I follow out of sight until the truck comes to a stop beside a ramshackle building. There are lights on inside and the two men go in.

A quick look toward the runway and one decision is made for me.

There's no plane.

I backtrack and wait at the abandoned building for Max. I scramble up the wall to the roof so I have a clear view of the area. If a plane approaches, I will see it. In a matter of minutes, both Max and a plane arrive simultaneously. I launch myself off the building, landing by Max's Explorer. The move is quick and from the look on Max's face, I may have taken ten years off his life.

"Jesus, Anna. Do you fucking fly now?"

Maybe.

"Go." I jump into the passenger seat. "A twin-engine plane just landed."

Max pushes the accelerator to the floor but his eyes are still wide, his breath coming in startled gasps.

We slow when we get within sight of the building where Culebra and Ramon are waiting. The approach of the Explorer is silenced by the noise from the plane. Max kills the engine and coasts to a stop behind a cluster of bushes. I expect Culebra and Ramon to come out to meet the plane. But instead, the pilot shuts down the engine and disappears into the building, too.

Max and I look at each other. He unclips his gun and motions to the car door. We let ourselves out quietly, approach in stealth mode. The door to the building is open, the light spilling out offering a clear view of three men inside.

Culebra's back is to us.

He turns, eyes narrowing.

I clamp down on my thoughts, hoping I haven't inadvertently given myself away.

He steps out before Max and I can take cover.

"Come out, Anna. You, too, Max. I could sense you were following. We've been waiting for you."

CHAPTER 17

M AX AND I LOOK AT EACH OTHER.

My sudden awareness that Culebra knew I was tracking him makes my first reaction, confusion, veer quickly to anger. "If you knew I was following you, why didn't you stop?"

"I'm sorry, Anna."

"You're *sorry*? If you wanted us to come with you, why didn't you simply ask Max and me? Why chase me away in Beso and then make me track you like a damned bloodhound?"

He doesn't react to my anger with anger of his own. Instead, his body and face reflect a willingness to endure whatever taunts I choose to fling his way. He stands quietly and waits.

Which, predictably, takes the wind out of my vitriolic sails and leaves me staring back at him feeling like a kid who just threw a tantrum in a toy shop.

After a moment, he says, "I know how angry you were at Christmas. Because I hid certain things from you. The anger is justified. I also know if I told you the reason Ramon came to see me, you'd feel obligated to help regardless of your personal feelings. I wanted to give you and Max a chance to decide on your own if you want to get involved."

He looks at me, dark eyes piercing and intent. "This is cartel business. It won't be pretty and it won't be easy. Once you hear the story, you can come with Ramon and me or go back home. Either way, I appreciate the trouble you've taken. You came after me. You've shown your loyalty and concern."

"But now that we're here, you intend to ask more of us than a show of loyalty and concern."

He lets a cold smile touch the corners of his eyes and lips. "I do. Yes."

At least now you're being honest. The same bitterness that sparked my outburst moments before is back.

Again, Culebra doesn't reply in kind. It's frustrating. I realize I'm spoiling for a fight, looking for an excuse to pull out and leave Culebra to his "cartel business." But Culebra knows me too well. He's not giving me the chance.

Ramon has come outside and stands beside him. In the doorway, the silhouette of the pilot is outlined against the bright interior. He has what is clearly recognizable as a rifle in his hands. It's cradled in his arms and not pointed at us. I suppose that's another good sign.

Culebra motions to the door. "Let's go inside. Please. We have much to discuss."

I look at Max. He shrugs and holsters his gun. We follow Culebra and Ramon into the building. Once we're inside, Culebra pulls the door closed and snaps the deadbolt.

"Is that to keep someone else out or to keep us in?" I ask.

"Both."

It's said with a half smile and hopeful spark of humor.

I don't smile back.

Culebra drops his eyes and the smile and takes his place at the head of a long table. The surface is scattered with maps and charts. He beckons for us to join him.

Max does. I take a moment to look around. The inside of

this place is bare wood—walls and floors. No furniture except for the table and a couple of folding chairs that look like they've spent a good deal of time in the elements. The paint is scoured and peeling. No windows. The light comes from a single, high-wattage bulb suspended from a ceiling joist, wires dangling down the side of one wall and plugged into the only outlet I can see.

That's it. Not much in the way of a hideout.

I take the step to the table. The pilot doesn't join us. He leans his thin frame against the wall opposite the door, his eyes shifting continuously from Max to me. I can't tell how old he is, his complexion is as scoured as the furniture, but his face is gaunt and severe, his lips pressed in a hard line that emphasizes the frown lines etched around his mouth. He has the animal magnetism of a Benicio Del Toro. The same hooded dark eyes, the same heavy eyelids. He's dressed in khaki pants and a black hoodie. I think *he* thinks he's generating an air of watchful vigilance when in fact, his posture screams "bomb with a short fuse." He hasn't leaned the rifle against the wall, either. It's still at the ready in his arms.

I keep him in my line of sight as I turn my attention to Culebra.

He and Ramon are talking with Max. When I look at Ramon, I remember how Max said he and Culebra met. Max found Culebra wandering in the desert. I found Ramon wandering in the desert. Somehow I doubt Ramon and I are headed for the same kind of relationship. He hasn't said a word to me. He hasn't even looked at me. Is it because I'm female or is it because he knows I'm vampire?

Culebra draws my attention with a wave of his hand. He points to something on the map. When I take my place beside Max, Culebra says, "We're headed here—outside Reynosa. About twelve hundred miles as the crow flies, almost to the Gulf."

"There's some fierce infighting going on in the area," Max says. "Between the old drug lords and members of Los Martillos."

I know the name. Everyone who lives on or near the border knows the name. Los Martillos are a band of ex-military thugs used as enforcers. Probably learned their trade at the same "school" as Culebra. "I hope that isn't what this is about," I say.

"Indirectly, it is."

Once again, a spark in my gut flares out as indignation. "You aren't seriously telling us that you're getting involved in drug shit again."

His eyes snap to mine. "It's not that simple."

Max holds up a hand in a conciliatory gesture. "Hear him out, Anna. We've been after some of these guys for a long time. Particularly Pablo Santiago. He has bounties on his head in Mexico and the United States. If there's a chance we could nail him or one of his cronies, it's worth a shot."

"What's worth a shot? We haven't heard what Culebra wants us to do."

Ramon may not completely understand the words passing between Max, Culebra and me, but there's certainly no misunderstanding my tone or expression. He barks something to Culebra. Culebra replies quietly and Ramon turns on his heels and stalks off to join the pilot.

I feel a flush of color creep up my neck. "Tell Ramon I know what *puta* means," I snap.

"I did," Culebra replies. "He's sorry."

Right. Neither Ramon's expression nor tone was apologetic.

"You might also remind him that I saved his life."

"I did that, too," Culebra says. "Listen, Anna, just hear me out. I was serious when I said I wouldn't force you to do anything you don't want to do. This isn't just about a battle between cartels. This is a family situation. Ramon's family. His wife and kids. They're in danger. He saved my life once. I owe it to him to try to save his."

"So what happened? His count turn up short? He steal a bag of coke?"

Culebra skewers me with eyes like steel knives. "Worse. He killed his boss's son."

Max whistles under his breath. "Santiago's son?"

"No. If he had done that, he'd already be dead," Culebra replies, his tone sharp. "No, this is the son of one of Santiago's lieutenants. A banking official in the government and an important link in the narco money chain. His son's death is causing problems for Santiago."

"So, what did the kid have to do with anything? Why'd Ramon kill him?" I ask.

Culebra casts a glance over at Ramon who responds with a nod.

"First you have to understand, growing up here is not the same as in the States. A good education is not available to all, prospects are few. One does what he must to provide for his family. Ramon's parents were poor farmers. When Ramon saw a chance to improve his situation, he took it."

I cut in with an impatient wave of my hand. "I don't know where this is going, but if you're about to tell me Ramon became a hired killer to put food on the table, I will tell you right now I don't care. I came because I thought *you* were in trouble. If it's not your life in danger, I'm out of here. I couldn't care less what happens to your cartel buddy."

A spark, dangerous, threatening, flashes in Culebra's eyes. He says so softly, I almost miss it, "So you pick and choose the monsters you fight now, huh? Your vow to protect the weak applies only to those you deem worthy."

An angry reply leaps to my lips, but I stifle it, aware that there are others here who don't know who or what I am. I turn my bitterness inward, projecting it to Culebra through my thoughts.

Don't do it, Culebra. Don't play the guilt card. You of all people know what I've done since accepting responsibility as the Chosen One. I sent my family half a world away. I hold my few human friends at arm's distance. I've given up a lot. I won't be coerced into helping a stranger who's in trouble because of his own stupid choices.

Max is unaware of what I've said to Culebra, but he interjects himself into the tense silence. "Maybe you should at least hear him out, Anna. If not for Ramon, then because this may be an opportunity to take a major player out of the game. Santiago is a big fish. Landing him would be a coup." He looks at Culebra. "For both our governments."

Resistance to getting involved still churns my stomach. "But he didn't kill Santiago's son," I remind Max. "How do you think going after this bank official will get you close to Santiago?"

"Because it's Santiago who is gunning for Ramon now," Culebra says. "Just as the boss came after me thirty years ago. Ramon inconvenienced Santiago. He doesn't care about the kid Ramon killed. The kid doesn't matter. He'll wipe out Ramon's entire family to send a message. Unless we can stop it."

Everyone in the room is looking at me. The pilot and Ramon with overt hostility, Culebra and Max with patience. As if they already know I'll give in.

I kick one of the chairs away from the table and sit, arms crossed over my chest.

"Okay, I'll listen. But this better be one motherfucker of a compelling story."

CHAPTER 18

CULEBRA CALLS RAMON TO JOIN US. *"DÍGALE."*

Ramon looks at me, frowning. *"¿Por qué? Ella no los ayuda."*

"Confíeen me. Tell her what you told me," Culebra insists. "Tell her your story."

Ramon shakes his head. His expression is stony, unconvinced by Culebra's urging.

"Anna can help us," Culebra says, more forcefully this time. "I want her to help us. You need to make her understand."

Ramon locks eyes with Culebra. He says something in Spanish that I translate as asking how I, a woman, could help. It is said with the condescending air of a man who is not used to asking help from a woman. Who is downright adverse to the idea.

I look from Max to Culebra. Both are looking at me as if they expect me to try to convince him. By doing what? I'm not about to share my true nature, but I was a bounty hunter long before I was made vampire. Maybe if I show

Ramon I can handle myself as well as any man, that I'm more than a pretty face, it would appease his macho sensibilities.

I stalk over to the pilot, hold out my hand for the rifle. Predictably, he straightens and pulls back, swinging the butt of the rifle toward me. Before he completes the arc, I've got both hands on the gun and with a twist of my hands, I've wrested it from his. He lunges toward me. I sidestep and he lands on the floor. With one foot on the small of his back, I toss the rifle onto the table.

For a moment, I think Ramon is still going to refuse. He's glaring at the pilot, at Culebra, at me.

"Fine," I snap, getting tired of the game. "If Ramon wants me to leave, I will."

Culebra holds up a hand to stop me. "Ramon?"

The pilot is climbing to his feet, red-faced and angry, when Ramon finally gives in with a rush of breath. He tosses the rifle back to the pilot and tells him to go outside.

The pilot does, with a parting glare to me that makes it clear I haven't made a new friend. Great. One more enemy to add to the list. I shoot Culebra a look that says this better be worth it.

When the door closes, Ramon parks his butt on the corner of the table and closes his eyes. For a moment. When he opens them again, they no longer focus on me but have that intent look of someone gazing inward to a place of shadow and pain.

He speaks, slowly, as if translating from his native language into English as he goes. "I had a son. Antonio. Only fifteen."

I think he's also speaking slowly because he's choosing his words carefully, so I will understand. With an effort, I push away my suspicions, clear my mind to listen.

"He was a quiet boy. A good student. He attended the same school as many of the sons of government officials. One of these boys, Rójan, was a . . ." He pauses, looks to Culebra. *"Matón."*

"Bully," Culebra says.

I nod.

"One day he and several others found my son alone in the schoolyard. They told him he was to be their 'bitch' and knocked him to the ground. They opened their pants, urinated on him." Ramon rubs a hand over his face. Refocuses to continue. "He tried to fight back, punching and kicking. But there were five of them. They said he needed to learn respect for his betters."

Another quick intake of breath. "The other boys held my son, pulled his pants down while Rójan, the *poquenõ bastardo*, raped him."

Ramon's voice catches, then turns cold. "My son was humiliated, his self-esteem destroyed. He didn't come to me. He knew Rójan was protected by his powerful family and would not suffer for his actions. So he withdrew. The shame built up inside him until he could no longer endure the pain. Within a month, he took his own life."

Ramon draws a deep breath, wipes his eyes with the back of his hand. "He left a note. Apologizing to us, his family, for what had been done to him. As if it had been his fault. As if he had shamed us. He *apologized*." He spits the word, his face hardening with rage. "I knew I had to avenge my son. At first, I wanted to kill Rójan's father. But then *sino*—" He looks to Culebra again.

"Fate," Culebra replies.

"*Sí.* Fate intervened. A few weeks after we buried Antonio, I was walking in the woods near our home. I heard a young woman crying. I found a couple lying in the shade. The boy was on top, but they were not making love. The girl was fighting and sobbing and begging him to stop. Her blouse was torn, her skirt pushed up around her waist. She was being raped. When I realized who the boy was, I was consumed by a fury that turned my blood to fire. It was Rójan."

Again he stops, composing himself, crossing his arms tightly across his chest, drawing deep breaths.

In spite of my suspicions, I am spellbound by his anguish. I understand it. I've lived it twice. Once, when I was made vampire through an act of rape. Again, when I found out my niece Trish was being abused by men who paid her mother to make videos of their sick acts, robbing a young girl of her innocence. All I could think about was exacting vengeance. I see the same hatred in Ramon's eyes now.

Culebra reads the emotions running through my mind. His eyes catch and hold mine. This is what he wanted me to hear—to understand.

I glance away to Max. His face betrays no emotion. He has heard Ramon's story or one like it many times before. I know in spite of the indifference he projects, his gut is churning the same as mine, the same as Culebra's. I also know he will do everything he can to exact justice for Ramon and his son. I know it because in spite of how I feel about him personally, Max is a good man.

Culebra touches Ramon's arm, nods at him to go on.

Ramon unfolds his arms, his shoulders relax a little, his back straightens. "I grabbed Rójan off the girl, held him while the girl got away. All the while, Rójan cursed me, threatening what his father could do to me, to my family. Threats I knew he could make good.

"It didn't matter. I punched him until he had no fight left. I took his belt, and used mine to bind his hands and feet to a tree. Then I slapped his face to arouse him. I showed him my knife. I told him what he had done to my son cost Antonio his life. I told him he would never rape anyone again. He merely laughed."

Ramon's voice turns cold. "Until I stabbed him. I stabbed him and watched as the life slowly ebbed from his body. Then I left him to die."

His eyes grow hard. "But it wasn't enough. I wanted him humiliated in death the way he humiliated my son in life. I thought when they found him like this, tied to a tree and stuck like the pig he was, he would be denied the noble death that befitted the son of an important government minister."

I find myself asking softly, "Someone found out that it

was you that killed him? Is that why your family is in danger?"

"*Sí.*" He wipes at his eyes again. "A few days later, I saw an article in the local paper. The police found the body of a young girl in a garbage dump. I recognized the photo. It was the girl who had been with Rójan. She was killed to silence her. With no witness to challenge the facts of Rójan's death, he was given a hero's funeral. It was said he died in a plane crash." Ramon spits at the ground. "He was called a hero.

"The girl must have told someone that Rójan had raped her. She may have even recognized me since I was often in town. I knew it was only a matter of time before the minister would seek his own revenge. I moved my family. But there is a price on their heads. I have to do something to save them. Get them out of the country." He stares intently at Max. "I am willing to help your government if they will protect my family."

Max exhales sharply, as if he'd been holding his breath during Ramon's story. The first physical reaction he's exhibited to Ramon's story. "We'll do what we can."

Culebra looks at me. But there's no question in his gaze. He knows my answer.

Shit. "I'm in."

How could I not be? My attacker is dead. The men who attacked Trish are either dead or in jail. What happened to Ramon's son had nothing to do with drugs and everything to do with human degradation. "Ramon, I am sorry for the loss of your son."

For the first time, Ramon's eyes are not full of uncertainty and disdain when they meet mine, but a glimmer of hope. He turns to the door. *"Consigue el plano listo para ir."*

He walks outside to ready the plane for takeoff. I turn to Culebra. I picked up something in his thoughts while Ramon was relating his story that makes me peer into his eyes.

"You lost someone in the same way?"

He smiles, a sad, slow tilting of the lips. "Every village has its bullies like Rójan. When I was twelve, my sister was attacked. She didn't survive."

There's more, I can tell by the way he's protecting his thoughts, not letting me read them. He doesn't give me a chance to ask about it, either, but with a pat on my arm leaves to join Ramon and the pilot.

Max is as quiet as I, lost in his thoughts the way I'm lost in mine. Culebra's insistence that we help Ramon makes sense now. We—Culebra, Ramon and I—share a terrible, common experience. We've all seen loved ones hurt by another's hand.

Max draws my attention with a wave of his hand, as if hit with a sudden thought.

"You'd better call Stephen before we take off," he says, pointing to his watch. "It's already late. Let him know—" He falters.

I sigh. "Yeah. Let him know what?" But I know Max is right. I dig my cell out of my pocket and ring Stephen. He picks up right away.

"Anna? Where are you? I've been worried."

"Sorry, Stephen. The job is going to take longer than I expected. I'm going out of town. I wish I could tell you how long, but I'm not sure."

"So, David and Tracey are going with you?"

Uh-oh. Something in his tone gives me pause. "Why do you ask?"

"You're not with them, are you?"

Ice is forming through the phone lines. To make matters worse, I feel Max's eyes on me. Fuck it. "No."

"Well, at least this time you're being honest. I talked to David an hour ago. Why would you lie to me? Why would you let me think you were with them?"

"I didn't lie to you. And if you'll recall, you hung up before I could tell you who I was with."

As soon as I say it, I know I've sunk myself deeper into the pit. Sure enough, Stephen counters with, "Well, here's your chance to set the record straight. Who are you with and what are you doing?"

From outside, the sound of the plane engine roars into life. I grab at it like a lifeline, an excuse to cut the conversation short. "I'm sorry, Stephen, I have to go. I'll call you when I can."

This time, before Stephen can respond, I disconnect. I look over at Max. He's giving me one of those "I told you so" looks. I give him one of those "fuck you" looks and narrow my eyes. "Don't say it. Not a fucking word."

CHAPTER 19

I HAVE NO IDEA WHAT KIND OF RESCUE PLAN CULEBRA and Ramon have in mind, or how Max and I will be involved. At this moment, it doesn't matter. Ramon's story compels me to help him.

Even the turbulence we hit as the small plane is buffeted by wind blowing off the hills doesn't bother me.

The acid churning my gut is not from the prospect of danger or the choppy ride. It's caused by the thought that I don't know if Stephen will be waiting for me when we get back. Why in the world didn't I tell him what I'm doing? It's like I have a chronic aversion to telling the truth even when there's no need to lie. Is it because he's human? Is it because Max is an unhappy reminder of what happens when I'm honest with a mortal partner?

I rest my head against the seat, close my eyes. My scorecard with boyfriends is pretty bleak. Human or supernatural, it doesn't seem to make a difference. I either piss them off, scare them away or kill them. Stephen deserved better. Of all of them, he was the best. I really liked him.

Liked him. I'm already thinking of him in past tense.

"Anna?"

I open one eye. Max has taken the seat next to me. I pull myself upright. "What?"

"We'll be landing in about thirty minutes. Are you all right?"

"Peachy. I've probably lost the nicest boyfriend I've ever had." I give him the fish eye. "Present company included."

He shrugs. "Maybe you have, maybe you haven't. Won't do you any good to obsess about it. We're going into a dangerous situation. Best get your head straight."

I bite back the sarcastic "no shit" comeback that almost springs from my lips and ask instead, "What's the plan?"

"My guess? When we land, we'll go straight to the safe house where Ramon has his family. We'll figure the rest from there."

"Does Ramon know about me?"

"That you're vampire? I'm not sure. He and Culebra have spent the flight talking but I get the impression it's more catching up than anything else. Those two were close once upon a time. There's a lot of history."

Max gets quiet for a moment. "You were thinking about Trish when Ramon spoke of what happened to his son, weren't you?"

Max was around during the time Trish came into my life. He knows what happened to her. He doesn't know what happened to me—not all of it—not about the rape that resulted in my becoming vampire. We were dating then and I couldn't bring myself to speak to him about it. I still can't.

I simply nod.

"I was, too," he says. "Is she doing well now?"

So well it makes me smile. "Yes. She and my folks were just here for a visit. They're selling the La Mesa house. France agrees with them."

He's quiet for a moment. "I know you'll miss them, but I'm glad it's worked out."

Silence settles around us. Well, silence in the sense that Max and I no longer talk. The drone and throb of the plane's twin engines fills the cabin with noise and vibration. This is a bare-bones transport plane. Six seats jammed together in an empty cargo space. Empty now. Since the pharmaceutical smell of cut cocaine and the earthy smell of marijuana lingers, there's no doubt that this plane's primary purpose is running drugs.

I look out the window, but even with vampire vision, I can't see much. There's no moon to cast even a shadow on the terrain below. It's a dark blur of black on black. Occasionally we pass over a cluster of lights from a village, but nothing that resembles a city. I think the pilot is purposely avoiding well-trafficked air space.

I remember from the map that the route was a straight shot across Mexico and that Reynosa was on the Rio Grande. I also remember from newspaper articles that it was a hotspot of cartel killings. Reynosa is like an 1880s Tombstone. I have the feeling we're heading right into our own gunfight at the OK Corral.

"Do you really think you have a chance of getting close to Santiago?" I ask Max after a minute.

He lifts his shoulders. "Depends on how badly he wants Ramon. He may send some men to do the actual killing but if he's really pissed, he may want to be there to make sure it gets done right."

"Are you going to alert your DEA buddies when we land?"

"Not right away. Not until I know we have a chance to get Santiago." He grins. "Besides, I have the best backup I could hope for. Culebra and a vampire with a hatred for people who abuse kids."

I snort. "I think that's the nicest thing you've ever said to me."

"Well, don't let it go to your head. It's probably the *last* nice thing I'll ever say to you."

Yeah. Before this trip is over, I'm sure I'll piss him off again. He's so easy to piss off and I'm so good at it.

* * *

IT'S NOT UNTIL WE COME IN FOR A LANDING THAT I realize how close to the ground we'd been flying. First a bright orange flicker appears suddenly out of the darkness in front of us. Then, we're descending, and the next moment, the wheels are scraping dirt. A cloud of dust rises like a ghostly fog, obscuring my view out the window. I assume the low altitude was to escape radar detection but frankly, I'm glad I didn't know how low we were flying. And doubly glad we had a pilot who knew the terrain.

We deplane while the engine is running at a dirt airstrip surrounded by dense brush. Dust hangs in the air and at the far end of the field, a second orange flicker dances in the darkness before it's quickly extinguished. A boy has thrown a tarp over what I can see now is a burning barrel of—I sniff. Oil. The boy is running back toward us now and the pilot waves a hand.

There's a building with open hangar doors and after we jump out, the pilot waits for the boy to climb aboard and then turns the plane toward the hangar.

Culebra and Ramon are walking to a battered Jeep parked a hundred yards away from the airstrip. Max and I follow. Ramon motions us inside and cranks the engine over.

I look toward the hangar. "The pilot isn't coming?"

"He'll wait for us here," Ramon answers.

It's a quiet ride. No conversation from the front seats or back. I glance at my watch. Ten. Max catches the gesture, mimics it.

"It's two hours later here," he says, slipping off his watch to adjust the time.

I do the same. Midnight. The witching hour.

We travel for thirty minutes down dirt roads with no discernable signs of life. We must be a good distance from Reynosa. No glimmer of city lights. I do catch the scent of water and hear the rush of currents. The Rio Grande is somewhere behind the thick curtain of vegetation we're skirting.

At last we come to a clearing. Squatting in the center is

a small clapboard cabin with boarded-up windows. Ramon swerves the Jeep into the dense brush alongside the cabin. Then he points to it. "We will stay here tonight."

I glance at Culebra. "Why would Ramon want to wait? I thought he was worried about his family's safety."

Ramon hears my question. He answers. "My wife will be frightened by the arrival of a vehicle this late at night. She has been through enough."

Like Ramon and Culebra, Max and I have to fight our way through the tangle of brush ensnaring the Jeep. Camouflage by nature, I guess. Max has his duffel bag in hand and once in the open, he charges after Ramon.

Culebra hangs back. *Anna, a word.*

I stop, turn to him.

I have not told Ramon that you are vampire.

Does he know you are a shape-shifter?

Culebra shakes his head. *No one from that part of my life knows. After the way I was treated by my own family, I wasn't going to take the chance.*

I nod. Keeping the secret of your true nature from humans, even those who love you, is something I understand only too well. *Shall I tell Max not to let anything slip?*

When you have a chance to do it without Ramon overhearing.

There's a sense of unease shimmering through his thoughts that startles me. *You don't trust Ramon? If that's true, what are we doing here?*

Culebra releases a breath. *It's not that I don't trust him. It's just that a lot of time has passed since I last saw him. Things change. People change.*

I don't understand, Culebra. If you have any doubts, why are you risking your life to help him?

Culebra looks away, toward the cabin. *I owe him a great debt. It is my obligation to pay it.*

When he turns back to me, his thoughts no longer radiate concern. *Let's get inside. We have much to discuss if we are to help Ramon and his family.*

I follow him toward the open cabin door. His attempt to

banish anxiety from his head was masterful but not entirely convincing. It leaves me troubled.

Ramon and Max have pried open the door to the cabin. When Culebra and I join them, they have an oil lantern burning on the table and are examining the contents of shelves lining the kitchen area of a very primitive one-room dwelling. A wood-burning stove, a small pile of wood beside it, a plank table, a freestanding sink with a pump handle are the only objects in the room. No chairs. No beds. No creature comforts of any kind. The structure is made of rough-hewn wood, floor, walls, ceiling. It's so small, the five of us make the place seem crowded.

Ramon pulls a coffeepot from one of the shelves and points at Max to grab a small burlap bag from another. When Max opens it, the rich smell of coffee fills the room. Max opens the belly of the stove and slips a log inside. He pulls a book of matches from an inside jacket pocket and strikes one. The wood catches fire immediately, the crackle and pop of dry tinder making me wonder how long it's been here.

I join Culebra to stand around the table while Ramon works the pump handle at the sink. At first, just a squeal of protesting pipes greets his efforts. Then a gush of brown water with the stink of sulfur.

My nose crinkles in disgust.

Ramon keeps pumping and gradually the water clears though the smell remains strong. He fills the percolator, dumps in some grounds, sets the pot on the stove. In a few minutes, the water boils, the coffee brews, the smell improves—a little.

Still, I think I'll pass on that coffee.

Max seems to agree. He unzips the duffel and pulls a couple of bottles of water from inside, holding one out to me.

I take it and drink. My digestive system won't be affected by bad water, but I draw the limits on bad coffee. "What else do you have in there?" I ask him, pointing to the duffel.

"Oh, this and that," he replies.

He turns away before I can ask again. I'm liking the

ambiguity. Makes me feel all warm and safe. Knowing Max, that duffel probably holds a small arsenal right along with the water.

A Boy Scout. Hell, better. When heading for a gunfight, who better to have with me than my own personal Wyatt Earp.

CHAPTER 20

ONCE THE CHUG AND GURGLE OF THE OLD PERCO-lator stops, Ramon pulls tin cups down from the back of one of the cabinets. When he looks over at Max and me, offering us mugs, we both hold up our hands in gestures of refusal. He pours two steaming mugs and he and Culebra gulp them down.

No reservation there about drinking the coffee.

The smell dissuaded me and I have the constitution of a—well, a vampire.

Culebra and Ramon have a brief conversation while they drink, after which Max, who understood, says to me, "Better get some rest. We're starting out at first light."

There are no beds, cots or even rugs in the barely furnished cabin. Luckily, I'm not high maintenance. Mimicking the others, I sink to the floor, lean my back against the wall and close my eyes. I let the human Anna relax, but leave vampire on alert.

Culebra's hint that Ramon may not be entirely trustworthy lingers in my head. Along with Max's earlier comment

about Ramon showing up to either warn Culebra about
some danger or to kill him. I should have asked Culebra
how Ramon found him. Had he kept in touch with his "old
friend"? Ramon told his story with an emotional intensity
that rang true, but I've told a few lies in my time. The best
lies always ring true.

I pass the night in that kind of half sleep that floats on
the surface of consciousness; the mind drifting but not letting go, the senses alert for the slightest stirring of physical
movement from inside or outside the cabin.

Not very restful. When dawn finally shows itself in pink
ribbons through chinks in the walls, it's a relief. I look over
at Max, and from the bleary-eyed way he meets my gaze,
I'd guess he's been awake all night, too.

Ramon climbs to his feet first and makes for the door.
Culebra and Max follow. From the sounds I pick up, they
each make for a different corner around the outside of the
cabin to relieve themselves.

Sometimes having super hearing is not such a blessing.

But because I have to pretend to be human, once they're
back, I head out. My system absorbs any kind of liquid directly into my bloodstream. There's nothing to excrete but
I wait a few minutes, shifting restlessly from one foot to the
other, then rejoin them. Culebra gives me a sly smile and I
roll my eyes.

Ramon makes another pot of coffee. I'm antsy to get
going. I would think he would be, too. But no one questions
it and after he and Culebra consume another pot, and Max
and I have finished off two more bottles of water, we're at
last trudging toward the Jeep.

Ramon once more takes the driver's seat, Culebra beside
him. Max and I climb into the back.

In the daylight, I see the river in dappled silver glimpses
through the brushes and trees to our right. We are following
its pathway west, away from Reynosa. While there is more
vegetation along the riverbank, the smell of desert heat and
abandonment is strong. We pass several cabins in various
stages of decay, as if one by one, their owners left for—what?

There's not much in this part of Mexico. Perhaps they moved closer to Reynosa. Or braved the currents of the Rio Grande to forge a new life across the border.

We continue to follow the river for two hours, a hot winter sun rising high in the sky. The humidity from the river and the desert heat combine to make the air so thick, you could drink it with a straw. Swarms of insects buzz around our heads. Ramon and Max are covered with a patina of sweat, attracting more insects. They alternate between swatting at them and wiping sweat out of their eyes.

Only Culebra and I are impervious to the swarm. Even mosquitoes refrain from biting a vampire—professional courtesy, I guess. I didn't realize shape-shifters had the same immunity.

I'm about to ask how much farther when Ramon brakes sharply, the Jeep skidding to a halt. He jumps out, grabs a heavy looking tree branch that has fallen near the trail and gives a tug. It pulls away, revealing an opening in the brush. He motions to Culebra to drive the Jeep through, pushing the branch into place when we're on the other side. Then he climbs back into the driver's seat and we're off-roading it through terrain even rougher than before.

I grab the roll bar to keep from bouncing out. Low-hanging branches pull and scrape at us, ruts as big across as tree trunks launch the Jeep airborne, then send it crashing back down to earth. I've jammed my jaws so tightly closed, my teeth ache. It's either that or take a chance they'll break with the jarring. I need my teeth. Don't know if there are vampire dentists. Every muscle in my body is drawn tight as a vise. When I look over at Max, he's got both hands around the roll bar. He looks a little green, like he may be getting carsick.

I don't say anything. If he's going to lose it, I don't want him looking in my direction.

Only Ramon seems oblivious to the Jeep's wild careening. His jaw is set, his eyes stare straight ahead. He's a man on a mission to save his family. I can't fault him for that.

I only wish I knew where the hell we were going.

We're not parallel to the river anymore. Gradually, the brush gets sparser, the ground more rocky. We start on an uphill climb. Low-growing bushes are crushed under the wheels of the Jeep, releasing the sweet smell of sage and musky scent of mesquite. The air becomes dryer, but not cooler. Max sheds his jacket, exposing the gun on his hip. Comfort wins over concealment.

We wind our way up and around a small hill.

"Where are we?" I ask Max.

"Somewhere I've never been before," he says. "The edges of the Chihuahuan Desert? Shit, I don't know. Even the banditos don't venture this far from civilization."

Culebra half turns in his seat. "We're almost there. Ramon chose the location for his safe house well."

Ramon ignores our conversation. White-knuckled hands gripping the wheel, his eyes focused straight ahead. I can only imagine what images are playing in his head. No matter how isolated a spot he chose, the fear that it wasn't isolated enough must be torturing him.

The ground levels off and we seem to be at the top of a mesa. There are a few trees here, oak and pinyon. Native grasses and low-growing creosote with lacy light green leaves, Yucca and mesquite cover the desert floor. Quite a difference from the more barren desert surrounding Beso de la Muerte.

Ramon is driving straight toward what looks, from my vantage point in the backseat, like the edge of the mesa. What the fuck? I get struck by a disturbing thought. What if Culebra was wrong and rather than going to help Ramon's family, Ramon is driving us all to oblivion. The *Thelma and Louise* way out. Maybe he made a deal to swap the safety of his family for his life and Culebra's.

I grip the roll bar tighter. I can grab Max and haul us both out before the Jeep goes over, but I can't grab Culebra, too.

I send out a frantic warning. *Culebra, I think he's going over the edge. Get ready to jump out.*

Culebra's thoughts reflect alarm. I grab Max's arm. He

turns toward me, his eyebrows raised. At the moment I've tightened my grip, ready to fling us both out, the Jeep slams to a stop.

Max's breath rushes out in a hiss. "What the fuck, Ramon?"

My sentiments exactly.

Ramon turns in the seat, surprise and confusion stamped on his face. He sees me grasping Max's arm and interprets Culebra's hand on the window as preparation for a bailout. He says something to Culebra in Spanish with a bewildered inflection in his voice that even I can interpret.

Max shakes out of my grip and starts to rub at his bicep. "Ouch. Next time you get the bright notion that we need to jump out of a moving vehicle, ask questions first, okay? Ramon just told Culebra that we're here. His family's safe house. Just over that bluff."

CHAPTER 21

OKAY, SO I GOT IT WRONG. TO HIDE MY EMBAR-
rassment, and because anger is my normal way of
dealing with being embarrassed, I lash out.

"Shit, Max, I thought he was driving us over the rim.
You did, too."

"Not until you grabbed me. What made you think he was
going kamikaze on us?"

"Oh, maybe the fact that he was driving straight for the
edge. And that it occurred to me he might have made a deal
with Santiago. His family's safety in exchange for his life
and Culebra's."

Culebra half turns in his seat but before he can say anything, Ramon jumps out of the Jeep. He heads for a patch
of brush that becomes camouflage netting when he pulls at
it. He motions to Max and Culebra. *"Ayúdeme."*

Max and Culebra join him. The three men grab the netting and pull it over the Jeep. It's sand colored and dotted
with bits of rock and brush. Ramon anchors it with more

rocks and stands back to brush dirt from his hands. He glances at his watch.

"Vengan conmigo," he says.

And runs straight toward the edge of the mesa. In an instant, bickering forgotten, Culebra, Max and I take off after him.

Ramon disappears just as we catch up. Like an optical illusion, the trail that looks, from the way Ramon vanished, like a steep drop-off actually levels off, hugging the side of a hill. It takes standing at the very brink to see that we're not looking at precipitous drop at all. Ramon is running ahead.

We plunge after him. Ramon moves with purpose. I catch up with him, eyes scanning, senses alert. I don't see anything that looks remotely like a house. Just a lot of brush and boulders. Once again, I wonder if Ramon isn't leading us into a trap.

Then I catch the scent. Human. Female. Somewhere off the trail.

Ramon calls out. "Maria! Gabriella!"

From around a bend in front of us, a woman's voice answers. *"¿Ramon? ¿Es tu?"*

And then Ramon and a woman are embracing. She appeared from the side of the trail like an apparition but there's nothing ghostly in the way she clings to her husband or he to her. Culebra and Max catch up.

When the woman sees Culebra, her hand flies to her mouth. *"¿Tomás?"*

And then she is hugging Culebra and crying and she, Ramon and Culebra are speaking all at once and so fast, the words are a blur in my head. She is darker than Ramon, sculpted cheekbones that are more Indian than Spanish. She is short, heavy hipped and stocky, dressed in a white shirt and jeans cinched at the waist with a wide leather belt. She has a big revolver in a holster clipped to her belt.

Max and I stand apart and watch. It's apparent she was waiting for Ramon—was this why he didn't want to start out last night? They had a prearranged time to meet? It would explain his crazy dash across the countryside.

Another movement from just out of sight to our right snaps me to attention. Max sees the reaction. "What is it?"

Before I can reply, another voice.

"¿Papa? Has vuelto para nosotros."

The words come from a girl, fourteen or fifteen, who steps into the path. She has a rifle slung over her shoulder. Her face is hidden by the wide brim of a hat she sweeps off at the sight of her father.

Ramon opens his arms to embrace the girl. *"¿Tu prometí que, no, mi preciosa?"*

Ramon hadn't mentioned having a daughter but clearly this girl is his. She inherited his hair color and eyes, his slender build. She's tall for her age and dressed like her mother in jeans, a white blouse.

Her mother watches, arms still around Culebra, her expression, her tears reflecting relief. Ramon turns his wife and daughter to face Max and me.

"This is my wife, Maria, and my daughter, Gabriella." To them he says, *"Son amigos de Tomás. llegaron para ayudarnos. Anna y Max."*

Max and I nod to them as Maria gestures for us to follow. She glances upward and I hear the drone of an aircraft in the distance. Ramon hears it, too, and his expression hardens. "Come. Quickly. It may be one of Santiago's."

Maria and the girl lead the way off the trail and into dense brush. There are low-growing bushes and pinyon pines that make the going slow. But they also provide solid cover. The airplane passes overhead and Max watches it through a canopy of branches. "No markings. Ramon might be right."

"Are they looking for him?" I ask.

"Could be. Or it could be a drug run."

Maria keeps going. Ramon catches up to his wife and daughter and takes the lead. We trek on for another twenty minutes before he stops. There is a small clearing just ahead with the remains of another abandoned cabin. I look around. The last time I remember seeing a more isolated piece of land was on a Navajo reservation. At least there, the natural beauty of Monument Valley made the isolation tolerable. Here, the emptiness presses in like deadweight. I'm overwhelmed with a sense of loneliness. This is where Ramon's wife and daughter are forced to hide?

But neither Ramon nor his wife or daughter seems to mind. They are smiling as Ramon bids us once more to follow him with a crook of a finger. We enter a door sagging precariously in a lopsided frame. He motions us to step around a pocked wooden table set in the middle of the floor. He reaches under the rim of the table and I hear the release of a lock. Then the hum of a motor. The table tilts down and away like a trapdoor to reveal a set of steps.

Maria and Gabriella lead the way down. Ramon and Culebra follow, then Max and me. I raise curious eyebrows to Max. "What the fuck?"

But we're at the bottom of the steps and as soon as Ramon sees we're down, he presses a button on a panel to his right beside yet another door. The motor hums again and the table flips upright and the platform once more snaps into place.

"Slick," I whisper to Max. "What now?"

Ramon is working the lock on the door. It's a keypad lock and his fingers move quickly over the numbers. But not quickly enough. I imagine he has no idea I've just memorized the combination. One can never be too careful.

The door swings open with a whoosh of pneumatics. Refrigerated air gusts out at us—fresh and smelling like spring. Lights flicker on, turning the inside bright as day. Ramon steps aside to allow his wife and daughter to pass, and then extends a hand to Culebra, Max and me.

"Welcome to my home."

A whistle escapes my lips at the same time a gasp of astonishment escapes Max's.

"Holy James Bond," I say. "Dr. No didn't have it this good."

CHAPTER 22

MAX, CULEBRA AND I ARE STANDING IN THE EN-trance to a cave. Well, more precisely, a cave-like structure. The walls are stone, but hewn stone, smoothed and beveled into diamond patterns that repeat floor, ceiling and walls. The chamber we're looking into is at least as big as the ground floor of my cottage, decorated with leather couches and big overstuffed recliners. There are plush rugs underfoot, original artwork on the walls, a bar of polished mahogany in the corner upon which rests crystal decanters filled with liquids that catch and reflect the lights directly overhead. On the opposite side, through an archway, I can see a kitchen and dining area. It's a big kitchen, with stainless-steel appliances and copper-bottomed pots hung from a rack suspended over a granite island. I look for a chef in a white hat and smock, but it appears that's the only detail missing in this *Architectural Digest*'s version of Wilma Flintstone's kitchen.

It's very quiet inside. So quiet, I wonder if I'm the only one who hears the distant, steady hum of a generator, so subtle it takes concentrating vampire hearing to detect it. That generator must be what supplies air and power to the place. Like a heart pumping blood and oxygen through a body.

Even Culebra is dumbstruck. His thoughts are as jumbled as mine.

Ramon moves to the bar. Picks up one of the decanters. "Mescal?"

It takes a minute to pull my brain back from the shock of what my eyes are seeing and to engage it again sufficiently to make my mouth work. "Yeah. A drink would be good." Then my legs get with the program and I'm at the bar.

Culebra and Max follow, both looking as dazed as I feel. Ramon pours from a crystal decanter with the label Scorpion Anejo Seven Star—I realize he's pouring the Dom Pérignon of mescals when I see the scorpion floating in the bottle and the flicker of eagerness in Culebra's eyes.

When we all have glasses in our hands, Ramon tips his toward us and says, *"Para todo mal, mezcal, y para todo bien también."*

Yeah, I've heard that toast before—from Culebra at his bar: for everything bad, mescal, and for everything good, too. Course we weren't drinking Scorpion Seven Star at the time.

We all clink glasses and the men drink. I'm more interested in taking another look at my surroundings than indulging in the rapturous moans of pleasure that follow the tasting. It's hard to take it all in.

"How did you do this?" I ask.

Ramon says, "With a lot of money and an army of engineers." He raises his glass to Max and me. "American engineers."

"How did you keep it a secret?" Max asks.

"With a lot of money," Ramon says again, "and a little coercion."

"You threatened the engineers if they told anyone?" I ask.

He shrugs. "Didn't take much. Everyone has something to protect. And they were well paid for their discretion."

"But this must have taken an army to construct," I say. "No one noticed?"

He smiles. Not warmly. "Silence has a price. Fortunately I could afford to pay it."

For a narco, business as usual. I get a queasy feeling in the pit of my stomach. I acted on impulse coming here. Ramon, standing in his elegant hideout, looks less like a father frightened for his family and more like the scumbag drug lord he is. Even his English has improved. Was his original bumbling an affect to gain my sympathy?

I lay the glass on the bar without taking a sip. "What now?"

Maria gestures toward the back wall of the cave. "Let me show you where to freshen up. Then we eat."

So she can speak English, too. And well.

We follow Maria through an archway and into a hall. There are four doors, two on each side. She opens the last one on the left for me. "There are fresh towels. Shower if you like. I think Gabriella has something that will fit you. I'll leave it on the bed."

Then she's ushering Max and Culebra to the opposite door. I watch as they disappear inside and Maria moves off down the hall. I close my own door and look around, checking first to see if there's an inside lock. There isn't.

This is a bedroom with the same diamond-patterned rock walls, ceiling and floor as the great room. This room, too, sports a plush rug, a woven mat of cotton this time, but no artwork. The bed is simple, covered with a colorful Mexican blanket, the headboard banked with throw pillows in red and yellow. There is a dresser on one side, a chest at the foot of the bed.

Both are empty.

I take a quick look around for cameras or microphones but don't find either. There is neither wainscoting nor floor-boards to conceal electronics.

I step into the bathroom. Small. Functional. A shower, a

vanity, a toilet. This door locks from the inside. I close and lock it before undressing.

After two days, a shower feels good. Maria has stocked the shower with good soap and shampoo. It smells of trees after a rain, like a growing forest with hints of pine. The bathroom is soon fragrant with it. I linger under the hot water before realizing I've been in here almost twenty minutes and the hot water is still hot. Ramon must have a hell of a water heater.

The best drug money can buy. Which most likely explains how they keep the place supplied with liquor and good toiletries. I imagine engineers aren't the only ones who can keep a secret for a price or a threat.

When I finally coax myself out, I towel dry and peek into the vanity. There are various types of remedies, for headaches, for colds. A comb and brush that looks unused. Several toothbrushes still in packages. A tube of toothpaste—Colgate. American. I take advantage of the chance to brush my teeth and use the comb and brush to detangle my hair. Then I steal a look into the bedroom.

Maria has left a long shift of pale green cotton on the bed. I slip it over my head. It falls to my ankles. It moves when I walk; the material is whisper soft and thin. I wonder if I look naked in the light. The thought makes me uncomfortable enough to take it off.

My jeans and T-shirt will have to do—even if they aren't the cleanest.

I hear the door open across the hall. In two steps, I'm at my door, too.

Max and Culebra are there, smelling of the same fragrant soap, freshly shaven, wet hair combed. They've changed into clean jeans (must be Ramon's—they are all about the same size, though Max's thighs clearly strain the seams of his pair) and lightweight Mexican guayabera shirts with colorful embroidery and pleating. Culebra's is light gray, Max's a blue that makes his eyes intense as the ocean.

Culebra looks past me into the bedroom. "Maria didn't bring you clean clothes?"

I follow his eyes to the shift on the bed. "I think it's a nightgown," I reply.

He grunts.

Max grins, looking around me, too. "Too girly for you?"

I close the door behind me with a decisive click.

Max sniffs the air. "Something smells good."

He lifts his nose and moves toward the great room, following the odor of meat and beans and grilled vegetables like a bloodhound on the scent of a rabbit. He heads straight for the kitchen, Culebra right on his heels.

Only I lag behind.

The table seats eight and is set with plates and utensils and a steaming stack of tortillas. There are three chairs in the same heavy dark wood as the table on one side, a long bench on the other, and two captain's chairs on each end. Ramon is already seated in one of the chairs, watching Maria as she moves around the kitchen. He has showered and changed, too, as has Maria. Still, the shower hasn't completely masked the smell coming off both Ramon and his wife. They've been busy in the last hour— and not just in the kitchen. The musk of their sex tickles my nose.

Maria looks up and sees us approaching. She frowns in a concerned way at me. "You didn't like the dress?"

I grope for a way to answer when Max pipes up, "Anna's not big on skirts. She's more the pants type."

Shit. He says it with a wink and I see clearly on both Ramon's and Maria's faces what they're thinking. I'm gay.

Maria recovers before Ramon. "I see. No problem. After we eat, I'll get you a pair of Gabriella's jeans. She may be a little shorter, but I think they'll fit. Now, sit. The food is almost ready."

Three words grab my attention: after we eat.

She's back arranging food in serving dishes and I look at Culebra. *What do I do?*

He purses his lips ever so slightly. *Maybe it's time to come clean.*

What?

Tell them you're on a strict liquid diet. For health reasons.

Oh, like that makes sense. Did you see the way they looked at me when Max said I wasn't big on skirts? Now I'm going to insult Maria by refusing to eat her food?

Got a better idea?

Maria is ready to serve and Ramon motions around the table. "Please. Sit. Eat."

I take the bench, Culebra and Max chairs, and Maria takes her place at the opposite end of the table.

"Where's Gabriella?" I ask.

"She's on watch. Outside." Maria answers. "One of us always takes watch."

An idea blossoms. "Has she eaten?"

"She will. When we've finished, I'll take her a plate."

I push myself up from the bench. "No. Let me relieve her. I'm not hungry and I'm sure she wants to be with her father."

Ramon looks startled but grateful. "Are you sure? You haven't eaten—"

"I'm sure. Is she just upstairs, in the cabin?"

"Yes."

"Then I'll go now. Send her right back to join you."

I'm at the door when Culebra's sardonic voice sounds off in my head. *Nice save.*

Ramon has crossed to open the door, and I step past him, releasing a sigh of relief when the door closes again behind me. Nice save indeed. You'd think I'd be used to dealing with humans forcing food on me, but it never gets any easier.

At the top of the stairs, I find Gabriella seated crosslegged on the floor of the shack, a laptop balanced on her knees. She has an iPod in her hand and earbuds in her ears. I can hear the beat of a rap song. It's loud enough that a tank could pull up in front of the cabin and fire off a shot before she'd hear it.

That's the way she's standing watch?

It's my first thought until I see that her eyes are on the

screen and projected there are four views of the grounds around, and leading to, the cabin.

She looks up in surprise when I appear from the subterranean stairway, and pulls the buds from her ears. "What are you doing here?"

I point to the laptop. "Nice setup. I didn't see one camera when we arrived, let alone four."

She smiles. "The best security system money can buy."

"Your English is as good as your mother's," I say.

She shrugs. "I go to school in the U.S. My mom and I spend a lot of time there." There's a pause while she seems to reconsider what she's just said. "At least we used to."

I point to the laptop. "I'm here to relieve you. I'll keep watch. You can join your family."

But she makes no move to get up. Her face is both youthful and mature—her smooth skin and wide eyes speak of her young years but the sadness dimming those eyes and the worry lines already forming around her mouth make her seem older, life-worn. I've seen the look before.

"I know about your brother. I'm sorry," I say.

She frowns. "My father told you?"

"It's why we're here."

She sniffs. "Then you've come on a fool's errand. It's too late for my brother."

"But not for you. We're going to make sure you and your mother are safe. That the men responsible for your brother's death are punished."

This time she laughs. "Well, that shouldn't be hard, should it? Seeing as how the one responsible is the one you came with."

Her bitterness is scathing. She can't mean Max; she couldn't know about him. She thinks Culebra had something to do with her brother's death? "You are mistaken. Cule—" I stop myself. "Tomás is a friend here to help."

"Tomás?" Her eyebrows arch in surprise. "I'm not talking about Tomás. I'm talking about my father."

CHAPTER 23

"MY FATHER IS THE REASON MY MOTHER AND I are living like animals in a cage." Gabriella turns away from me, looks out through the ruined doorway. "He is the reason my brother killed himself. Antonio could never be what my father pushed him to be. That last outrage was the breaking point. My father wanted him to fight back against the bullies tormenting him. When he wouldn't, my father made it clear he thought Antonio a disgrace, a weakling. And then he took matters into his own hands."

I'm trying to reconcile the story she is telling with the one her father told us. According to Ramon, Antonio never told anyone what happened to him. "Did your brother talk to you about what had been done to him? It sounds like you knew what happened to Antonio before you read his note?"

"What note?"

I stop, take a mental step back. Perhaps Gabriella didn't know about the note. Ramon may have wanted to protect his daughter from the truth about the details of Antonio's rape. I certainly have no intention of being the one to break it to her.

"I may have misunderstood. It's not important anyway. What is important is that we're going to make sure you and your mother are safe."

Gabriella shakes her head and hands me the laptop. "Good luck with that," she says, standing up. "My father is a hard-ass narco. If he can't protect us, what chance do you think you have?"

She starts for the stairway, then stops, looking back at me. "I'm going to get something to eat. My mother loves to cook. At home, we have someone who cooks for us. I think she actually likes being here because she feels like she's taking care of us again. Oh well. At least if we die, she'll die happy." She's winding the cord for the earbuds around her iPod and when she's done, she stuffs the thing into her jeans. "Don't mention the iPod, okay? My father is paranoid. He thinks any electronic device can be bugged."

I nod that her secret is safe. She takes a step toward the stairway.

"Gabriella?"

She stops again and turns around.

"You seemed really happy to see your father an hour ago. What's changed?"

"I thought he came back to take us home. He hasn't. Another promise broken."

I raise my eyebrows and shake my head.

Her footsteps echo on the steps and then I hear the soft swish as the door opens into the living area. I've pushed the lever that returns the table to its position in the middle of the cabin and perch myself on the edge.

Gabriella's cynicism lingers in my head. I've often wondered how the members of a gangster's family square their lifestyle with the means by which it's obtained. I have no idea how Ramon's family lived before but if this hideaway is any indication, they must have had it pretty good. Gabriella is obviously well educated. Her teeth and skin flawless. Before they went into hiding, did she ever give a second thought to the bloodshed going on around her? Or was she immune because of who she was—or more precisely, because of who her father was?

That didn't save her brother, though, did it? Even a hard-ass narco answers to somebody.

A click and a whirring sound emanate from beneath the table as the mechanism hums again to life. I jump away just as the table tilts inward, exposing the stairway.

Max trudges into view. He's holding a plate brimming with tortillas, beans, meat and vegetables. More importantly, he's carrying two bottles of Dos Equis. We set the table upright again and take seats slouching against the wall facing the door. I balance the laptop on my knees while Max balances his plate on his.

Max hands me one of the beers. "Brought you some food. Maria insisted. But I guess you can't eat it, can you? Guess I'll have to take care of it. Wouldn't want Maria to think you didn't like her cooking any more than you liked her taste in clothes."

I punch his arm. "Nice going in there. They think I'm gay. In a good Catholic country like Mexico, I'm sure they feel real comfortable around me now."

"More comfortable than they'd be if they knew what you really are?" He's shoveling meat and beans into a tortilla.

"Didn't you eat downstairs?" I ask. The smell makes my mouth water.

He takes a huge bite. My eyes trail the path from plate to mouth like a dog panting for table scraps.

"Yep. But damn, this is good. Maria is one hell of a cook."

Great. I let him eat, finding a little consolation in my beer. After a moment, I ask, "What are they talking about?"

"Downstairs? Nothing important. Family stuff."

"So what happens now? When do we go after Santiago?"

"Ramon told Culebra we'd talk tonight, after Maria and Gabriella go to bed."

"Gabriella blames her father for Antonio's death. She's pretty antagonistic toward him."

"She's a teenager," Max says. "She's supposed to be antagonistic. It's her job."

"Maybe. But it seemed more than teenage angst. She said something about Ramon wanting Antonio to avenge himself against the bullies and when he wouldn't, Ramon called him a disgrace, a weakling. And took matters into his own hands."

Max takes a break from eating to look at me. "You think Ramon's killing Rójan was premeditated?"

"I don't know. But Gabriella seems to think so. She didn't know anything about a suicide note, either. I'm not sure she knew he had been raped. In her mind, Antonio killed himself because he couldn't live up to his father's 'standards.'"

Max lifts his shoulder and takes another bite. "You should probably let Culebra know. He seems to take everything Ramon says at face value."

His words remind me of my conversation with Culebra the first night. "Maybe not." I fill him in on the fact that Ramon does not know I'm vampire nor does he know Culebra is a shape-shifter. And that Culebra thought it best not to divulge our natures to Ramon.

Max has the same reaction I had. "Then what are we doing? Why did Culebra drag us into this thing if he doesn't trust Ramon?"

My turn to shrug. "Culebra owes Ramon some kind of blood debt. One he feels obligated to repay. Besides, this is your big chance to get intel on Santiago, right? I'd think it wouldn't matter to you how."

"True." He drags a tortilla across the plate, scooping up bits of meat and beans and with a look of pure contentment, slips the food into his mouth. When he sees me watching him, he smacks his lips appreciatively and grins.

Show-off. "I think you missed a bean. Maybe licking the plate would be more efficient?"

Max sniffs, still grinning. "Jealousy is such an ugly emotion." He lays the plate on the table and looks out the door at the early evening sun blazing its lazy path across the winter sky. "We've got a lot of time to kill."

I stand and hand him the laptop. "I'm going downstairs to take a nap. May as well rest while I can. I'll bring the plate back to Maria and tell her how wonderful lunch was. You can stand guard."

Max rubs his stomach. "Shit. I ate too much. Maybe I should go down for that nap."

"Nope. I called it first." I reach under the rim of the table and activate the lever. "You can jog around the cabin—work off a few of those calories. Those jeans look a little tight on you. Wouldn't want you splitting any seams."

He raises an eyebrow. "It's not me," he says. "Ramon doesn't have my manly physique."

"Yeah. Right."

Max steps closer, too close.

"I can think of another way to work off a few calories."

"Are you nuts?" I push him away with both hands. "You'd better lay off the mescal. We're not a couple. Haven't been for a long time. I have a boyfriend, Stephen, remember?"

"Maybe you do and maybe you don't."

His obvious glee at the thought that my days with Stephen are numbered makes me angry enough to tell him exactly what I'm thinking. "Stephen is not like you. He doesn't judge me. He knows I didn't choose to become a vampire. He loves me in spite of it."

Max sniffs. "Does he? Is that why you didn't tell him where you were going or who you were with? You saved his ass because you're a vampire. He's grateful. Now. Just wait until he has to live with it."

"I saved your ass, too." The words come out in a growl. "And you weren't very grateful, were you? Thanks for reminding me, Max. You're a real prick."

I'm down the stairs quicker than Max can come up with a response. At the bottom, I work the combination and when the door opens, I'm facing three pairs of startled eyes.

Shit. I forgot. I should have knocked. Now they know I know the combination.

Too late. And right now, I'm too aggravated with Max to

care what they know. I hand Maria the plate. "Thank you. The food was delicious." I take a quick glance around. "Where's Gabriella?"

Maria takes the plate. "She went to her room. Is Max keeping watch?"

"Yes. And if you don't mind, I'd like to lie down for a while. We didn't get much sleep last night."

Ramon looks ready to ask me how I got the door open, but Culebra comes to my rescue. "Taking a nap is a good idea. We'll be up late tonight. You get some rest. Ramon, Maria and I still have much to catch up on." He smiles at them and for the moment, at least, they are caught up in his good humor.

Culebra can feel that I'm angry with Max, but he doesn't intrude on my thoughts to ask why. I nod and make my escape, leaving them sitting around the table.

Just a warm, happy, cozy little family reunion.

What a fucking joke.

CHAPTER 24

THIS TIME, MARIA LEFT ME A PAIR OF JEANS AND A white long-sleeved blouse with a scoop neck and embroidery around the cuffs and hem. The clothes are laid out neatly on the bed. The dress or nightgown or whatever the hell that was is gone. I move Maria's latest offering to the chest at the foot of the bed, intending to shower again after I take a nap. Now I strip out of my well-worn clothes and toss all except my belt into the trash basket in the bathroom. I won't be packing anything to take with me. Then I crawl naked under the blankets.

It's cool and dark in the room.

I close my eyes.

Max's face is imprinted on the back of my eyelids. He's laughing. He's gotten to me and he knows it.

But he's wrong about Stephen. Stephen won't leave me because I'm vampire. The way Max did. If Stephen leaves me it's because I came on this stupid campaign without telling him where I was going or what I was doing.

Why did I do that? Stephen could have handled the truth.

Probably would have applauded my loyalty. Instead I kept it from him.

I press my fingertips against my eyes until sharp pinpoints of light explode behind my eyelids, obliterating Max's sneering face and replacing it with shards of white light that spin like a mirrored pinwheel.

Fuck you, Max. I'm not going to think about losing Stephen anymore. He'll either be waiting for me when I get back . . .

Or he won't.

I'M AWAKENED BY A TAPPING ON THE BEDROOM DOOR.

I glance at my watch.

It's late—after eleven. I've been asleep for almost six hours?

"Yes?" I call through the door.

"We're waiting for you. Are you all right?"

It's Max. "I'm fine." Shithead. "Give me ten minutes."

I hear him move away down the hall. It's a good thing he didn't let himself into the room. I would have had his head.

I roll out of bed, mind numb from sleep. Too long. I slept too long. I should have had Culebra wake me after an hour or so.

A scalding hot shower with a brisk icy follow-up clears my head, snaps me back. Gabriella's clothes fit. I feel refreshed, rested for the first time in two days.

When I walk into the living area, Culebra, Ramon and Max are gathered at the bar; Ramon and Culebra are behind it, Max on the other side. He indicates I should join him. Reluctantly, I do. It would be too obvious if I ignored him. Even as hard as I'm trying to keep a lid on my aggravation, Culebra feels it. He raises curious eyebrows but doesn't push with a question.

Ramon runs his eyes over my clothes. "Are you more comfortable now?"

I nod. "Thank Gabriella for me." There is a map laid out

on the bar. I point to it. "Is that a map of Santiago's village?"

Max turns toward me. "This is a topographical map of the area. We're looking for a way to get to the village where Santiago is said to be living. A way that will not expose us to the villagers or to Santiago's air patrols."

I don't so much as glance his way but stay focused on the map. "Where is the village?"

Ramon places a finger on a point that, judging from the legend, seems to be about ten miles east of us. But the area does not look to be mountainous, just flat desert.

"Not going to be easy," I say. "To approach unnoticed."

"We can't take the Jeep," Culebra says, nodding. "Too noisy. But Ramon says there is vegetation so we'll have cover. We go on foot."

Ramon looks at me, then away. I read the skepticism on his face before he says, "It will be too difficult for a woman. Anna should stay here."

He's talking to the men, naturally.

"Don't worry about Anna." Max says before I can speak up. "She's tougher than she looks."

I stay quiet. I'm not about to defend myself again to Ramon. If my little display of bravado with the pilot didn't convince him, nothing will. Besides, it might be better if he doesn't want me to come with them. I can move far faster and with more stealth on my own. Tracking this trio should be a piece of cake. I look at Culebra and open my thoughts.

Culebra understands. *You may be right.* He lets a frown pull at the corners of his mouth and says out loud, "Perhaps Anna should stay here. We'll move faster without a woman holding us back."

I almost smile.

Then Max sends an astonished "what the fuck" expression Culebra's way that is sure to be followed with some kind of spoiler about how strong and fast and what a good tracker I am. Was he listening at all when I told him Ramon shouldn't know about me? Or has he been hitting the mescal again? I take matters into my own hands.

By smacking him across the face. Hard.

He yelps, hand on his cheek, and turns fire-flashing eyes toward me. "What the hell."

"I know what you're doing. Don't think you can make up with me. I don't want to go anywhere with you. You boys think you can do better on your own? Be my guest."

Ramon lowers his head and says to Culebra, *"Pensé que ella era homosexual. ¿Son amantes?"*

"Evidentemente no más," Culebra replies dryly.

Max finally catches on, though the anger blazing from his eyes at my smacking him is real enough. *"La perra se queda aquí,"* he snaps.

The bitch stays here.

Cute, Max. Nice way to get into character.

The three proceed to plot their course as if I've left the room. I plop myself into a chair to pout. And listen. When all the plans are made and they are ready to leave, that's my cue to jump out of the chair and glare. "I'm going to my room," I snap and flounce off.

No one, not even Culebra, bothers to say good-bye.

CHAPTER 25

I LEAVE THE BEDROOM DOOR OPEN JUST A CRACK SO I can listen to what's happening in the living room. There is a rustling of activity as supplies are gathered, backpacks filled, weapons made ready. At one point, Ramon enters his wife's room. I assume to let her know that they are leaving. She follows him back to the living room, voice tense as she says her good-byes.

Neither Max nor Culebra venture into my room. Max is still offended by the slap; Culebra knows we will be in touch as soon as they leave and I follow.

Finally, I hear the pneumatic whoosh of the door being opened. Maria calls a last "*vayan con dios*," reverently, as if the three were embarking on a religious crusade. All I have to do now is wait for her to go back to bed and I can be on my way, too.

So, I wait.

Maria is walking around the living area. It sounds as if she's straightening up, glasses clinking, papers rustling.

Come on, Maria. You can do all that tomorrow morning. Go to bed.

But she doesn't.

In another minute, the smell of coffee drifts back.

Shit. She's making coffee. What's she planning to do? Hold a vigil until her man gets back?

Finally she goes into her bedroom and closes the door. Now's my chance. I exit my room and tiptoe past her door, heading for the living room. Then I'm through the living area and ready to work the code to open the door to the staircase. Hopefully they haven't changed it after my unexpected and stupid appearance yesterday.

Suddenly, I hear her bedroom door open once again and footsteps approach.

My fingers fly over the keypad. I've just hit Enter when I hear another sound. The door slides open, but I hardly notice. At my back, the unmistakable ratchet of a pump-action shotgun being primed to fire freezes me to the spot.

"Turn around. Slowly."

I do. I don't intend to see what a shotgun would do to me or to find out how long it takes me to recover from such a wound.

Maria has the gun leveled at my torso.

"What are you doing, Maria?"

"Ramon said you might try to follow. He was right. He wants you to stay here."

"But I came to help. How can I help if I'm here?"

Maria sniffs. "You are a woman. How could you help? You would only be a distraction. What is to be done is men's work."

"And you know what is to be done?"

"I know enough. Ramon is wise in these ways. He and Tomás will do what is necessary."

"And Max."

Another disdainful sniff. "Ramon knows what Max is. *Un policía contra narcótraficant.* He is alive only because he is Tomás's friend. He will stay alive only as long as he is useful. If you and he are indeed lovers, I think you will soon be wearing *ropa de luto*."

I don't recognize the expression. "What does that mean?"

"Mourning clothes," she says.

An icy finger touches the back of my neck. I have to get out of here. Maria is still gripping the trigger of the shotgun. I need to get it away from her without waking Gabriella. If she's like her mother, she's likely to come out guns blazing at the sound of a shotgun blast.

"Can I sit down?" I ask. "That shotgun scares me."

She jabs in the direction of the couch. I back toward it, keeping Maria in my line of sight. I'm hoping she wants to secure the door and sure enough, she half turns to the keyboard, trying to keep the shotgun level on me at the same time she works the code.

I don't give her a chance to do, either. I'm on her in less than a heartbeat, wrenching the gun from her and pushing her down onto the floor. I put a finger to her lips. "No noise. Wouldn't want to wake your daughter."

She glares at me. *"Puta."*

That again. "How do you communicate with Ramon?"

She looks like she's not going to answer so I tickle her chin with the barrel of the shotgun. "I said I didn't want to wake your daughter. I didn't say I wouldn't."

Harsh, maybe. But it works. "Cell phone."

"Where is it?"

She clamps her jaws tight but her eyes betray her. They flicker toward the table. I grab her arm, yank her to her feet and pull her with me. The cell phone is on the counter separating the kitchen from the dining area. I drop it to the floor, crush it with my heel and toss it onto the counter.

"Does Gabriella have a phone?"

She shakes her head. "No. Cell phones are a danger to us—too easy to trace. We have only the one. She is not allowed."

Knowing Gabriella, knowing teenagers, I suspect she

might have a phone her folks don't know about. Like the iPod. But there's nothing I can do about that. I push Maria down into one of the chairs and look around for something to tie her up with. I don't see anything promising. In the kitchen area there are some towels hanging from a wooden spool. I grab up two, tear them into strips and bind her hands and feet.

"Who are you working for?" she asks, twisting her head to watch as I secure the knots. "Are you with Santiago? Has he hired you to kill us?"

For the first time, her voice shakes a bit, her eyes grow big. She is afraid.

I jam the last piece of towel into her mouth. "No. Tomás spoke the truth when he told Ramon we were here to help. All of us. It's too bad your husband didn't believe it."

I give the strip of towel a tug to make sure it is tight across her mouth. I don't want her calling out to her daughter as soon as I'm gone. I bend down so we are eye level. "I will tell you this. If any harm comes to any of my friends because of Ramon, you may be the one wearing *ropa de luto*."

She believes me. The panic in her eyes confirms it.

She struggles to speak through the gag but nothing comes through but garbled sounds.

This time, I make it out the door. I wish I could think of a way of disabling the keypad. Keep Maria and Gabriella locked inside. A quick examination of the lock doesn't yield any simple or obvious ways to do it. So I resort to another simple and obvious way—I punch a fist through the mechanism. I suppose there might be a failsafe somewhere inside, but Maria won't be able to get to it until she's untied. And if Gabriella is a typical teen, it may be hours before she gets up and finds her mother.

So now I'm off. Up the stairway, out through the cabin. It's quiet and dark in the clearing. No breeze, a sprinkling of stars overhead, a crescent moon. I let vampire surface, listen for sounds of the men moving through the brush. I sniff the air. Thanks to Maria's puttering, they have a sixty-minute lead, but I know the direction they'll be traveling.

The ground I run over is rock strewn and covered with low brush. I startle small creatures—rats, snakes, rabbits—in my path. Insects scurry or fly away. From just out of sight, a bigger predator hunts, taking off after the vermin I send scampering in his direction.

Say thank you, vampire growls.

In ten minutes, I pick up the scent. Max, first, the most familiar, then Culebra and Ramon. They move with purpose, not as quietly as I, and it's not hard to catch up.

I slow down, the human Anna pushes a reluctant vampire back into vigilance mode. It's my turn to take up the pursuit.

The men move steadily eastward. I recall bits of their conversation from earlier. Santiago is living on the outskirts of a village far from Reynosa. He has bought and paid for the village, supplying the residents with money and food in exchange for their silence and cooperation. Anyone suspected of not cooperating has already been disposed of.

He is planning to run his business from this remote location until the heat dies down. The latest round of violence has spilled across the border. The murder of an American tourist caught in the cross fire between narco factions raised the ire of both the *Federales* and U.S. cops. Ground and air patrols have increased, suspected drug houses closed down, the usual avenues open to money laundering unavailable because of closer government scrutiny.

Ramon said this is why Santiago wants him dead. The boy he killed was the son of a government official who facilitated the exchange of dirty money for clean. He oversaw the chains of *casas de cambios*, money exchange houses, moving billions of narco dollars through the system. The man now refuses to reopen the channels until he gets his revenge. Until Rójan's killer is dead.

If Max, Culebra and Ramon continue at this rate, it will take them well past daybreak to reach the village. They'll have to camp somewhere on the route to wait for the cover of darkness to get close. I can reach the village much faster.

I send a message to Culebra. *I'm here.*

I thought I'd hear from you sooner.

Ran into a little trouble with Maria. She tried to keep me at the cave.

Why would she do that? Culebra's tone indicates surprise.

Ramon, I answer simply. *You should tell Max that Ramon doesn't trust him. He should be on his guard.*

Culebra's surprise turns into concern. *Why would he distrust the one man who can get his family to safety?*

Don't know. Didn't stick around to ask. Listen, I'm going on ahead to take a look around the village. See if I can pick out where Santiago is hiding.

We won't make it before sunrise, Culebra says, echoing my thoughts, impatient that he has to stay behind. *We'll have to take cover on the trail.*

I'll come back as soon as I can.

Culebra closes our mental communication conduit. What lingers after is the definite trace of bitterness that he can't shape-shift and come with me. There's just a touch of jealousy there, too.

Makes me smile.

CHAPTER 26

THE VILLAGE IS MORE PRIMITIVE THAN I IMAGINED. It's like something from the nineteenth century. A well stands in the middle of a courtyard from which four dirt roads radiate outward like the points of a compass. There are no more than a dozen houses—shacks really—scattered off the roads. Simple wooden structures each with a patchwork garden in front and chickens pecking in pens on the sides. The only vehicles I see are two ancient trucks with wooden beds parked side by side near the one brick structure in town. A church—a tiny church with a steepled roof and bell tower.

Good cover for a drug kingpin used to living in luxury. It's unlikely the cops on either side of the border would think to search for him in a place like this.

Still, I can't imagine Santiago living like a peasant in one of those shacks. There must be more to this village.

Or one of those simple structures has an underground mansion like Ramon's underground cave. Money makes all things possible. Big money works miracles.

I keep to the shadows, out of sight of prying eyes. The presence of a stranger, especially a *gringa*, would certainly attract attention. So I circle the village in a wide arc, keeping to the trees and whatever scrub brush I can use for cover.

It's fast approaching dawn. The village is still asleep, no stirrings at all from any of the houses. There are several more shacks separated from the cluster around the courtyard. They look no different from the others. No big black Escalades parked in front, no AK-47 gun-toting toadies standing guard, nothing that shouts major narco kingpin in residence here.

Well, this scouting trip has been a bust.

And I have to wait until nightfall for Culebra.

I hunker down in a cluster of bushes, hoping the green leafy ground cover under my ass isn't poison oak or ivy. Vampire or no, an itch is an itch. I burrow in like a fox until I'm sure no casual passerby can spot me. I have a semiclear view to the center of the village and a better view of the shacks on the outskirts.

Nothing to do now but wait.

And think.

Is Ramon really launching this preemptive strike to protect his family from Santiago's wrath? Or is it something else? How much does Maria know about the death of Rójan? About Ramon's part in it? She seems to take his word as law. Gabriella is far less accepting. She hasn't romanticized her father the way Maria has. Still, they are blood. It would be a mistake to look on her as an ally.

I wonder if Maria would have shot me to keep me at the cave simply because Ramon told her to. I'm glad I told Culebra to keep an eye on Ramon and to protect Max. I can't shake the feeling that Culebra is more a pawn in this game than a partner. And I believed Maria when she said Max was expendable. What she and Ramon don't realize is that Max and Culebra are a formidable pair. More than a match for Ramon now that they have been warned.

The far-off sound of a motor snaps me to attention. It's

full light out now. A plume of dust rises from the eastern radial of the roads stretching from the well. The timbre and decibel level of the engine marks it as a big vehicle—a truck, maybe. I lean forward to get a better look.

And pull back immediately. From my left, from one of the shacks closest to my hiding place, a man sticks his head out a window. He watches the truck approach and when it has reached the center of the village and come to a stop by the well, he leans back inside and yells.

"Las muchachas. Ahora."

The door opens. A man steps out first, an AK-47 strapped bandolier style across his chest by a loose cord. He's barrel-chested and squat, hair secured by a handkerchief tied around his head. He wears sweatpants and a T-shirt straining over a big belly. He's barefoot.

The toadie I've been looking for?

He has a cigarette in his hand and he waves it in a come-along motion. He stands beside the door and barks something sharp.

As if propelled from behind, three young women stumble out. They blink at the light and clutch at blankets thrown over their shoulders. They are barefoot and dirty, hair un-kempt, faces smudged. None of them could be older than sixteen. They cower together, eyes on the toadie. He gets behind them and uses the stock of the rifle still tied across his chest to move them forward.

"Muévan, putas," he says.

They remain close, moving as one, trying to keep as far away from the guard as they dare. He keeps prodding them toward the well and the waiting truck.

The arrival of the truck has awakened a few of the inhab-itants and curious faces poke from windows and doors. As soon as they see who is behind the wheel, see who is ap-proaching from the shack with the girls, they disappear back inside like wisps of smoke.

The driver's door opens and a man who could be the toadie's twin—overweight, dirty T-shirt, jeans hung so low I can't imagine what's holding them up—jumps to the ground. They embrace, patting each other on the back, mumbling something in Spanish too rapidly for me to catch. Then they go to the back of the panel truck and the driver opens the rear doors.

"*¿Cuatro este vez, huh?*"

"*Al jefe le crece el apetito por las chicas. Esta aburrido,*" the toadie replies with a laugh.

I understand the boss is bored but he wants *four* this time? Four what?

In a moment, I know. The driver yells something through the open doors and four girls appear from inside. Roughly, the driver drags one after the other to the ground and shoves them toward the waiting toadie. The girls are all dressed in simple dresses, sandals on their feet. They are thin, young, younger even than the three standing in the front of the truck, and big-eyed with fear.

The toadie steps up to each, and in turn, lifts a chin, cups a breast, runs a hand up between legs and pinches. The startled girls yelp and pull back. The toadie grins and spits out his cigarette.

"*El Jefe estará contento,*" he says. He jabs a thumb toward the front of the truck where the other three girls wait, their faces drawn with uncertainty. "*La basura está lista para hechar afuera.*"

The garbage is ready to be taken out. My guts churn as the two pigs laugh. Another round of backslapping and jokes aimed at the "education" the new girls are about to receive and then the guard moves the new arrivals back toward the shack.

The driver watches a moment, then he snaps at the three to come to the back of the truck. He lifts each one into the back, a hand snaking under the blanket of the first, pulling it down to expose the breasts of the second and finally ripping the blanket completely off the third. He bends that one back against the bumper, grinding himself into her until she cries for him to stop. He laughs and turns her around, using a hand under her ass to propel her roughly into the truck. "*Más adelante, chica,*" he says, slamming the door.

CHAPTER 27

I CAN'T WRAP MY HEAD AROUND WHAT I JUST WIT-
nessed. The new girls can't be more than twelve or thir-
teen. Are they being fed like takeout to someone in that
shack and then thrown out like garbage when he's ready for
the next course?

Is that someone Santiago?

This is the person Culebra swore allegiance to? That Ramon works for?

As soon as the truck with the girls departs, a van pulls
into the village and stops in front of the church. This time,
the villagers begin drifting outside. My rage extends to
them, too, the ones who withdrew quickly when they saw
what was happening.

Or does this happen every week? Every day? Are they
afraid for their own wives and daughters? Is that why they
raise no objection?

I remember what Ramon said. The village has been
bought and paid for.

I now have a decision to make. Do I go after the truck? I could free the girls, see they make it to safety. Kill the driver.

Then what?

There is most likely someone waiting for the truck to return. I could make the driver talk and tell me where and when.

I peek out. The bell in the steeple begins to ring. The villagers move toward the open church door, including the toadie, who shuts and locks the door to the shack where he brought the girls. Three men are hauling bags from the back of the van and bringing them into the church.

I can't remember. Is it Sunday? Are the villagers going to mass? They actually have a priest in this devil's playground? Where was the priest when the girls were being abused by the toadie and his buddy?

The bags being unloaded are too big and heavy-looking to hold communion wafers. Should I move closer?

I look toward the shack where the girls were taken. The door remains closed. It's quiet inside. I'm torn between attempting to get a look inside the church and rescuing those girls. Part of me wants to burst in, haul the girls out before the pig gets his hands on them. But the saner, logical part of me says there's another reason I'm here.

The village courtyard is deserted. The church bell has stopped ringing. Whatever was being delivered, is now inside the church. Everyone in the village seems to be inside, too. The van stands open and empty. I can do more good in the long run if I go after the truck that took the girls and get the driver to tell me what's going on.

If I'm going to get away, it will have to be now.

I slip out of my hiding place, pulling brush tamped down back into place. I keep an eye out for any strays, but everyone seems to have marched like good little ants into the church. I only have to scurry a little deeper into the brush before I can safely pick up speed. I run parallel to the road, watching for the truck.

It hasn't gone far.

The truck has been pulled off to the side of the road. I don't have to use vampire hearing to know what is going on. The driver has climbed into the back, the cries of his victim shattering the early morning quiet. When I leap inside, I can scarcely believe what I see.

Two of the girls are lying in pools of blood, their throats slashed. The third is barely visible under the half-naked body of the man on top of her. He is pushing at her and grunting, a knife at her cheek.

I feel my control slipping. Fight to get it back.

You need the man. Take control, Anna.

It's too late. The smell of spilled blood turns my mind as black as night. Vampire roars in blood lust and rage. I can't hold back.

The driver turns to look at what beast screams in a human voice but with such inhuman fury. His eyes widen and he pulls away from the girl, backing himself into a corner. His member shrivels and the sharp smell of urine staining the front of his pants is evidence that his fear has made him lose control.

I approach like a stalking tiger.

He holds out the knife.

As if that flimsy blade is any match for vampire. It takes the merest flick to break his hand at the wrist and fling the knife away.

He screams.

I want him to scream. I want to break every bone in his body, tear limbs one by one, until there are only pieces left and I can suck the life juices from them.

I make him cower in that corner. Make him wait for the pain to come.

But vampire is too caught up in the feast she is about to devour. She doesn't see until it is too late.

The girl. She is on her feet. She snatches the knife from where it fell on the floor. Too fast and too filled with rage even for vampire, she lunges before I can stop her. The knife slashes across the man's throat. The arterial spray covers my face, and its smell and texture is too compelling. His body spasms. With a glance back at the girl, I grab him, hold him to my chest, bury my face in his neck and drink.

CHAPTER 28

R EALIZATION AND REASON RETURN WITH A JOLT.
The human Anna comes back in an eye blink, horror at what vampire—at what I have done.

Shit. I sit back on my haunches, wiping blood from my face with the sleeve of the pristine white shirt Maria gave me.

Pristine no more.

What do I do now?

A sound, a small, mewling whimper makes me jerk around.

The girl, the one attacked who became attacker, sits beside the bodies of the slain girls, crying softly.

Surprise that she's still here, that she didn't run away in horror when she saw me feed, that she's not screaming, shakes me.

She looks up when she feels my eyes on her. Her expression doesn't change. There's no fear, no tensing of her body in preparation for fight or flight. There's only resignation in her gaze. As if surrounded by so much death, she accepts that hers is inevitable.

After all that's been done to her, does she welcome it?

I don't know what to do. I rack my brain for some phrase to offer comfort, to offer assurance that I mean her no harm.

"No te hará daño. Soy amigo. ¿Habla Inglés?"

Even as I say the words, I mean no harm, I wonder how she can believe it after what she saw me do.

But she only shrugs and replies, *"Sí."*

Relief washes over me. At least we have a chance to communicate.

She wipes at her eyes with the corner of the blanket she's pulled back around her trembling body. But she says nothing. She's waiting for me.

I place a hand on the center of my chest. "My name is Anna. What's yours?"

She squares her shoulders, sits up straighter. "Adelita."

Still no emotion. She doesn't seem to care what I am or what I did. She asks no questions.

Better not to push. She is calm. I will be, too.

"That's a beautiful name. You are very brave, Adelita. Now we need to move this truck off the road and hide it until we can decide what to do. I have some friends not far from here who will help us. You are barefoot. Do you think you could walk if I gave you my shoes?"

She shakes her head. "I will take his," she says, pointing to the man, spitting the words as if having to mention him raises bile in her throat.

I am sitting closest to him so I reach over and untie the shoelaces on what looks like a brand-new pair of Nikes. Thankfully, they are clean inside. I hold them out to Adelita. "He has surprisingly small feet for a pig," I say.

She understands and a slight smile touches the corners of her mouth. She holds up a thumb and forefinger and squeezes them close. "He was small in many respects," she says.

She slips the shoes on her feet and laces them. She has delicate features, brown eyes and hair. The small smile she showed me before is gone, her lips pinched tight. But it gave me a hint of the pretty girl she must have been.

I wish I had clothes to offer her but I didn't exactly pack for this trip. I motion to the open door and climb out. She follows, trying to manage the blanket. It's too coarse too wrap like a sarong.

"Maybe I can fix it a little," I offer, holding out a hand.

I think she may object, but surprisingly, she simply hands the blanket to me and stands naked and still.

Maybe she's been through so much, she can't imagine things could possibly get worse.

Her frail body is mottled with bruises.

I think I guessed right.

I fold the blanket in two and rip a hole in the middle with my teeth. When I hand it back, she slips it over her head, and it falls around her like a poncho, the ends reaching almost to the ground. There is a roll of twine and some duct tape lying in a heap by the door. I measure out a length of twine and snap it off. She winds it around her waist, tucking the sides of the blanket close so her body is covered.

She nods her thanks.

And waits for me to take the lead once more.

We walk to the front of the truck and I peek inside. The keys are in the ignition. "Get in. We'll move the truck so it can't be seen if someone comes by."

She crosses to the passenger side and slips in. The windows have been rolled up and the cab smells of sour breath and sweat-stained clothes, nauseating reminders of the dead man in back.

For the first time, the young girl, the raped and beaten little girl, cannot control the responses of her horrified mind and body. She flings open the door, leans out and retches.

I don't move. Don't offer a comforting hand. Don't utter false comforting words.

Nothing I say or do could make things better. She's been through hell. Maybe her body's way of coping is to purge. Vomit out some of the misery and despair and make room for something better. Maybe with the emptiness can come a little hope.

Maybe.

But for now, I leave her alone. After a moment, she stops. Her breathing becomes more regular. She remains leaning out of the truck.

I look around the cab. There's not much here—a pack of cigarettes and some matches, a half-empty bottle of water, a rag stuffed behind the seats. The rag is dirty and reeks of oil and gasoline, but it's all we have. At least it doesn't carry the scent of the dead man. I hand it to her along with the water bottle. Adelita takes them, rinses her mouth with water and spits, wipes her mouth and nose, and releases a deep breath.

"Gracias," she says, straightening in the seat, slamming the car door closed. She drops the rag to the floor and turns a tear-streaked face to mine. "We can go now."

CHAPTER 29

I CRANK THE ENGINE OVER AND PULL THE TRUCK BACK
onto the road.

"I need to ask you a few questions," I say. "Are you up
to it?"

"Yes."

"Who were you with in the village?"

"I don't know for sure. No one ever said his name. They
called him *El Jefe*."

"How did you and the others end up there?"

A catch in her breath. "Some men came to my school.
They said they had work that would pay well. They said we
would be gone only a week and would be brought back to our
village after. They said we would be treated with respect."

Her voice drops off. When I glance over, she's pressed
the palms of her hands against streaming eyes.

"I'm sorry to have to—"

"No." She regains herself quickly, wipes away the tears
with the back of her hand. "I want to help. What do you
need to know?"

"How long have you been gone from your village?"

"Longer than a week. Three weeks, I think. I lost track of time."

"The men who took you, do you know where they come from?"

"Near San Fernando. They spoke of it often during the drive. How they were anxious to return there when they finished delivering us. How they hated these trips because the 'cargo' was so much trouble. Running drugs was a lot easier."

Adelita has been staring straight ahead as she speaks, her voice steady but without nuance. She could be reciting a school lesson or repeating a tedious anecdote told to her by a tiresome old relative.

I look around as we drive. There are few places to hide the truck and I begin to worry how long we have before someone comes looking for it.

Time for another plan.

Off to the left about one hundred yards there is an outcropping of rock. I leave the road and head toward it.

Adelita glances over. "What are you doing?"

"I can't see any way to hide the truck. I don't know how much time we have before it's missed. If the driver's friends come looking, I want them to find an accident that will convince them no one escaped. I may need to siphon gasoline from the truck to start a fire."

She nods that she understands. "There is gasoline in a plastic jug in back. I don't know how much is in it."

"I'll check."

The truck bounces and rattles over the desert floor, making conversation impossible. It takes effort just to lock your jaw and grind your teeth together to prevent the jarring from shaking anything loose.

As we approach the rocks, I slow down and stop. "I want you to get out here. I'll see what's in the back that we can use."

"I want to help," she says.

"I know. And you will. But I can take care of this. You should sit here in the shade and rest."

She draws in a breath as if to argue, but I reach across her and open the passenger door. "Please. Trust me. Do as I ask."

And after a moment, she does. She climbs slowly out of the cab and finds a shady place under a scrub oak. I wait until she's settled to put the truck in gear once more and head for the rocks.

When I'm ten yards out, I stop again. I don't relish going into the back of the truck, but I know what I have to do. When I open the doors, the smell of blood hits me with the force of a blow. It's hot inside and close and the harsh buzz of flies already drawn to the bodies makes the atmosphere even more unpleasant.

Even vampire is repelled. But it's vampire strength I need so I call her forth. Reluctantly, I climb into the back of truck. I don't look at the girls. Not yet. The driver I heave onto my shoulders and jump to the ground. I take him to the cab and prop his body into the seat. Then I return to the back just long enough to find the gas can Adelita mentioned. I give it a shake. It's almost full.

Now comes the hard part. I have to make it look to the casual observer that there are three bodies here, not two. I hate touching their bodies. It seems disrespectful. But I drag them together so they're near the door and almost on top of each other. As if they died trying to get out. I sprinkle gasoline over the bodies, whispering an apology to the girls. I am about to burn away their very existence. The only offering I can make is the promise to avenge their deaths.

I slam the back doors closed, snap the padlock. There's a small porthole window in one side of the doors. I use my elbow and smash it in. I don't want to take the chance that the fire might be snuffed out for lack of oxygen. I want it to burn long and hard.

I carry the can to the cab. I push the dead man over and squeeze in next to him. I soak him and the cab in gasoline. Then I turn the ignition and put the truck in reverse.

I see Adelita in the rearview mirror. She is watching, concern and uncertainty on her face. I take one of the cigarettes from the pack in back of the seat, carefully light it, throw the match out the window. When I judge I am far enough away to create the right impact, I change gears, jam the accelerator to the floor and the truck leaps forward.

I open the door, ready to jump out but stupidly, I have miscalculated. The truck hits the rocks before I can jump with enough force to crumble the hood and shatter the windshield. I bounce forward against the steering wheel, the sickening crack of a rib making me recoil with pain. The cigarette falls from my lips and the cab becomes an inferno. I throw myself sideways out of the burning cab and roll away.

The ball of flame leaps skyward. I hear Adelita running toward me before I see her. From her vantage, she could not tell if I escaped the inferno. When she sees me climb to my feet, her relief is physical. She grabs my shoulders and hugs me to her, speaking in Spanish and crying until her body shakes.

Against the pain of broken ribs, I put my arms around her and hug back just as fiercely.

CHAPTER 30

A FTER A MOMENT, I PUSH ADELITA GENTLY AWAY. "We need to get out of here. I'm sure they'll spot the fire in the village. We can't be here when they come to see what happened."

She steps back. "Where are we to go?"

I take her hand and lead her back to and across the road, going as quickly as I can. I feel the broken bone begin to knit, but the process would be much less painful if I could just stop and let the magic of vampiric healing work unfettered. Instead, the constant tug and pull of keeping up a brisk pace makes me wince with every step.

Adelita sees it. She stops abruptly. "You are hurt."

"Never mind. It's nothing. We can't stop now. My friends are not far. We need to get to them as quickly as possible."

She frowns but I turn away and keep going deeper into the brush. Already I hear the rumble of a motor approaching from the direction of the village. Adelita can't hear it, but I can. If I were by myself, I'd wait and see who they sent out. See if the fire coaxed Santiago from his hiding place. But I can't risk Adelita's safety. If anyone spotted her, she'd most likely be blamed for the accident. My hope is that I can get her back to her home or at least have Max send her to a safe house while we finish what we came to do.

Adelita and I continue toward the spot where the three men hunkered down to await nightfall. It's hot, dirty work, pushing through bushes that catch and scrape at our skin and arms. There are clouds of pesky no-see-ums that rise from under trampling feet and swarm around our heads and into our eyes. I guess we traveled farther in the truck than I realized. Finally, we're at a point where I think I can reach Culebra telepathically, and I draw Adelita to a stop.

"We'll rest here a minute," I tell Adelita. Seems more plausible then telling her we're stopping so I can contact my shape-shifter friend via a mind meld.

Adelita's look of sympathy says she figures I want to stop because my ribs hurt, and she doesn't argue. She does hear the engine from the approaching vehicle now and takes cover. She makes herself as small as possible by folding her body against the thickest clump of bushes she can find. There is fear shadowing her eyes again. I mimic her action and place a finger to my lips.

The sound of a truck engine draws closer to the scene of the "accident." I put off trying to communicate with Culebra so I can listen to the flurry of activity—doors opening, footsteps running, excited yelling. I understand some of the conversation. First there is confusion as to how the driver, a new guy, could have left the road and hit the rocks. Then anger that he must have been drunk or high. Finally, a furious round of arguing as to who would be the unlucky one to break the news to *El Jefe*. He won't be happy that he lost a truck or that the driver cost *El Jefe* the income he would have gotten from the girls when they were put to work back in town.

That last bit brings a bitter smile to my lips. Obviously *El Jefe* didn't know that the new guy had his own plan for the girls. Rape and murder. He's probably better off dead. So is Toadie if he is the unlucky one who got him the job. I remember how they glad-handed each other in the village.

I catch Adelita watching me with a curious expression on her face. She can't hear what I hear. She must be wondering why I've grown so still, head tilted in the direction of the road. She doesn't ask questions, though, only waits for me to indicate that it's safe to continue our trek. Under normal circumstances seeing me become vampire should have sent her racing in the opposite direction. Instead, here she is, quietly waiting to follow my lead. Her faith in me is extraordinary.

After ten minutes or so, the men return to their truck and head back to the village. The smoke rising from the burned vehicle thins out, and I wonder if I should go back and see how completely it burned. Hopefully, there is too little left to make it obvious two bodies and not three were in the back. If we were in a city, a forensic team would scope it out in a heartbeat. Since I doubt Horatio Caine and his crew are vacationing anywhere near this dump, we may just get away with it.

Time to see if I can reach Culebra.

I open the conduit. *Culebra? Are you awake?*

The answer comes back immediately. *Yes. Where are you? Did you find Santiago?*

I'm close. I don't know about Santiago. There is someone hiding in that village. But he never came out. I have a girl with me who may be able to help. I'm hoping Max has a picture in that bag of tricks he brought.

A girl?

I give him a brief recap, including what I found when I followed the truck and how Adelita and I took care of the problem.

There is silence for a moment. Then, he says, *I saw the smoke.*

I thought you'd be asleep.

He makes a sound like the huffing of a breath. *We should*

be. But something has got Ramon in a state. He's watching Max and me like we're going to bolt. His nervousness is putting us all on edge.

He didn't get a phone call, did he? I'm thinking of Maria. Gabriella would have awakened eventually to find her mother bound and gagged and me gone. If Gabriella did indeed have a cell phone like I suspected, Maria would have lost no time in contacting Ramon and telling him I was on their trail.

I don't think so. But who can tell? With these new phones, she might have sent him a text and I'd never know. In any case, are you coming in?

I glance over at Adelita. She's watching me intently again, as if *I* might be planning to bolt. I smile at her and stretch, as if working kinks out of my legs. She gives me a tiny smile back.

What does Ramon plan to do when it gets dark? I ask then.

He hasn't said. I think he and I should get as close to the village as we can, scope it out. Leave Max behind as backup in case we get into trouble. Can you tell me where Santiago may be hiding?

I explain the layout of the village, tell him where I saw the girls taken.

Were there many guards? Culebra asks.

No. And that's surprising. I only saw one armed man. He had an AK-47. If Santiago was there, you'd think he'd have an army to protect him.

We can't be sure he doesn't. Well, what do you want to do?

I glance again at Adelita. She is leaning against one of the bushes, her head has fallen to her chest. I think the poor kid is asleep. I check my watch.

There's only three more hours of daylight. I'll wait for you and Ramon to leave camp. Let Max know that I'm here. Have you warned him about Ramon?

Didn't have a chance. I told you Ramon is watching us. That's another reason I want Max to stay behind when we go to the village tonight. If Ramon and I get separated, I don't want Max to become a target. I feel better knowing you will be with him.

Let me know when you've left for the village.

Culebra closes the link between us abruptly, as if someone may have called to him. I scoot myself over to where Adelita is sleeping and work my way into the brush beside her. She looks so small and fragile, so defenseless. Another surge of bitter rage against the men who abused her turns my blood hot. When I gather her to my chest, she gives one jerky start. I touch her hair gently and draw her head down to rest on my shoulder and she settles against me. Her breathing again becomes deep and regular. I wonder how long it's been since she felt safe enough to fall asleep?

CHAPTER 31

Adelita stirs and jolts awake, dragging me back to consciousness with her. She pushes away from me with a sharp cry. She flails her fists and screams out for me to let her go.

I tighten my arms around her. "Shhh, baby," I whisper. "It's all right. You're safe."

It takes a minute, but slowly, Adelita's mind clears as she looks up at me and realizes who is holding her. Her body relaxes, her fists drop. She sobs against my shoulder. I let her cry, get it out of her system, while my senses strain to catch any movement from the direction of camp to indicate they heard Adelita's scream. My gut twists with pain for the girl. Just as vampire blood ignites with thoughts of revenge toward those who are responsible.

I take a quick glance at my watch. It's after midnight. Hopefully Culebra and Ramon have already left for the village. Before I can try to contact Culebra, the sound of footfalls moving slowly and carefully through the brush toward us reaches my ears.

I hold a finger to my lips and Adelita's eyes grow big. She swallows back her sobs, a hand pressed to her mouth. I push her gently away and stand up.

I catch his scent before I see him. Relief washes over me. I smile at Adelita. "It's okay. It's my friend."

Max doesn't have the advantage of super hearing and smell so I head out to meet him before he bursts commando style into our clearing and scares Adelita to death. I meet him about twenty yards out and seeing me pop up unexpectedly right in his path gives Max the start I was afraid he'd give Adelita.

He drops his gun hand and exhales sharply. "Jesus, Anna. Where did you come from?" Then he stops and looks at me. *Really* looks at me.

"You've got blood all over you."

I raise a hand to my face self-consciously. I'd forgotten.

Max holsters his gun, pulls a handkerchief from his pocket. "Here. At least wipe your face off."

I take the handkerchief, spit on it and scrub at my face. The cloth comes away stained. When I try to return it to Max, he pushes it back at me. "Keep it. Do I want to know whose blood it is?"

"I'll tell you later. Have Culebra and Ramon left for the village?"

"About an hour ago. I expect them back anytime. Were you coming to give us a report?"

"Already gave it to Culebra."

He shoots me a puzzled frown. "How long have you been here?"

"Since this afternoon."

"Then why—?"

"Come on. I have someone I want you to meet."

Max has a perplexed look on his face, but he follows me. When I get back to the place I left Adelita, my heart leaps with alarm. She's not where I left her.

Max is looking around. "Meet who? There's no one here."

I peer into the bushes, catch her scent, the scent of blood, and follow it to her hiding place. "It's all right. Max is a friend."

I had no idea how the sight of an unfamiliar man would affect Adelita. She's trembling, unable to stand or talk, eyes fixed on Max. Her skin is torn where she forced herself into thick brush, rough bark and sharp branches gouging at her.

I squat so she and I are at eye level. "He will not hurt you. He is here to help get you to safety."

I hold out my hands to her. At first, I think she will refuse to come out, the nightmare of her captivity turning any man not known to her into a new enemy.

But she turns her gaze away from Max and focuses on me. She takes my hand and lets me tear away at the brush holding her until I've managed to make a hole big enough for her to free herself without tearing more skin. I pull her gently to her feet with me.

We walk back to Max.

His eyes widen when he sees the girl, bruised, torn, bleeding, dressed in the remnants of that old blanket. He also sees the fear in her eyes. He makes no move to come closer.

"This is Adelita, Max. She escaped from the village. She is very brave." I touch Adelita's arm. "This is my friend Max. He will help get you to safety."

Max begins to speak softly to Adelita in Spanish. She nods and after a moment, replies to something he asked her. She still has not let go of my hand. They talk for several minutes and then Max says to me, "Let's go back to camp. I have food and water. She looks like she could use something to eat."

Max walks ahead and beside me, Adelita matches my stride without hesitation. She does not take her eyes off Max, though, nor does she let go of my hand. It's no surprise that she doesn't react to the coldness of my skin. I doubt she notices. Shock and fear have turned her own hand to ice.

It's a short walk to the small clearing where the men spent the night. Calling it a "camp" is overstating it. No tents. No campfire. The only indication that anyone was here is Max's duffel shoved under a twisted mesquite. He retrieves it and unzips one of the pockets, pulling a couple of protein bars out of it. He hands them to Adelita.

For the first time since Max joined us, she lets go of my hand. She rips at the paper and wolfs down the first bite so quickly, she starts to choke. I'm at her side in an instant, taking the bars from her hand, breaking off small bits that she eats slowly once she has caught her breath.

Max pulls a bottle of water from the bag next. He hands it to me and I open it and when Adelita has finished the first bar, offer her a drink.

"My god," Max whispers to me while we watch her eat. "Did Santiago do this to her?"

I tell him the same thing I told Culebra—that I didn't know. And that Adelita never heard a name except *El Jefe*. I also tell him about the other girls, the two dead, the four delivered to this *El Jefe* like takeout. What happened when I found the driver and the truck.

"Must be Santiago and his crew," Max says when I finish. "Sounds twisted enough."

Adelita has finished the bars and is sipping at the water. A little color has returned to her cheeks, but her eyes remain wary, watchful. Max hunkers down and when I do, too, Adelita follows our lead.

"When do you expect Culebra and Ramon to return?" I ask.

"They plan to stay on lookout until dawn—or until they know for sure if Santiago is in the village."

"Then what?"

"Then we go in after him."

"Did Culebra tell you—?"

"That Ramon doesn't trust me? Yes. It's not a big surprise, though. The story of my coming along out of friendship for Culebra was a little thin. He may think I'm here solely to bust him."

"There's more, too. Maria wasn't going to let me follow last night. Did Culebra tell you that, too?"

He looks surprised. "No. Didn't have much time alone without Ramon. Did she try to stop you?"

"With a big shotgun."

He looks at me, eyebrows raised. "Is she still breathing?"

"Of course she is. I just incapacitated her. Gabriella would have freed her as soon as the girl woke up. I didn't like some of the things Maria was saying. I get the feeling Ramon has a bigger agenda than he's letting on."

Before Max can respond, I catch a sound approaching through the brush, rapid footsteps coming toward us.

I hold up a hand for Max to be quiet.

More than two sets of footsteps.

I jump up, startling Adelita into jumping up, too.

Max is on his feet, gun drawn. "What is it?"

I grab Adelita's hand, force it into Max's. "Get her out of here. I'll hold them off."

"Them? You're sure it's not Culebra and Ramon?"

"Not unless they've grown a dozen more pairs of legs."

Adelita pulls free of Max, stumbles to my side. I look over her head to Max. "Get her out of here. Get to the Jeep, take her across the border. If they catch her again, they'll kill her."

Max doesn't hesitate even for a moment. He scoops Adelita into his arms. "I'll be back as soon as I can. Do you still have your cell?"

"Turned it off. I don't think I have much battery life left."

"I should get back to the river in six hours." He looks at his watch. "Turn it on at eight a.m. I can trace you."

Adelita is staring at me with the blank-eyed look of a wounded animal. She looks like a child in Max's arms. I stroke her hair. "You will be safe. You can't stay here. The men from the village are coming."

She closes her eyes for an instant, then releases a long slow breath as if the fight has left her. Max tightens his arms around her. He nods just once to me and in the next moment, the two are gone.

CHAPTER 32

MAX MOVES ALMOST AS SILENTLY AS I DO through the brush. In a minute, all I hear are the approaching footsteps of what I guess to be a dozen men. I grab Max's duffel and head back toward the rocks and the burned-out truck.

I do nothing to hide my tracks. I want whoever is coming to find an easy trail to follow. One set of footprints. I want them to come after me.

It takes me far less time to reach the rocks than it will for those following. Gives me time to find a vantage point to use as lookout. While I wait, I open Max's bag of tricks.

I was wrong. He doesn't have a *small* arsenal inside, he has a big arsenal inside. Grenades, flares, a couple of handguns, a small case with a disassembled rifle and a sniper's scope.

Boy Scout, indeed. Prepared to earn a murder badge.

In the side pouches are several more of those protein bars and the last two bottles of water.

I chug half of one, splash water onto the handkerchief

and try again to scrub at my face. I can't imagine how I appeared to Adelita—my face and clothes so soaked in blood.

Maybe the fact that it was one of her tormentor's blood made it less horrific.

From what I gather from the sounds, the men have reached the place where Ramon, Culebra and Max stayed the night. I listen intently but the men don't appear to be talking. They must be a well-trained gang of thugs, not wanting to give away their location. I imagine them searching the ground, finding the discarded wrappers and the empty water bottles. Now comes the tricky part.

Will they see where Max and I found Adelita hiding in the thicket, or will my more obvious tracks draw them away?

In a moment, I have my answer. They start in my direction.

Good.

A glance at my watch.

All I have to do now is keep them occupied for eight hours.

I wait until they reach the side of the road. I want to see who is leading the hunting party. They gather and stop in the cover of brush, whispering and pointing toward the rocks, the beams of a half dozen LED flashlights crisscrossing in front of them.

Then they step into the road.

It's no surprise when I recognize the man in front, or when I hear his familiar voice call out.

"Come on out, Max," Ramon says. "We have Culebra. It will go easier on both of you if you come out now."

He doesn't mention me. Either he hasn't yet been in contact with Maria or he doesn't want to let Max know that I've followed.

I consider my options. I could pick them off one by one with the rifle in Max's bag.

No. Better to lead them on a merry chase away from the village, give Max more time to get away.

One thing I can do, though. Finish the job I started this morning.

I grab one of the grenades. Pull the pin. Toss it onto the burned-out bed of the truck.

The flash of the grenade flying through the air is caught by the searching flashlights. The men dive back into the brush.

The grenade explodes, flinging bits of wood from the truck's side panels and charred bodies in a wide arc and reigniting the fuel that was left in the gas tank.

Now not even Horatio Caine could piece together what's left.

A cry goes up from the group. Excited exclamations in Spanish. Evidently a piece of wood from the truck flew straight into one of the men. He staggers out into the road, flanked on either side by two buddies trying to drag him back into the brush. He's fighting them. There's a long, slender splinter no wider than an arrow projecting from his chest in front and out his back. The two trying to get him out of the road give up quickly and leave him to take cover again. The wounded man makes it no more than three or four steps before he collapses.

I don't know how he keeps going but he raises himself onto his knees, grasps the wooden spear with two hands and pulls.

His scream hangs in the air longer than it takes the blood to drain from his body.

I watch the man die, feeling nothing, my mind a blank slate. No. That isn't entirely true. I do have a thought.

One down . . .

CHAPTER 33

THERE'S MORE MURMURING GOING ON BEHIND the cover of brush at the side of the road. The gist seems to be an argument between the men who want to continue after Max (or who they *think* is Max) and the ones who think they should go back for reinforcements.

Ramon is clear what he wants to do. I hear him arguing that it's only one man for god's sake. But the counterargument is pretty compelling.

It's one of their own lying in a pool of blood in the middle of the road.

I don't wait to see who's going to win. I grab the duffel and start running away from the rocks and in a direction away from the village. If Ramon wins the argument, I want to leave a trail for him to follow. Tracks and when the ground gets rocky, small branches scattered along the way. I want it to look like a man running for his life.

After about fifteen minutes, I stop to listen.

I don't hear anything.

Shit.

They aren't following. My plan to get them going in the wrong direction so I could double back to the village isn't working. I guess the fear that Max had more grenades in that duffel convinced them they needed to amp up the firepower, too.

Damn it. At least it gives Max and Adelita more time to get away.

I backtrack along my own trail, this time not crossing back into the brush, but continuing along the road, careful to keep out of sight. It doesn't take long to overtake Ramon and his gang. Ramon is once more in the lead but he walks like a man rigid with anger that he couldn't convince the others to follow him after Max.

They're moving along the road, on the opposite side from me. To a man, they keep swiveling their heads and flashlights back the way they've come, on alert for an ambush from behind.

I pick up speed. I can easily beat them to the village. If I'm lucky, I can reach out to Culebra, find out where they're holding him, cut him loose before Ramon makes it back. One vampire can outrun an army of men.

And I do. I reach the outskirts of the village in minutes. It's very quiet, though something is different from the first time I approached the village. A lookout is posted near the well. He's in the shadows, but the glowing tip of a cigarette gives him away. I make my way around him soundlessly to the shack where I saw Adelita and the girls.

There's a guard here now, too. Squatting down with his back against the wall of the shack, rifle resting on his lap. I send out a mental probe.

Culebra?

I'm here.

He doesn't sound hurt or scared. He sounds pissed. *What happened?*

Fucking Ramon. Coldcocked me as soon as we got to the village.

How'd he do that? I thought you were suspicious of him?

Not suspicious enough, obviously. Or on my guard the way I should have been. Where are you?

About fifty feet from the shack, in some bushes.

Is Max with you? He didn't get Max, too, did he?

No. I give him a *Reader's Digest* version of what happened. About how I sent him away with Adelita so she would be safe. *He's going to come back, but it will be eight hours at least.*

I let a minute go by before asking. *I know there are more girls. Are they with you?*

No. The anger is back, radiating through his thoughts. *They moved them to another shack. He's with them.*

Santiago?

Not the Santiago we're after. His bastard brother, Luis.

Who the hell is Luis?

A decoy. Culebra's mind radiates dark anger. *A trap set by Ramon.*

Why? What happened to protecting his family?

He is protecting his family. Santiago made him a deal he couldn't refuse. Me in exchange for the life of his wife and daughter.

Santiago wants you? After all this time? You must have really pissed him off.

When Culebra doesn't answer right away, I get the feeling there's something more he's hiding about his past. Something he wants to keep hidden. There'll be time to find out what it is later.

So, shape-shift. Get yourself out of there. The men heading back for the village will leave again to go after Max. I've laid a false trail. When Max gets back, we'll go in after the girls. I'm not leaving them. I saw what they did to Adelita.

Culebra remains shut down. Whether he's considering what I said or coming up with his own plan isn't coming through. Finally he says, *I'm staying put. At least for the time being. I might pick up something from Luis or the guards that gives us an idea where his brother is. We've got nothing but time until Max gets back anyway. May as well see if I can learn something useful.*

What if Ramon comes back and decides to kill you?

Culebra's dry chuckle resonates in his head, transmits itself to me.

Then I shape-shift and bite his ass.

NOTHING FOR ME TO DO NOW BUT WAIT. I TRUDGE back to the same spot I occupied this morning—well, yesterday morning actually—and crawl back inside my little burrow. In thirty minutes I hear Ramon and his troops come into the village. The men disperse, Ramon barking a sharp order that they have fifteen minutes to get supplies and get their asses back to the well. I watch to see if he's going to the shack where Culebra is being held, but he goes instead to where Culebra said Luis Santiago and the girls were hiding.

The guard snaps to attention when Ramon approaches. Ramon ignores him and pushes open the door to stalk inside. His anger is apparent and the guard doesn't challenge or question him—in fact he doesn't even greet him, just ducks out of Ramon's way.

I can't hear what's being said behind the door Ramon slammed on his way inside. Gives me a chance to decide what I'm doing next.

Culebra?

Yes.

When the men start out again, I'm going to follow them for a while. Make sure they pick the trail I laid and not Max's. He's gotten a pretty good head start but hopefully they're not adding a bloodhound to their posse.

Culebra's rasping chuckle comes through once again.

Haven't seen any bloodhounds around.

Ramon appears just then and heads for Culebra's shack.

Uh-oh, I say. *Ramon is on the way.*

I feel it as Culebra's thoughts turn dark and dangerous. *Stay tuned in,* he says. *I'll try to find out what he has planned.*

Ramon heads for the shack, his gait as stiff and angry as

it was before. He greets this guard with as much arrogance as he did the other, too.

"Mueve el culo," he barks. Move your ass.

The guard jumps to his feet, stands at attention. But he needn't have bothered. Ramon whips past him without a backward glance.

In a moment, Culebra has opened a mental conduit that allows me to hear what is going on. Ramon must have struck Culebra because a wave of pain colors his thoughts bloodred. Ramon and he are talking in Spanish, but Culebra's interpretation comes through to me in English. It's a trick of this telepathy thing. No language barriers.

I don't know where Max would go. Or why he left.

You are lying.

Another gasp from Culebra. And another. Ramon keeps hitting him until I feel Culebra's thoughts grow dim. I'm just about to jump up and pull him out of there when Culebra sends me a message.

Don't. Make sure they follow the false trail. Ramon won't kill me. He has orders to bring me to his brother alive.

The beating goes on.

Let me stop this, Culebra. I can kill all these motherfuckers and we'll leave with the girls.

No. Culebra's answer is quick and heated. *We need to find Santiago or I'll never be safe. Go. Please.*

Vampire stirs, feeling Culebra's pain, not understanding why I don't unleash her to save our friend.

But the human Anna understands.

I fight my way out of my bramble hiding place and take off down the trail to the rocks. Culebra's pain follows me but I know he's right. It's the only way. I'll lay the false trail farther and farther from the village. By the time Ramon and his thugs realize they're chasing a ghost, I will have Culebra and the girls to safety.

CHAPTER 34

M Y THOUGHTS ARE FOCUSED ON ONE THING— take this trail deeper and deeper into the desert and farther and farther away from the village. If Ramon wonders why Max would come this way instead of heading back toward the road, I'm hoping he attributes it to Max being disoriented. He heard Max say in the Jeep that he'd never been in this part of Mexico before.

I run, fast, leaving as much damage as I can in my wake. Environmentalists would rank me with off-road vehicles and dirt bikes on the list of forces destructive to the Earth's gentle crust. I kick, pull and crush whatever is underfoot.

When I gauge I've gone ten miles or so, I stop and look back. The meandering path of destruction looks good. A little obvious, maybe, but I'm hoping Ramon either isn't smart enough or is too angry to make that distinction. And it's dark. Ramon will only see what his flashlights allow.

Now to get back. This time, I make a wide arc away from the trail I just laid and run like a light-footed cat instead of a charging rhinoceros. I doubt Ramon will be able to tell anything except that the trail suddenly stops. Let him waste time trying to figure it out.

I almost get caught. I hear Ramon and his party as they arrive across the road from the rocks and burned-out truck. I have to dive for cover in some brush. I end up sharing the space with a startled rattlesnake that curls and hisses at me.

Culebra? I ask hopefully.

The snake's only response is to rattle threateningly and slither backward away from me.

Away from me.

Vampire is smiling. Not Culebra.

Ramon leads his gang toward the rocks and has soon picked up "Max's" trail. I wait until they are well on their way to leave my hiding place and take off for the village.

As soon as I'm in communications range with Culebra, I open my thoughts, hoping Ramon didn't do any permanent damage.

His reply is weak but coherent. *You're back.*

Are you all right?

Depends on your description of all right. But maybe you should check with Ramon. I think I broke his knuckles with my face.

The husky sound of Culebra's labored breathing as he attempts to laugh wipes the urge to smile off my face. *You don't sound well. I'm coming in to get you.*

No. As quick as before. Adamant. *I'm in no danger now. Luis and his guards will be coming here to eat at daybreak. They might let something slip that will give away his brother's location.*

Are you sure you'll be all right?

Yes. I told you. They have orders not to kill me.

But it's all right to beat him senseless. Reluctantly, I settle back into my den. By this time, I've actually made a nice little indentation for myself. Max's duffel is secure behind me. A glance at my watch shows there's still three hours until dawn, four until Max is due to call. I'm glad I had time to tell Max about Maria. She may be waiting in ambush on the path to the Jeep. If she and Gabriella were able to get out through that damaged door, that is.

I scoot down, curling into a ball, and rest my head against the duffel. Stephen's face pops into my head. I've been gone how long? He's probably in Washington already. I can't call him. I have no idea how much battery power I have left in my cell. I can't waste any to check. Besides, what would I say? Hadn't I already come to the conclusion that going to Washington was out of the question for me?

Can't dwell on something I can do nothing about. Four hours. This may be the last time I have to question Culebra about his past. I reach out to him.

I'm here, he replies with an echo of sarcasm that asks, where else would I be?

Tell me why Santiago still has it out for you?

At first, I think he's not going to answer. Or he's ignoring me. There's no open communication link between us. All I can do is wait for him to make up his mind.

At last he does.

I did more than kill for Santiago. His tone is heavy with recrimination and regret. *I told you I was hungry for money and power. So an opportunity came along—one Julio found out about—and I jumped at the chance to participate.*

Another pause. I *feel* Culebra steeling himself to go on. At last he does.

It was a gun deal. Julio had a contact in the ATF. An extremely well-paid contact. A cache of guns that was to go to another government organization was hijacked with this mole's help and brought across the border. Eighteen hundred automatic rifles and handguns. And we delivered them into Santiago's hands.

Julio was a hero. Until it was discovered that Julio's "mole" was an undercover agent. The deal was a sting to track the guns to Santiago and the other cartel heads. We started getting hit with raids on our homes, on our businesses. The ATF came looking for the guns.

They underestimated how quickly we were able to dis-

tribute and hide those guns. They found nothing. But the ATF interference caused a serious setback to the drug operation. For months, we were stopped from using our normal supply routes for fear of being raided. The Federales *increased patrols, closed down the money houses, followed us night and day. Even our families were harassed.*

Santiago blamed Julio. A whisper campaign started. Rumors that Julio knew the guns would be traced. That he'd made a deal with the ATF—safe passage to the U.S. for him and his family if he ratted on Santiago. And collect a huge bounty.

There is so much sadness, so much regret in Culebra's tone that it hurts my heart. His mind closes for an instant. I ask, *What happened to Julio?*

Another long moment of silence. *Santiago had him killed. I was spared because Julio never gave up my part in the operation. He was tortured, but he never gave me up. In spite of it, Santiago had his suspicions. Julio and I were so close. But he decided he couldn't lose two of his best executioners, so he chose to let me live. That time.*

He pauses another long moment. I wait for him to continue, wondering how I could have condemned him on Christmas Eve without hearing the whole story.

Sorry that I did.

How does Ramon figure into all this? I ask finally.

Ramon was from my village. My only friend. Remember my sister? The one I said was murdered? It happened right before I decided to leave my village. It was a gang of local thugs. They picked her up on her way home from school. Took her to an abandoned building. Tortured her, raped her. We found her body a week later in a pile of garbage.

The words stop abruptly. Culebra goes still and silent. Then, *I vowed revenge. Ramon said he would help me. We set out to find the gang. It wasn't hard. We simply hung around the schoolyard waiting for another innocent girl to be targeted. We didn't have long to wait.*

Less than a week after my sister was murdered, they went after another girl. Ramon and I followed them to an old barn on a piece of property long deserted. There were three of them.

It wasn't hard to kill them. Ramon and I called them out of the barn, said we were Federales. *They were kids, not more than sixteen. The idiot* cabrónes *came out with their hands up! Ramon and I shot them where they stood. We let the girl go. She had no problem promising to keep our secret. Ramon and I waited until she had run away, then we dragged the bodies inside the barn. I found my sister's locket and trophies the boys had taken from other girls. There were six trophies. For six girls. I realized then the villagers had to have known what was going on. And yet they did nothing to protect their children. They kept the secret because of shame or guilt or pride.*

It made me sick to live among such cowards. My parents had already made it clear I was a freak, un bestia. *I now held them in contempt, too. I left soon after that.*

His voice leaves an echo in my mind as the words stop. *So helping you avenge your sister is why you felt you owed Ramon a debt?*

Yes. And because I brought him into Santiago's operation when he, too, fled the village. I took him under my wing the way Julio did me.

Do you know why he's turned on you now?

Another empty silence. I wait.

I believe he is trying to save his own skin, Culebra says. *He made a mistake killing that minister's son. Money is more important to Santiago than blood. There is a bounty on Ramon's head now, and on the heads of his wife and daughter. It couldn't have been a hard decision for him to make—trading my life for theirs. I would have done the same thing.*

I don't believe it. But I make no comment. Instead, *I'm not sure I understand. What could Ramon offer Santiago?*

Knowledge that I'm alive. That I was involved in the gun operation. Ramon was the only other person who knew of my involvement with Julio and the ATF sting. One of the first things I did when I recovered from being shot was to give Max the locations of the hidden guns. They were able to recover some of them and round up a few of Santiago's lieutenants.

But not Santiago or the big boss?

A sharp laugh. *They were too smart. They've always been too smart.*

So you did a good thing, right? You saved a lot of innocent lives by getting those guns back.

A sound like a small sob makes the hair stir on my arms. *Not good enough. They didn't find all the guns. I am haunted by the ghosts of those who have been raped, robbed and killed with the weapons they didn't find.*

You did what you could.

I didn't do enough.

The link between us closes abruptly. Through my lacy curtain of leaves, I see why. Men are moving toward his shack, talking softly among themselves. I see two guards I recognize from before and in the lead, someone I don't. A short, fat man I can only guess is Luis Santiago.

CHAPTER 35

LUIS DISAPPEARS INTO THE SHACK, FOLLOWED BY his toadies. I want to rush in, kill the guards, make Luis talk. But I'll wait for Culebra to try it his way. Maybe he's right and the guards will let something slip. They don't expect Culebra to live long enough to pass anything he hears on to anyone else. And they sure as hell don't know he has telepathic abilities. They may speak freely among themselves.

In the meantime, this may be my chance to get to the girls.

I leave my hiding place and make my way to the shack where Ramon went to see Luis. There is no guard outside. It surprises me and makes me wary. I look toward the shacks surrounding Luis'. But no heads appear in the windows, no observers in the doorways, no rifles peeking over the tops of the thatched roofs. The shack appears to be completely unprotected.

There's only one way to approach the shack and that's from the front. It doesn't make sense that they would leave the four girls by themselves. There must be a guard inside.

I pick up a rock and send it skittering through the doorway. Then a second. I'm still shielded by a wall of dense brush so I hunker down to see if the rocks will draw someone out.

Nothing happens.

No one comes to investigate. No shouts from within. Nothing.

Glancing around once more to be sure I'm not being observed, I sprint with vampire speed to the doorway and disappear inside. I flatten myself against the wall and wait to listen for the sounds that would signify life inside the shack.

It's dark and close and smells of unwashed male and sex. The door opens to one room with another just off the back. I detect only the dull thudding of four heartbeats from that room. They left the girls alone.

Should make this easy.

I call out softly as I make my way into the room where the girls are. There's no answer. Once I push back the blanket hung over the door, I see why.

The four girls are lying diagonally across the bed. Their hands and feet are tied, their mouths gagged. When I approach, I smell the harsh pungency of chloroform.

No wonder they weren't worried about leaving the girls unguarded.

They're unconscious.

CHAPTER 36

S HIT.
        I go to the first girl, slap her cheeks to see if I can
bring her around. She moans, but doesn't come to. Neither
do any of the others. I could drag them out of the shack but
in this condition, I don't know what I'd do with them. And
I don't know when Luis will be back. I may be able to carry
two at a time, but if they wake up while in my arms and
start making noise, we'll be discovered.

Shit.

A glance at my watch. Still two hours before Max is due
to call. And then how long will it take him to get here after
that? How long will Ramon keep following my false trail
before he decides to give it up and return to the village?

Time is not on my side.

I step to the window and look out. Three shacks over is
the little church. Is there a priest? Could I persuade him to
hide the girls until reinforcements arrive?

Persuasion is one of my special abilities.

I jump out of the window and scoot around the back of the shacks to the back of the church. There is a narrow wooden door. I try it and the door opens to my touch. I close it quietly behind me and look around.

This is the tiniest church I've ever seen. And the strangest. There is no altar, no crucifix, no statues, no candles. No scent of the beeswax my mother's altar society used to polish pews.

No surprise, that, since there are no pews to polish.

It's just an open room with a long table down the center. Weights and plastic wrap and duct tape are on one end. The rest of the table is bare now. But its use is obvious. White powder residue dusts the surface.

The only thing worshiped in this building is *llello*.

So that bell I heard the first day I scouted this village of the damned was a call to work, not a call to worship.

Nice camouflage. A plane patrolling overhead would see a cute little church, not a cocaine production line.

I look around. There's another door off to the side where the altar should be. I push through it. Inside is a closet and a small cabinet. This looks like the vestibule where a priest would hang his garments and store the communion wafers and wine. I guess in another lifetime, this actually was a church. The lock on the cabinet is broken and when I look inside, it's empty. Dusty cobwebs drape the corners.

What now?

I realize I haven't heard anything from Culebra. I send out a probe, not in words exactly, but an exploratory query to see if I can pick up on his thoughts. Nothing comes through. The conduit is open but cloaked.

At least I don't pick up on any pain. Perhaps he's busy listening to Luis and his buddies.

Shit. Shit. Shit.

My brain is a whirlwind of uncertainty. I leave the vestibule, closing the door behind me. Obviously, there hasn't been a cocaine shipment delivered in the last day or this place would be jumping with activity. Could I stow the girls in here? Would Luis and his thugs think to look in the church? Or would they assume the girls ran off? How much time would it buy me?

Okay, I've got to ask Culebra some questions.

This time when I attempt to contact him, I make it deliberate and forceful.

He lets me in. His *What is it?* is not so much abrupt as concerned.

How long do you think Luis will stay in your shack?

Ten, fifteen minutes. They're finishing breakfast.

Have you learned anything useful?

No, damn it. All the fat pig has on his mind is how long the girls will be under. He hasn't dipped his wick yet and he's getting impatient. Ramon's failure to bring Max back upset his plans. He thought he'd have two trophies to offer his brother by now and an afternoon to reward himself with his new "playmates." But no hint where Santiago is.

Okay. I'm in the church—which really isn't. It's where Luis packages his coke for export. But there's no cocaine here now. Was there any mention of when the next shipment is due?

No. Sorry. No talk of business at all. Just fucking.

His tone is acid tinged and angry. His thoughts are mixed—he's rethinking his not wanting me to come in and kill the whole bunch. The hell with finding Santiago.

Say the word, I respond.

He pauses a heartbeat. *No. I need to do this my way. Stopping Santiago is more important. What are you going to do until Max calls?*

I'm going to move the girls into the church.

It might work. I doubt they'll think of looking so close.

My thoughts, too.

Better make it quick, though. Another pause, as if he's listening again to the conversation going on in the other room. *They're finishing up. Talking about getting back.*

I'll let you know when it's done.

The conduit closes and I waste no time beating it back to the shack.

The girls are still out. I lift the first, deadweight in my arms. I lower her to the ground through the window and repeat the operation until all four are outside. I heft two at a time over my shoulders and run to the back of the church, squeezing through the door. I lay them out on the floor of the vestibule. They just barely fit. I remove the ropes from their hands and feet and the gags from their mouths.

Then I close the door and perch myself on the table to wait for Luis to discover the girls are gone . . . for hell to break loose.

CHAPTER 37

C ULEBRA HAD IT PEGGED JUST RIGHT. FIFTEEN MIN-
utes later, I hear the men outside Luis' shack. I brace
myself for the yells that should follow when they check that
back room.

But nothing happens. I smell tobacco and pot and realize
the men are gathered in front of the shack, enjoying a little
after-breakfast smoke. Even Luis has joined his men, sharing a joke that has something to do with what his brother
plans for Culebra when he gets his hands on him.

I sit up straighter. They're saying Santiago will most
likely kill Culebra—like Culebra did to the minister's son.

Culebra is being blamed for killing the minister's son?
How could that be?

The laughter and crude talk continue for the time it takes
a joint to burn down to a cinder. I start to think I must have
misunderstood. Culebra was long gone when Ramon lost
his son and took his revenge. It's not possible anyone could
have thought Culebra committed the murder.

Is it?

Jesus, is that part of Ramon's trap?

The yell I've been expecting erupts, bringing me out of my thoughts with a start. I cross to the tiny window in front and peek out.

Luis is in the doorway, screaming at his men—upbraiding them for leaving the girls unattended—calling for the man who administered the drug that was supposed to knock them out.

A man slinks forward, mumbling that he doesn't understand how they could have walked away.

Luis draws a revolver from his belt and shoots him—the wound a tiny rose blooming on the bridge of his nose that explodes in a spray of blood and brain matter out the back of his skull.

The men standing beside and behind him are spattered with gore. They recoil.

Luis keeps screaming, waving the revolver. *"Busquen las cabronas. Ya. O le mataré a todos."*

As one, they disperse, running in different directions like rats startled by a cobra.

No one approaches the church.

Yet.

There are six men that I can see—they run from shack to shack, hauling men and families out as they search their homes. They gather the villagers by the well and Luis stands guard over them while the search goes on.

One comes close to the door of the church. I hug the wall behind the door as he looks inside. If he makes a move for the vestibule, I'll kill him. He doesn't. He slams the door behind him and continues to the next shack.

They hit Culebra's shack, too. But since he's alone inside with a guard, they leave him. He reaches out.

You got the girls out, I see.

A disturbing thought strikes me, knotting my stomach. *Luis is going nuts. He killed the man responsible for chloroforming the girls. He's gathering the villagers by the well. You don't think he'll—*

The sound of a gunshot brings an abrupt halt to our dialogue. My heart thuds against my ribs as I peek out once again.

Luis has one of the villagers by the arm. The man slumps into him, bleeding from a wound in his lower thigh. He lets him fall to the ground, goes to the next. Shoots him in the leg, too, and moves on. The screams of the wounded men pierce my heart.

Jesus, Culebra. He's shooting all the men. Wounding them but not killing them.

A spark of dark humor comes through. *Of course not. Can't deplete his workforce by killing them, can he?*

What the fuck should I do?

Nothing. Culebra's tone is obstinate, resolute. *There's nothing you can do. Protect the girls.*

I won't him let him shoot the children. If he starts shooting the children—

Then do what you must.

I watch in disbelief and wait for the shooting to stop. It does, ten rounds later. All the men lie on the ground, moaning, bleeding, their wives and children cowering around them. The smell of spilled blood reaches me inside the church, makes vampire urges flex and chafe to be set free.

Luis, satisfied at last that the villagers knew nothing of how the girls escaped, turns and starts back to his shack. His guards stand by wide-eyed with fear at what Luis will do next. He stops at the door and barks an order that sends them scurrying around the perimeter of the village to expand the search. They leave eagerly, anxious for any excuse to put distance between themselves and their rabid boss.

No one comes near the church again.

I should have stopped him, I tell Culebra.

And then what? We'd be no better off. We don't want Luis, we want his brother. When Ramon comes back and we have Max on our side, then we act.

I think you want Ramon more than you want Santiago, I say quietly.

He doesn't deny it. His thoughts are suddenly closed to me.

Why?

His mind doesn't reopen to me for a full minute. Then, *I heard something Ramon said to one of the guards. When he was beating me. He took credit for killing my family. For leaving me to die in that burning car.*

I thought you said it was the boss.

I wasn't there when my family was killed. I always figured it was the boss. I didn't see who was in the car when I was shot. But today, I learned the truth. I heard it from Ramon's own lips.

I think of hearing Luis tell his men that Culebra was responsible for the minister's death. How his brother would kill him. Ramon was setting him up again. *Culebra, there's more—*

A sound from the direction of the vestibule. A scraping, like a person struggling to stand up. A moan.

Culebra, I have to go. The girls are coming to.

The next instant he's gone and I'm rushing to the vestibule. When I open the door, one of the girls is on her feet, wild-eyed and looking around frantically. I see it in her eyes—she's looking for a weapon. When she sees me and realizes it isn't Luis or one of his men, her expression shifts to confusion. But the instinct to fight remains strong. She backs into a corner, her fists balled at her side.

I hold up my hands. "I won't hurt you," I whisper in Spanish. I put a finger to my lips and glance toward the window. "You must be quiet. *El Jefe* is looking for you."

The name ignites fear in her eyes but also understanding. She hasn't been here long enough to have been reduced to the state Adelita was. Her clothes are still intact on her small frame, her hair still shiny and held back from her childlike face with a barrette. She can't be more than fourteen.

The others begin to regain consciousness, too. One retches from the effects of the drug, her shoulders heaving. I hold her hair away from her face. The girl who first awoke steps beside me and takes my place, holding the sick girl's head and crooning softly to her.

She calls her *hermana*—sister. This one can't be more than twelve.

Revulsion comes in waves of red-hot fury. I want Luis to find us so I can tear him to pieces in front of this child's eyes.

Not yet, Anna. Culebra has honed in on my emotions. *You will get your chance, I promise you.*

Luis is mine.

He is yours.

The young girl has stopped heaving. The older sister hugs her to her chest, whispering that they must be quiet. All four now huddle together, eyes on me.

I want nothing more than to give them the assurance they seek. That I can wake them from this nightmare and get them to safety.

I need a plan. And I need a diversion.

I need Max.

CHAPTER 38

IT'S FULL DAYLIGHT NOW AND I LOOK AT MY WATCH.
Ten minutes before I can turn on my cell and try to reach
Max. A glance around at the girls looking to me for salva-
tion makes my heart feel heavy in my chest. How long can
we hide here before someone thinks to look more closely in
the church?

At eight, I switch on the cell. The power indicator reads
two bars. Less than half power. I pull up Max's number and
press Send.

He picks up right away. "Are you all right?"

"Did you get Adelita to safety?"

There's just the slightest hesitation, but it's enough to
jump start my heart. "Max? Where's Adelita?"

He snaps back. "Relax, Anna. She's okay. She's in a safe
house on the U.S. side of the river."

I let out a breath. "Good. Here's the situation. I got four
girls away from Santiago's brother, Luis, and we're hiding
in a church building in the village. I don't know how much

time we have before they look for us in the one place they haven't searched. It might not be long."

"Where's Culebra?"

I tell him quickly and succinctly what's happening to Culebra. What I don't tell him is that Ramon was one of the bastards that attacked him all those years ago. Some news is better left delivered in person. I finish up with, "How long before you get to us?"

"I'm already on the way. Do you have the duffel?"

"You mean the one with the arsenal inside? Yes. Nice thinking, by the way."

"I should reach you in four hours. I'll contact you when I get close."

"No Maria sightings?"

"No. You must have done a good job on that door. Shut your phone down now. Conserve power."

He says good-bye and disconnects. I do the same, noticing I'm down to just one bar now as I power the phone off.

The girls have been watching me whisper into the phone. They don't say a word when I shove it into my pocket, waiting, I guess, for me to give them some kind of signal that we can leave now.

Instead, I tell them something that makes their faces grow even tauter with concern. I have to leave them. I need to get the duffel. The weapons inside may be their best hope yet to making it out alive.

The older girl has assumed the role of protector. She listens to what I tell them I must do. My Spanish must be getting better, because she nods and pulls the others into a close circle. "We will be waiting for your return," she says. In English. "I will keep them quiet. Please hurry. We have been without food and water since yesterday morning. I don't know how much longer the little ones can last."

At fourteen or so, she is the oldest of the four by two or three years. She is the most physically developed, her sister and the others are barely into puberty. The tear-streaked faces of "the little ones" burn into my brain. Luis' appetite has not only grown, it's gotten more perverse. I look around the church, trying to understand how men can perpetuate such horror on children.

No answer comes.

This used to be a place of worship. My head spins at the paradox. God created men like Luis in his own image? Then maybe god created this vampire to be his retribution.

CHAPTER 39

I T'S GROWN VERY QUIET IN THE VILLAGE. THE WOM-
en have taken their men back into their shacks. There is
just the occasional muffled cry as a wound is being tended.
I can only imagine the primitive tools they're using to ex-
tract those bullets.

Should I feel sympathy? I can't. Bastards let little girls
be tortured under their noses. I hope it hurts like hell.

I look out the window. The body of Luis' dead henchman lies unattended in the dirt. Flies drone around like the
corpse in a cloud. A pack of mangy dogs materialize from
the brush around the village. They sniff the body, take ten-
tative nips as if testing to see if there is any life left, any
movement that could signal a threat. After a while, two of
them work in concert, grabbing the ankles, yanking the
body to the side of the well out of my view.

Away from the lone man standing outside the nearest
shack.

Luis' guard, the only one not searching the perimeter for
the girls, stands at attention beside the door to the shack.

Trying to ignore the dogs. But he can't ignore the sound. He can hear as well as I the noise the dogs make as they tear into the flesh of Luis' victim. His eyes swivel back and forth. Sweat trickles down his face, stains the collar of his shirt. He doesn't try to wipe it away. He doesn't move at all, afraid maybe to incur Luis' wrath like the man being torn apart on the other side of the well—especially if the wrath takes the form of a bullet to the brain.

I'm glad the girls are huddled in back. They can't see or hear this.

When I think it's safe, I climb out of the back window and drop silently to the ground. I have only to make it a few feet before reaching cover. Then I'm scurrying through the brush like a desert coyote, eyes, ears and nose alert for the return of Ramon and his men or the approach of Luis' search party. Those cowards seem to have disappeared. Maybe the idea of facing repercussions for not being able to find the girls made running away a more favorable option.

The duffel remains where I left it. Culebra's shack is within sight, but I don't take time to reach out to him. I'll let him know that Max is on the way when I've gotten back to the girls.

I lift the duffel carefully, hold it against my chest to keep the guns inside from shifting around. It's so quiet around me, even the slightest sound might draw attention.

Then I'm racing back to the church. When I reach the back window, I lower the duffel silently to the floor and climb in after it.

The four girls are just where I left them, clinging to each other, breathless with fear. The older girl's eyes flicker with relief when she sees me.

I zip open the duffel to see if there are any more of the protein bars inside. There are only two left. I hand them to her. *"Éste es todo. Tu tienes que compartirlos con las otras."* When she's taken them and is dividing them, I ask, *"¿Como se llama?"*

She waits until the three have started to eat, before she

answers, "Esmeralda." She points to each girl in turn, "Francisca, Dorotea, my sister, Peppi."

"Do any of the others speak English?"

Peppi alone looks up from her bar. She has been eating slowly, one tiny bite at a time. "*Sí.* Yes. A little."

I rummage in the bag to see how much water is left. One bottle. Shit. I think back to a few hours ago when I used a bottle to wash the blood from my face. A stupid waste of water. Water these girls need. With a sigh of self-recrimination, I pull the last bottle out and hand it to Esmeralda. "This is all the water."

She understands and opens the bottle. She tells the girls in Spanish, "Take just a sip. We must make this last."

There are no groans of protest, just grateful smiles. Each in turn tips the bottle to parched lips and swallows a mouthful. When they pass it back to Esmeralda, she recaps the bottle without taking a drink herself. She hasn't eaten her bar, either, but has rewrapped it and slipped it into a pocket in her skirt.

She reads the question in my expression. "I don't need it. They might." Her eyes turn to the girls.

She is saving hers for the little ones. "You need to be strong for them. At least take some water."

"You haven't."

And there's a very good reason for that but telling her what it is might make going back to Luis seem a better bargain than staying here with a vampire.

"I drank a bottle earlier," I lie. "I'm fine. Please. At least take a sip."

She seems ready to argue but then, since I don't appear ready to give in, she opens the water bottle and brings it to her lips. As if I can't tell she's not really taking a drink. Then she carefully recaps the bottle, and stares at me until I give her a grudging nod.

She's stubborn. She reminds me of me.

I like her.

Nothing to do but hunker down and wait for Max and hope he gets here before any of the villagers realize no one has yet made a thorough search of the church for the missing girls. The fact that Luis' men couldn't move fast enough to get away from him is working in our favor. Hiding in plain sight does sometimes work.

Esmeralda has the three girls gathered around her like a mother chicken with her peeps. They are all so quiet, so withdrawn. Since they arrived less than twenty-four hours ago, and Luis has had other things to occupy his mind, maybe I'll be able to get them away before their nightmare becomes worse than being kidnapped and drugged.

And what Luis had planned for them is infinitely worse.

CHAPTER 40

I 'VE NEVER SEEN CHILDREN SO CALM AND SILENT. I
guess that's what happens when you're scared to death.
I'm the one who has to remind myself not to keep checking
my watch, not to get up and pace to the window. Luis'
shack faces the church directly and if the guard sees a
flicker of a shadow or a face at that window, he's sure to
come investigate.

My whole body burns with the need to do something.
Waiting has never been easy—not when I was human, especially not now as a vampire. David used to hate doing
surveillance with me. I'd get so antsy, he'd say I was like a
maggot in shit. Crude but accurate. I couldn't sit still.

What happens when Max gets here? As long as Ramon
hasn't returned, the answer is easy. I "question" Luis about
the whereabouts of his brother while Max frees Culebra.
Then we get the hell out of here. Get the girls to safety,
come back to mop up.

If what Culebra says is true about Ramon, he's as dead
as the Santiago brothers.

I'm sure Culebra will insist. As will I.

Peppi is whispering something to her sister. Esmeralda looks over at me. "She has to go to the bathroom."

The little girl has a look of embarrassment on her face.

"It's okay, Peppi," I whisper. "Go behind the vestibule door."

Esmeralda helps her sister to her feet and points to the door. Peppi scoots around her, glancing back at us as if ashamed her body has betrayed her.

"What about the others?" I ask Esmeralda.

She asks, but the other girls shake their heads. I think they are afraid to move away from her protective arms.

"Are you all from the same place?" I ask Esmeralda when Peppi has returned and settled down once again near her sister.

"Yes. A village not far from here."

I think of Adelita's story. "Were you brought here with the promise of jobs?"

Esmeralda's face grows dark with anger. "Jobs? No. We were kidnapped from a schoolyard. In the middle of the day. In front of our teachers. They stood by and watched, too frightened of the narcos to fight to save us."

"Did you know the men who took you?"

"Yes. The men in our village grow *amapolas* . . . um, poppies. When the men came, we thought it was for the *opio*. The drugs. But they took us instead. For *El Jefe*."

She is quiet for a moment. "I begged them not to take the little ones. They laughed and said I could come along, too, if I wanted to take care of them. They didn't know Peppi was my sister. But the way they said I could come along, the way they laughed, I knew what they were going to do. I had to stay with the *niños*. To try to protect them. But I failed."

"No. You were very brave. And we will get them out of here. Someone is coming soon to help us. We need only be patient for a little while longer."

As soon as I speak the words, the thought "from my lips to god's ear" leaps to mind. Must be the influence of our setting. The look of hope on Esmeralda's face burns like a torch. I hope my promise to her doesn't prove to be as empty as this forsaken church.

THE HOURS PASS WITH SLOW-MOTION AGONY. I CAN'T think of anything else to ask Esmeralda and she, too, stays silent. She doesn't ask me who I am or why I'm here. I glance down at my bloodstained shirt. Perhaps she's afraid of the answers. Her eyes follow me each time I walk to the back window and I feel her watching when I return my seat. She's put her trust in me, but that doesn't mean she's going to relax her vigilance. All that's important to her is that she and the girls are alive and unmolested. In her eyes, I read her resolve to fight for them. Against anyone.

The village is quiet, too. I keep expecting the search party to return or Ramon and his men to come back. I wonder what Luis is doing in his shack—probably devising ways to torture the men if they come back empty-handed. Or jerking off to mental images of four little girls.

Finally, finally, I hear footsteps approach. One set of footsteps. I jump up so fast, vampire fast, everyone gasps. I curse myself for the blunder, put a finger to my lips. Only I can hear the stealthy approach from outside. I want to be sure it's Max before the footsteps come any closer.

I move to the back door, open it a crack to test the wind.

Max's scent.

Relief washes over me like a tidal wave.

I look back at the girls. They know someone is outside. Fear is stark on their faces. "It's okay," I whisper. "It's my friend."

I wait for Max to get to the door, then push it open. He slips inside. He's dressed in camos, a large backpack over his shoulders, a rifle strapped across his chest.

He and I look at each other a moment. Then his eyes go to the girls. He takes off the backpack and opens it. This time there's a water bottle and protein bar for each girl.

The food and water are accepted eagerly. Even Esmeralda drinks this time and unwraps her bar gratefully.

We watch the girls eat and drink.

"I'm glad you're here," I say.

Max is quiet for a moment. "I'm sorry about what happened before. If you love Stephen, I hope it works out for you. I don't know why I did or said what I did."

God, that conversation seems so long ago. And so utterly irrelevant now. Not that I intend to let Max off so easily. I allow a smile. "Maybe you really *are* a prick. Ever thought of that?"

"Every minute of every day."

He has a wistful tone to his voice that makes me stare hard at him. "Who are you and what did you do with the real Max?"

His face reddens a little. A sound from outside cuts our conversation short. Once again, I've picked up what human ears cannot. I signal Max and the girls to be quiet.

After another second, though, it's unnecessary because the cacophony of cries and gunshots is explosive enough for us all to hear. We freeze.

I gather from the excited calls to Luis to come outside that Ramon and his men have returned.

I peek out the front window.

Ramon says he did not return empty-handed.

The shouts bring Luis to the door of his shack. Ramon and his men are gathered in a circle near the well.

"Esta son para muchachas," Ramon says. *"Le trajimos una sorpresa. Un premio de la consolación."*

He is offering a consolation prize for Luis' lost girls.

A consolation prize?

Luis steps forward. *"Enséñame,"* he says, hand on the gun at his waist.

Ramon steps aside and one of his men pushes a figure behind him to the front.

All the air rushes out of my body. My heart pounds so violently, I'm sure everyone can hear it. I whirl on Max with rage bubbling in white-hot fury to the surface.

"What the fuck have you done, Max?"

He shoulders me aside to look out.

He pales. "I don't know how she got here. You have to believe me, Anna. I don't know how she could have followed me."

I shove him away, back against the table, with such force, he stumbles and falls. The table scrapes loudly against the wooden floor. I don't care about the noise.

I whirl and look outside again.

One of Ramon's men has pushed her to the ground and Luis is circling her like a lion with wounded prey.

Ramon grabs her hair and yanks her face upward.

"Oh god, no." The words hiss out, my heart pounding. "Adelita."

CHAPTER 41

I WATCH LUIS. IF HIS HAND SO MUCH AS TWITCHES on that gun, I'm going out after Adelita. He's questioning his men, asking how they found her and where. He points to her clothes, clean jeans and a sweatshirt, asks her how she got away. How she could have escaped the burned-out truck. Why she came back.

His eyes search the perimeter of the village, asking is she alone?

He fires off one question after another, not waiting for answers. Ramon tries to interrupt, offering assurances that she is alone, that they found no one else. Just a dead-end trail that stopped so quickly, it was as if an angel had reached down and spirited Max away.

Luis doesn't look convinced. He approaches Ramon and draws his gun, putting the barrel against Ramon's forehead.

Kill him. I wish it so hard, the nails on my balled fists draw blood.

But Ramon pleads for his life, begs Luis to ask his men.

They will confirm his story. There was no sign of Max. They found Adelita right outside the village.

Luis lowers the gun a fraction, asks if Ramon found any trace of the six men who went in search of the other girls—the ones spirited away from his shack like Max was evidently spirited away—*"No por ángel,"* he spits. *"Por el diablo mismo."*

By the devil.

I let a smile touch my lips. I've been called worse.

Ramon looks around. He finds the body of the murdered guard, dragged away to the far side of the well, recoils at the sight and sound of the dogs ripping at it. He meets Luis' eyes. Shakes his head. *"Lo juro. No vi a nadie."*

Luis drops his gun hand. He fires off a rapid-fire directive that has Ramon and his men looking at each other with puzzled expressions.

Ramon frowns. He has been told that all of his men will be required to work the shipment arriving today. Not just the villagers. *"¿Por qué?"* he asks.

Luis smiles. *"Usted sabrá pronto bastante."*

Max, too, has been listening. "Why would the villagers not be able to work?" he asks me. "What has Luis done to them?"

I watch as the men disperse, quietly, slinking away as if hoping Luis does not notice and call them back. Only Ramon, Luis and Adelita remain. I ignore Max, waiting to see what happens next. Luis reaches down and hauls Adelita to her feet. He pulls her close to him, clutches her chin in a pinch so hard, I think I see bruises start to form.

"Afortunado para ti, estoy corto seis trabajadores," he says. *"Ramon, átala aquí hasta que llegue el carro."*

He is telling her she is lucky that he is down six workers. I allow a little relief to loosen some of the knots in my shoulders as Ramon ties her to a post near the well. Then he and Luis disappear into Luis' shack.

I draw a breath. It may be a temporary reprieve, but at least I can keep an eye on her. If Luis had dragged her inside his shack, it would have given us no time to formulate an escape plan. I shut my eyes in frustration and concern. Now we have five girls to protect.

I'm ready to face Max.

Once again, my nails bite into the palms of my hand. It's the only way I can keep my anger under control. Even my voice shakes with the effort when I ask, "How did she get here?"

Max can sense how close to rage I am. He closes his eyes for a minute, just as I did before, and passes a hand over his face. "There can be only one way. I didn't think to check."

"Check what?"

"I didn't take the Jeep back to the States. I took the Explorer. I picked it up at the airstrip. There is a tarp over the cargo space in back. Adelita begged me to bring her with me when I came back to get you. I said no. She may have hidden in the back."

"May have?"

"I thought I'd convinced her that we could take care of it. I promised her we would."

I feel the pressure building again, the need to rip something apart or scream. Instead, I center myself, focus on drawing strength from deep inside. "Care of what? What exactly did you promise, Max?"

"When we were in the border station, I showed her some pictures of cartel members, to see if she could identify who attacked her. She identified Luis. She also identified the man who came to her village. The one who kidnapped her."

I know before he says it.

"Ramon."

He nods. "She went crazy when she saw his picture. Said she had to stop him from kidnapping any more girls. I promised her that we would stop him—you and I. She agreed to stay at the border station until we got back."

"But she didn't. How could you have not known she was in the back of the car?"

Max releases a breath. "On the way here, I thought I heard something—a noise—from the back." He lowers his eyes. "I just figured something had shifted. You've seen the back of my truck. I keep tools in the back. And other stuff. When I didn't hear anything again, I forgot about it." He holds out his hands. "Anna, how could I have known she stowed away? She told me she'd wait for us."

My eyes drift out through the window to Adelita, tied like an animal to the well. I'm not ready to concede that Max was not to blame for her being here. Part of me admires her courage and determination. Part of me wants to shake her until her teeth rattle.

She has not uttered a sound since arriving at the village. Her face is turned toward the direction of the dogs, the sound of them worrying at the corpse and snapping at each other hangs heavy and grotesquely on the still morning air. She must be so scared.

"Anna?"

Max's voice pulls me back. I shift my gaze to him.

"Luis said they're expecting a shipment today. We have to get the girls out of here."

He's right.

Luis didn't say when the truck was due, but what if Ramon gathers the troops and directs them to the church to wait? Our luck is running out.

Esmeralda appears suddenly at our side. She, too, heard all that transpired outside and understood the conversation between Max and me. Her grasp of the situation is evident in the shadow of fear that darkens her eyes. "What are we going to do?" she asks.

I look up at Max. "You take the girls. Get as far away as you can." A tiny pause. "And you will make sure they stay put this time, right?"

A spark flares in Max's eyes. "I've already had one new asshole ripped today. Don't need another one." He jabs a finger in my direction. "And you?"

"I'm going to wait for the shipment to arrive. When the men are busy unloading the truck, I'll free Culebra. Then we take care of Ramon."

Max hefts the backpack. "What about Luis?"

"Get the girls to safety. Meet us back where you camped out that first night. We'll bring Luis there."

"Just you and Culebra? There must be twenty men in the village now that Ramon is back."

I allow a growl to erupt from the pit of my rage. I lean close so that only Max can hear. "Good thing I'm hungry."

CHAPTER 42

ESMERALDA HAS THE GIRLS UP AND GATHERED around her. She whispers how important it is that they be very quiet. Max climbs out the back window first and I lift the girls one at a time to his waiting arms. I focus all my attention on listening, making sure no one is approaching the church until they are all safely hunkered down outside. Then I signal Max to move out.

Esmeralda grabs my hand and kisses it.

I touch her cheek.

Then they are gone.

I still have Max's duffel and I open it and take inventory. There are two grenades, the guns and plenty of ammunition. Too bad Max didn't pack real explosives—dynamite or C4. It would be an easy way to take care of both the drugs and the men—rig a bomb.

The fact that I don't know how to rig a bomb I view as a minor impediment. And make a note to do some research on that when I get home.

I listen but don't yet hear the approach of a vehicle signaling the arrival of the drugs. Time to alert Culebra and get him ready to act when I say the word.

I open my thoughts to him and he's there.

What's going on? I haven't heard from you for hours. Did Max make it?

Come and gone, I reply.

What do you mean gone?

Just left with the girls.

So, it's just you and me.

How many men with you?

Three now. Two just came back. They think Luis is loco. They said that fucking all that young pussy has softened his brain. They found out what he did to the villagers when he discovered the new girls had gone missing. They plan to go along with him until the truck gets here, then get the hell out the first opportunity they get.

Think they all feel that way?

At least the ones who went out with Ramon looking for Max. They aren't too crazy about Ramon, either. Think he's planning something. Trust is not big among these thugs.

I let a beat go by before changing the subject. *How are you holding up?*

Fine. I'm done waiting for these cogidas locas *to tell us where Santiago is. I say we get one or two of them somewhere alone and make them talk.*

My thoughts exactly. There is one complication. I tell him about Adelita following Max and how she came back to stop Ramon. That it was Ramon who kidnapped her from her village. I also tell him that right now she's tied next to the well and that Luis will probably kill her after he uses her to help process the shipment coming in today.

Brave girl, Culebra says. *Stupid, but brave. But you have no intention of letting him kill her.*

Not a chance. I'm thinking we let her work for the narcos. Then when the truck gets ready to leave, we lob one of Max's grenades into it. That will take care of one problem. If we're lucky, most of the men will be inside, too. Ramon, you can take care of. Once I've got Adelita safe, we'll take her and Luis and meet Max. Can you get free?

Just tell me when.

Culebra falls quiet and I do, too. More waiting. More nervous energy building up with no way to release the pressure. I wish I could let Adelita know I'm here and that we'll get her out when the time comes. I take out one of the grenades and toss it hand to hand, feeling its round heft, listening to the safety ring jingle against the fuse. This tiny activity brings some relief, some promise of action to come.

While vampire rests quietly inside.

She is not restless or anxious. She is patient.

And hungry.

CHAPTER 43

LUIS IS THE ONE WHO ALERTS ME THAT THE TRUCK is on its way. He comes out of his shack, a cell phone at his ear and Ramon at his heels, and heads for Adelita. In a minute, he's cut the rope binding her to the post and is dragging her toward the church.

I remembered the first time I watched the village from my hiding place in the brush. How the church bells called the villagers to what I mistakenly thought was worship. I'm in the same place now, the duffel safe beside me, watching the same procession of men, women and children answer the peal of the bells. The difference this time, though, is that half the men are limping, their leg wounds bound by clumsy bandages, their faces drawn and pale from the pain.

I've removed all traces of the girls' presence from the church. The empty water bottles, the wrappers from the protein bars. Even used a rag from the duffel to scrub away Peppi's urine stain before moving back to the other side of the village.

The only bad thing about moving is that I can't see Adelita now that she is inside the church. I can listen though. If I hear anything that sounds like Luis is abusing her, the plan to wait goes up in smoke. So far, it's quiet.

What I do have is a clear view of the torn body of Luis' henchman. The dogs have left, slinking back into the brush, leaving only the bloody, stinking mess of internal organs exposed to sun and heat. If I were capable of it, I would have gagged at the smell. There is blood and then there is blood.

In a few minutes, I hear the truck. I signal Culebra. *The truck is coming. I have no idea how long it will take to package the drugs so be ready to get out when I tell you.*

His response sounds like a hiss of anticipation. It makes me smile.

The truck pulls into the space between the well and the church. Two men jump out and one whistles a shrill greeting. By the time they've opened the back, three other men have joined them. Ramon's men. I can tell because they aren't limping. Yet.

The five men each shoulder a bag marked *harina*—flour—and head into the church. Only one man is sent back outside to stand guard. The door closes.

No sound of casual chatter drifts out from inside the church. Only the occasional sharp bark of an order or harsh hacking cough from a breath drawn too deeply. I didn't see any protective masks among the detritus of plastic bags and duct tape left from one delivery to another. Evidently Luis doesn't worry about his workers getting high on his supply. Maybe that's part of their pay. All the cocaine you can inhale while working. I think of the children. My stomach roils.

I hope Adelita is careful enough to stay alert. She has no idea I'm here or that I'm planning to rescue her. But she needs to be able to move on her own when I tell her.

How long does it take to process five twenty-five pound sacks of cocaine? I have no idea. It strikes me that I know someone who does. I also realize I no longer hold Culebra's past against him. It's with a sense of relief that I reach out to him.

Is it time?

He sounds so eager I find myself smiling. *Not yet. I have a question. How long does it take to package a hundred and twenty-five pounds of cocaine?*

That's about sixty kilos. Depends on whether they're cutting it or just packaging it pure to be cut later.

I didn't see anything around to cut it with, unless one of those bags wasn't cocaine after all.

Unlikely. With everyone in the village working, I'd say not more than two hours. They can move pretty fast if they're just weighing and packaging it.

Then we have two more hours to wait.

What then?

Once you hear the grenade explode, make your getaway. Meet me behind the church. How many men are with you?

Just one. That same hissing sound comes through that I heard before. *I'll bite him enough times to make sure he's down. May not kill him unless he dies from shock. He may. I plan to let him see me shift.*

I like your style.

I like yours, too. You may not know it, but cocaine is highly flammable. That truck should go up like a bomb.

That's what I'm hoping.

We lapse into a comfortable silence. Then Culebra asks, *How do you expect to get Adelita away from Luis?*

I'm hoping when he hears the explosion, he sends his goons out to check what happened. I figure he won't keep more than one or two men with him. I'll take care of them and get Adelita free. We're meeting Max back at the campsite. I plan to bring Luis with us. What happens to Ramon is up to you.

Good, Culebra says. *I want to watch Ramon die.* A pause. *What about Luis?*

No hesitation. *Max can have first crack at him. Make Luis tell him where his brother is hiding. I figure I owe Max that much. He wants a big fish. I plan to see he gets a big fish. After that, Luis is mine.*

Luis won't be easy to crack.

The memory of finding Adelita being raped in the back of that truck, the image of Luis going from villager to villager and shooting them as casually as if swatting mosquitoes, the faces of the four young girls he had delivered like takeout for his pleasure . . . these things run through my mind before I answer.

Not easy for Max to crack maybe, I say. *But not hard for me. He'll talk for me.*

CHAPTER 44

I T'S MORE DIFFICULT THAN EVER TO WAIT. THE thought that Adelita is being used as slave labor makes me long to get her out of that church. I wish I could have gotten a message to her. She doesn't know I'm here. She doesn't know I'm watching her. She must be feeling such terror, such hopelessness. She came back to do one thing—make Ramon pay. Keep him from taking other innocents the way he took her. She'll think she failed.

Did Ramon recognize Adelita when he caught her sneaking up on the village? Or has Ramon kidnapped so many girls, the faces blur in his memory? Did she tell him who she was?

I have to take a step back. I'm working myself into the kind of state that makes vampire want to claw and chew her way free. I have to keep her in check, at least until I've disposed of the truck and gotten Adelita to safety. When Culebra has Ramon and I have Luis is the time to allow vengeance and anger out to play.

At last, the door to the church opens and a man steps out,

beckoning the guard inside. In a moment, there is a flurry of activity as the villagers begin moving pallets of small, wrapped parcels to the truck.

Culebra?

I'm here.

They're loading the truck. When you hear the explosion, make your move.

His eagerness to attack comes through in a fiery wave of anticipation that sizzles in my head.

Meet you at the camp.

I wish I could watch Culebra shape-shift into a rattlesnake and see the guard's expression when the snake attacks. But a bigger part of me is anxious to get into position to exact some retribution of my own.

I take both grenades from the duffel and secure them by hooking the handles over my belt. The irony that I'm wearing Gabriella's clothes while plotting revenge against her father is not lost on me. I wonder what Gabriella would think if she knew what her father had done—the girls, some younger than she is, that he's procured for his boss.

Shit. Maybe she already does.

I watch as the men load the truck. When there are fewer trips being made back and forth, I figure they're close to being finished. I leave my hiding place and start out for the road. I'd been going over in my head the best place to attack. I tear across the desert floor.

Not far from where I found Adelita that first day, there's a bend in the road. Two tall, bushy mesquite trees grow, one on each side, to form a canopy over the spot. I stash the duffel beside one of the trees and scramble like a monkey up the trunk to test the strength of branches intertwined in the middle, looking for one capable of supporting my weight. When I find the right spot, I stretch my body flat, like a cat hunting a bird, and peer down through the leaves to check it out.

Perfect. I won't even have to lob the grenade. Just pull the pin and let it drop.

I'm ready. The sound of the truck engine cranking to life

in the village sends my heart into overdrive. The only draw-back to my plan is that I left before the last of the cocaine was loaded. I don't know how many of Ramon's men chose to leave with the truck.

Or how many Luis would allow to leave.

The sputter of the truck engine idling makes me feel the same thrill that I felt from Culebra when I told him it was almost time. Every nerve in my body tingles. I push my face down into the leaves to make sure I have a clear shot when the truck passes underneath. I grab one of the gre-nades off my belt and hold it ready.

I don't know how fast the truck will be going and it oc-curs to me that the concussion from the explosion might dislodge me. No problem. I'm high enough not to be blown apart, and that's the most important thing. A fall to the ground won't kill me.

I focus on the sounds from the village. The truck engine idling, rough at first, then smoothing out. The clutch en-gages. I feel the vibration as the truck rolls onto the dirt road.

The truck picks up speed and my heart races with excite-ment. I allow a smile. I see a plume of dust draw closer, hear the wheels hum. It takes about five minutes before the truck rolls into view. Another two to approach the bend.

I gauge the trajectory, squeeze the handle, pull the gre-nade pin, wait for the canvas top of the truck bed to move into place directly underneath me.

I open my hand, let the grenade fall.

CHAPTER 45

NOTHING HAPPENS THE WAY I EXPECT. I IMAGINED the truck would go up in a fiery explosion, the way the one I found Adelita in did. It's what happens on television. It's what I counted on.

Not so much.

The grenade hits the top of the canvas, bounces. My breath catches. Is it going to bounce off? No. It settles between the cab and the canvas. When it explodes, the cab takes the brunt of the blast, glass from the rear window explodes out and through the front, taking the bodies of the driver and his passenger with it. They hit the ground twenty feet away, bloody, not moving.

But the panel bed of the truck remains intact. Licks of flame tickle the edges of the canvas. Nobody runs out the back so I assume Luis kept all of the men at the village.

I drop down from my perch. Maybe I need to add an accelerant. Adelita's tormentor had a gas can in his truck.

I make my way around to the back. It would be too much

to hope there's a full gas can here, too. When I pull back the tarp, all I see are the hundreds of small plastic and duct-taped packages.

No sound yet from the village but I have no doubt the men are heading here at a run. Quick. Think.

What did Culebra say? Processed cocaine is highly flammable. I jump inside, start ripping a dozen packages apart and shake the powder loose.

I need a rag. Nothing I can see. I rip the sleeves off my blouse. I tie the ends together to form a long rope. Stick one end in the gas tank, bury the other under the cocaine.

One grenade left. This has to work.

Stepping back, I squeeze the handle, pull the pin, toss the grenade into the back.

This time, the resulting explosion is all I'd hoped for. The cocaine goes up with a loud whoosh. Flames zoom along the rope into the gas tank. The blast lifts the back of the truck off the ground and then erupts in a giant fireball.

Very satisfying. Except for one thing. I'm standing too close. The skin on my face and arms grows hot and tight. I jump back, fingers flying to explore the damage. Blisters are already forming. Followed seconds later by the pain.

Fuck. Not the first time I've been burned. Not the worst burn, either. But it hurts like a son of a bitch.

No time to worry about me. I hear the sound of a vehicle approach from the village. I hadn't seen another vehicle in all the time I was hiding there. Must have been hidden in the dense brush behind the village or in one of the shacks. Hardly matters *where* it came from; it's almost here.

I grab the duffel from under the tree. Consider climbing back up to ambush the men coming from the village. But I need to get back to Adelita. Hopefully Luis sent most of his men to check out the explosions. Leaves fewer men between Adelita and me.

But I don't wait to see. I start back at a run, not parallel to the road, but in an arc away from it so I'll come out behind the church. I make it back to the village in minutes, far quicker than the time it will take the vehicle to get from the village to the site of the explosion. When I'm right behind the church, still hidden by brush, I stop and listen.

There's a lot of noise coming from the direction of the well. I recognize Luis' voice and Ramon's. Shouting with an edge of hysteria and mounting anger. Recriminations fly back and forth. They don't even know what happened and they're snapping at each other like a couple of mongrels.

When I make my way to the back door of the church and peek up to look through the window, the place is empty. I knew it would be too much to ask to find Adelita alone inside.

I scoot back into the brush. If she's not in the church, she must be in Luis' shack.

Before I plan my attack, it's time to see how Culebra is doing.

He picks up on the first mental ring.

Where are you?

It might be my imagination, but his voice sounds more sibilant than usual.

Near the church, I reply. *I'm going to get Adelita now. I think she's in Luis' shack. Ramon and Luis are by the well. Can you keep them busy for a few minutes?*

I think I can manage it.

Will you tell me when to go?

He laughs. Coldly. *I won't have to. You'll know.*

The ice in his tone makes my blood quicken.

He's right. In moments, there's a cry from outside. Ramon. I glance out the window. Ramon is hopping on one foot, clutching his right ankle. Luis looks on, horrified, as the biggest rattlesnake I've ever seen slithers toward him. The snake is horror-movie size, its tongue dancing on the air, a death rattle trailing behind.

Luis doesn't have a weapon and Ramon's revolver lies in the dirt a dozen yards away where he dropped it when he was bitten. All Luis can do is stare. And back away.

If it weren't so important to get to Adelita, I'd watch to

see where Culebra bites him. I hope it's in the balls. I drag myself away from the window and steal out the back door. The fact that no one came running at Ramon's cry tells me they've either been sent by Luis to investigate the explosion or are cowering in their shacks, afraid of what Luis is doing to Ramon.

I move silently to the rear of Luis' shack and peek in. The small window opens to that back room where I found Esmeralda and the little ones bound and drugged. There's no sign of Adelita.

No sign of a guard, either. I debate whether to take a weapon but one-on-one, vampire can move faster and quieter and do more damage than any weapon. I leave the duffel on the ground and slip inside.

Luis is still yelling for help so I assume Culebra hasn't attacked him yet. Ramon, on the other hand, is screaming in pain and fear. When I sidle up to the open doorway that separates the two rooms, I finally see Adelita.

She's at the doorway that opens to the courtyard, watching what's happening near the well. A guard is holding her by the arm with one hand; he has a gun in the other. He tracks the slithering path of the huge snake advancing relentlessly toward Luis, his eyes registering horror. Luis is yelling at him to shoot it, but the guard is too afraid to leave the shack. The revolver hangs uselessly at this side.

Lightning fast, I grab the gun away from the guard and bring the butt down hard on the back of his head. There's a sickening crunch of gun metal on skull and he hits the ground. He didn't see it coming, his expression reflects no surprise, no pain. His eyes simply go blank. I stuff the revolver in the waistband of my jeans, grab his ankles and yank him back out of Luis' line of sight.

Not that Luis is looking. His gaze remains fastened on the snake.

But Adelita releases a sharp breath. Her hand flies to her mouth, smothering first the startled cry as the guard goes down and then the relieved cry when she recognizes who knocked him out.

She shouldn't be too relieved. I plan to let her know at the first opportunity how stupid it was to sneak into Max's car and to end up, once again, Luis' prisoner.

But first things first. I place a finger over my lips and motion abruptly for her to follow me. We move slowly away from the door. At the doorway to the back room, I lean close and bark, "We'll go out through the window."

She nods, avoiding my eyes. She must hear the anger in my voice.

Good.

I drop down first, holding a hand up for Adelita to grab as she lowers herself to the ground. I keep hold of that hand and, snatching up the duffel, lead her into the brush and away from the shack. She comes along quietly. As relieved as I am that she's unhurt, that's how furious I am that she put herself in the position to be hurt in the first place.

When I think we're safely far enough away, I draw her to a stop beside me. "I have to go back," I tell her. "You stay here. Right here. Do you understand?"

"Go back? Why?"

"To help another friend."

"Is it Max? If it is, I want to help."

"No."

She flinches, the word hitting her like a slap.

"You cannot help. You shouldn't even be here. Now this time, listen to me. Stay right here. I won't be long."

Her jaw sets. "Do you know what my name means?"

The question comes out of the blue. I stare at her, then throw up my hands. "Fuck, Adelita. What kind of question is that?"

"Do you?" she insists, digging in mental heels. She doesn't drop her gaze or look away.

I give in. "No. What does it mean?"

"Warrior." She says it with pride. "I am not a child. I want Ramon to pay for what he did to me and to the two girls who died in that truck. You can't stop me from going back."

Her tenacity is admirable. Completely and ridiculously absurd, but admirable.

"How do you propose to get Ramon?" I ask. "You have no weapon. You are one against his army."

She points to the guard's gun, tucked into my belt. "I'll take that."

I'd forgotten the revolver. It was a reflex action to take it when the guard fell. "Do you know how to shoot?"

"Yes."

But her eyes betray her.

I shake my head. "No. You don't. I can't stand here and argue with you, Adelita. If you want to help, please just be here when I get back. We may have to move fast. I promise, we will punish Ramon for what he did to you. He is being punished now."

Her eyes widen. "You mean the snake? Do you think god sent the snake? Is it possible?"

That god sent the snake? Hardly. But if it will get her to concede to my wishes, I'll play along. "Maybe. But I think it's also a message that you need to protect yourself. You've escaped Luis twice now. You might not be so lucky the third time."

I imagine the thoughts spinning behind those dark eyes. "You may be right. Perhaps god wants me to save other girls from men like Luis. Maybe if I tell my story . . ."

"That's it." My skin is crawling with the need to get back to Culebra. To get Luis and Ramon away from the village before the men return with tales of the lost drug shipment. "We'll get you interviews in all the newspapers. But right now, I have to get back to the village. You'll be safe if you stay right here. I won't be long. I promise."

Finally, a solemn smile touches her lips. "I promise, too. I will wait here for you to return."

I'm so relieved, I want to kiss her.

But then she follows up with, "Maybe you should leave the gun? In case someone comes looking for me?"

My eyes narrow. "Don't fuck with me, Adelita. Stay

right here." I let vampire surface, just enough to make my eyes turn—slit like a cat's and yellow. Threatening.

She gulps. And backs down. "I will wait here."

This time I believe her.

I snatch the duffel, run back through the brush, blood hot with anticipation, eager to take my turn with Ramon and Luis.

CHAPTER 46

Luis is still crying like a little girl and Ramon is still squealing like the pig he is. Culebra has wound his heavy, sinewy coils around Luis' legs and is spitting into his face with a tongue darting from a head as big as a Rottweiler.

I take a moment to enjoy Luis' terror before I reach out to Culebra. *I'm back. Looks like your snake act is making Luis apoplectic. He may stroke out before you have the chance to kill him.*

There's no response. It dawns on me that I'm not sure if our mental connection works when Culebra is in his other form. Maybe I need to speak out loud—

You could have stayed away a little longer. He hisses the words. *Things are just getting interesting.*

—or maybe Culebra is enjoying himself, too.

I step out of the shadows and go first to grab up Ramon's gun before he remembers he dropped it. He looks startled to see me and I realize he hasn't been in contact with Maria after all. For an instant, he forgets about his swollen ankle and stares, mouth open.

Then concern darkens his face and turns his mouth hard. "You. How did you get away?" Concern veers to anger. "Maria. Did you hurt her?"

"Not as much as she wanted to hurt me," I snap back. "But I guess that was your idea, wasn't it? To have her threaten to shoot me if I tried to leave."

"What about Gabriella? If you did anything to hurt her—"

"Ramon!" Luis yells. *"Cállate la boca!"*

We both turn to Luis, the snake's head now perilously close to his. He says, *"¿Quién es esta mujer?"*

Culebra swivels his head and I swear he winks at me. Then Ramon is explaining who I am and that Max and I are friends of Tomás.

At the mention of Tomás, Luis unleashes a torrent of Spanish, telling Ramon to go get the guard in Tomás' shack and to bring the guard back here to shoot this fucking snake. And for Ramon to shoot Tomás while he's there, the hell with what his brother wants.

Ramon hobbles off with a backward glance. I have his revolver dangling at my side but he doesn't try to take it from me. He doesn't seem to want to get any closer than he has to. Maybe he thinks I've forgotten I have it and if I remember, I'll shoot him.

They think they're still in charge, Culebra says with glee in his tone. *I think I'll go show Ramon how wrong they are.*

Culebra begins to loosen his coils, drawing himself down from Luis' body. I watch the process with interest. If I didn't know the true nature of that huge reptile, I'd be scurrying up the nearest tree. As for Luis, he goes weak-kneed with relief when the snake untangles itself and frees him. He sinks to the ground, face pale with fear; his dark eyes stand out like black Chinese checker marbles on a granite slab.

Pathetic wretch. I have to stifle a laugh.

Culebra slithers off into the brush after Ramon. I get

CHAPTER 47

L UIS STARES AT MAX. IF EVER AN EXPRESSION REGIS-
tered a "now who the fuck is this?" look, it's his.

Max and Adelita join me. "How did you get back so
quickly?" I ask.

"Hitched a ride with the *Federales*. They picked us up in
a helicopter near Ramon's place. Before you ask, the girls
are safe. Then they brought me back." He shoots Adelita a
stern look. "Alone, this time."

Adelita isn't looking at Max. I'm not sure she heard him.
Her eyes are on Luis. She steps toward him, but I grab her
arm and pull her back.

"I know what you want to do," I say quietly. "But we
need him alive. At least for now."

Max looks around. "Where is everybody?"

"Cule—ah—Tomás should be back any minute. With
Ramon."

Luis squares his shoulders. "Ramon will have killed him
by now." He squints at Max. "So you are the American pig
after my brother."

Max raises his eyebrows. "I guess I am. And you are the *pendejo* brother he tethered like a goat out here in the middle of nowhere to lure the lions."

"You will never catch Pablo. He's too smart and his army too strong. You and your bitch and the traitor Tomás are dead." His eyes flick to Adelita and he moistens his lips with his tongue. "You, chica, I may keep around for a while. You will have to do until I find those four *pequeña putas* who ran away. I don't know how you got away from the burning truck, or escaped from my shack, but here you are again. It is fate."

This time when Adelita jumps toward Luis, I don't hold her back. She's on him like a wild woman, spitting and clawing until his face is running with blood. He's twisting against the ropes, trying to protect himself, but he's helpless to do anything but scream at us to stop her.

The blood has me mesmerized. I find myself licking my lips the way Luis did his a few moments before.

Then Max touches my arm.

I look at him. He nods toward Adelita. Vampire retreats and I put my arms around Adelita's waist and lift her back and away.

She squirms and fights against my grip, but I'm much stronger and when she's caught her breath and starts to calm down, I turn her to face me and cradle her in my arms.

Luis moans. His face is a mess. Adelita caught his right eye with a fingernail, there's a long gash radiating from the corner and it's red-rimmed and weeping. Makes me hug her tighter.

Adelita grows still, resting her head against my chest. Then she straightens and steps free, not looking at Max or me. She stands with her back to Luis. Her shoulders shake and I think she's crying, but I let her have her moment. She's one tough kid.

Luis, for once, has no vitriol to spout. His eyes are squeezed shut and he draws shaky breaths through clenched teeth. He's in pain and it's a joy to see.

Max leans toward me. "We should get out of here. Where's Culebra?"

A good question. *Culebra?*

His answer comes back. *On my way.*

As if on cue, there's movement from the perimeter of the village and Culebra and Ramon appear. Ramon is stumbling like a drunk. His right ankle is bound by a crude bandage that looks like it's made from strips of a sheet. His hands are tied behind his back with rope. His eyes are glazed, his gait unsteady.

Culebra is walking close behind him—*walking* behind him. He is back in human form and has a rifle in his hand. He is smiling.

Does Ramon know—

Culebra answers before I complete the question. *That I'm the one that bit him? No. Not yet.*

Luis doesn't see Ramon and Culebra until they are right in front of him. When he does, the color drains from his face, making the blood from his wounds stand out in slashes of crimson like paint on a canvas.

Ramon doesn't notice. He's busy trying to stay on his feet. He doesn't look good.

Is he going to be all right? I ask Culebra. Not that I care. But he may have information we need.

I only bit him once, Culebra answers. His glance goes to Luis and he says out loud, "Looks like *he* got into a fight with a panther." He hooks an eyebrow in my direction. *Or a vampire.*

I jab a thumb in Adelita's direction. "Not a panther. A wildcat."

Adelita turns at the sound of Culebra's voice. Her posture straightens when she spies Ramon. Her smile is bitter as she assesses his condition. "Another pig," she spits.

I hadn't had a chance to ask Adelita the question I considered earlier. I jab a thumb toward Ramon. "Did he recognize you when he found you outside the village?"

Ramon catches the question and his eyes go to Adelita. "Why would I know you?" he asks.

Adelita's eyes go hard at his answer and I think for an instant she will go after him the way she did Luis. "Does that answer your question?" she says to me, taking two steps forward to shove him with both hands.

Ramon loses his balance and tips back, unable to break his fall. Adelita takes the heel of her foot and presses it into his injured ankle. He cries out, writhing in pain.

"You kidnapped me from my village." She punctuates each word with a grinding of her heel. Then she steps back to stand beside Max and me. "He'll remember me now, I think."

"No wonder you like her," Culebra says to me. "She's just like you."

Max looks around. "We'd better get out of here. Luis' men may come back at any time. With reinforcements."

Luis lifts his head. "You'll never get away. My men know every inch of the area. And when I tell Pablo what you've done, there won't be a place on this fucking earth where you'll be safe."

"And when do you plan to tell Pablo?" Max looks at Ramon. "I think I know of a place Pablo won't find us. Isn't that right, Ramon?"

Culebra has pulled Ramon roughly to his feet. Ramon has no more fight in him. His face is drawn with pain and resignation. "I would like to see Maria and Gabriella," he says simply.

Max strides to Luis and cuts the rope binding him to the post. Before Luis can take a step, he's replaced one restraint with another, handcuffs.

"What are you doing?"

"Do you think we're leaving you?" Max says. "You can't be that stupid."

"Stop!" he screams. "You have no authority here. This is kidnapping."

Adelita moves again. Fast as quicksilver, she's darted to Luis and with strength I wouldn't have expected from such a small girl, she's backhanded him across the face so hard, he stumbles backward. *"¿Usted habla del secuestro? ¿Cómo atrévase le?"*

Max and Culebra watch, grim smiles touching their mouths. She's asking how he dares to talk of kidnapping.

I smile, too, before taking Adelita's hand to pull her back once again. "Easy, girl. He has a long walk ahead of him. Plenty of time for him to ponder the irony. The kidnapper kidnapped."

Adelita spits in his direction but does back up with me.

Luis coughs and works his jaw, a trickle of blood glistening at the right corner of his mouth. He glares at Adelita but has the good sense to keep quiet.

Max motions Culebra to join us, leaving Ramon and Luis a few feet away at the well. He lowers his voice so they can't hear. "We're going to have to make good time. It's a four-hour hike back to Ramon's little hideaway. Once we get there, we'll contact the pilot and make arrangements to get Ramon and Luis into custody. I'll have our guys waiting at the San Diego/Tijuana border to make the arrest."

"You're not taking them at Reynosa?" I ask.

Max shakes his head. "Can't trust that Luis' men won't be waiting for us there. Better to put some distance between us and the cartel."

I glance toward Ramon, leaning heavily against the well for support. "Will he make it?"

Culebra follows up with an even better question. "Do we need him?"

Max considers the question, then directs another at me. "What about Maria and Gabriella? Do you think they'll be a problem if we show up without Ramon?"

"Not for long," I answer shortly. "It's odd that Maria hasn't gotten in touch with Ramon. She must have figured a way to get out by now."

"Which means, maybe she didn't want to get in touch with him." Culebra glances at Ramon. "Maybe she and Gabriella are ready to be free."

Max shrugs. "Seems the majority opinion is that we

leave Ramon. Now we have to decide if we leave him alive or dead."

Adelita has been listening. She steps forward. *"Muerto,"* she whispers with a grim smile. *"Yo lo haré."*

She wants Ramon dead and she's volunteering to do it.

I echo her sentiment. "Dead. Or he's likely to let Luis' troops know who to look for when they get back."

Max nods his agreement. Culebra's lips curl. "It is decided." He looks at Adelita. "But I will be the one to carry out the execution. He murdered my family." He turns to Max. "You take Luis and Adelita." Then he narrows his eyes at me. "Anna, will you stay?"

Adelita's eyes burn into me. Scenes of the hell she's endured seem to shine through. It takes me a nanosecond to reply. "Hell, yes."

CHAPTER 48

IT TAKES LONGER TO CONVINCE ADELITA TO LEAVE Culebra and me with Ramon and to go on with Max and Luis. She argues that she has a reason to want Ramon dead, too, and should be allowed to witness his execution. Her voice is low and urgent.

She appeals to me rather than Max or Culebra and I know why. She saw me with the driver in the truck. She knows my taste for vengeance is strong.

But as much as I understand her feelings, as much as I sympathize with her, she has seen enough death in her short life. Her nightmares will be riddled with blood and terror as it is. She has had no control over what happened to her up to this moment. Time alters perspective. If she participates in killing Ramon, consciously or unconsciously, she may come to feel responsible for his death. She has been abused, but she's not a killer—yet.

That's a burden she doesn't need.

That's a burden best shouldered by me.

That's a burden I've already accepted.

Max lets me talk with her and after a time, when Adelita reluctantly accepts that she should go, I nod to him.

He approaches, dipping a hand into his backpack. "I almost forgot. I brought something for you."

He pulls a clean, white T-shirt out of the bag and hands it to me. "Figured you were ready for a change of clothes."

I glance down at my blouse, frayed around the arms where I tore off the sleeves, covered with blood, so dirty it's hard to imagine it's original pristine whiteness. Wonder if Gabriella wants it back?

I take the T-shirt, smile a thank-you and slip the tee over my head, working the blouse off and letting it slip to the ground. Then I work my arms into the sleeves and tug it into place.

I feel better already.

Max motions to Adelita, then crooks a finger at me. "You'll follow?"

"We'll be right behind you."

Max leads Adelita into the brush, staying close in case she takes a notion to change her mind. Luis, tethered by a short length of rope, walks ahead. He has been quiet during the exchange. Perhaps afraid if he says anything, he will meet the same fate as Ramon.

Ramon, for his part, is quiet as well. It's as if he's no longer in the present, but gazes unfocused at a scene only he can see. Culebra and I wait until we can no longer hear Max and Adelita. Then we approach.

Culebra prods Ramon with the barrel of his rifle. "I heard you," he says.

Ramon raises his head, his eyes clear. "You heard what?"

"I know the part you played in the death of my family. I know you tried to kill me."

Ramon looks away. "It was a long time ago."

"You did it to take my place with Santiago."

A shrug. "You would have done the same."

"And now?" Culebra asks. "What do you gain from my death now?"

Ramon is leaning heavily against the well, trying to take the weight off his injured ankle. I don't let him, leveraging my own body against his so he stumbles onto both feet again. He winces and whistles with the pain. *"Puta,"* he hisses.

"Answer Culebra's question."

"I needed someone to serve up as Rójan's killer. Someone Santiago would believe still held a grudge."

"Why would Santiago believe Culebra killed Rójan?" I ask. "He's been gone fifteen years."

"We killed his family. Blood vengeance runs deep." Ramon sniffs. "Killing Rójan wounded Santiago where it hurt the most. He lost money. And Santiago would believe me because I said it. Especially when I confirm his suspicion that Tomás *had* worked with Julio to set up that gun deal. Twice he has cost Pablo Santiago money. Your friend *Culebra* would be dead so he could not dispute it. I would have killed him as a show of loyalty and been back in Pablo's good graces." His voice drops. "I would have avenged my son."

"And assuaged your guilt?" I think back to what Gabriella told me. "Your own daughter holds you responsible for Antonio's death. Did you know that?"

"She is a girl. She does not understand how it is with men. They have to be strong. To stand up for themselves. Antonio was weak."

Something in his tone sends an icy finger up my spine. "Was any of the story you told us about your son true?"

Ramon blinks over at me. "What difference does it make?"

Culebra catches the meaning of my question. "Did Rójan do any of the things you accused him of?" He speaks slowly, coldly, deliberately.

Ramon's eyes shoot fire. "He pissed on my son. *Pissed* on him. It was an outrage and Antonio should have killed him for that. He wouldn't. So I did."

Culebra and I look at each other, understanding dawning with brutal clarity. Ramon made up a story designed to suck us in. And it did.

Culebra opens his thoughts, his mind a black void of despair. *Do we need to know anything else?*

Do you think he knows where Santiago is hiding?

Culebra shakes his head. *I think Luis is the only one who knows. Ramon has not had Pablo Santiago's trust since he killed Rójan. I doubt Pablo was so quick to accept Ramon's version of what happened. But when Ramon cooked up the story that I killed the boy to get even with Santiago for killing my family, and the finance minister was demanding blood for blood, I became the perfect scapegoat. He sweetened the pot by reminding Pablo of the gun sting. I told you, money is more important than blood to Santiago. He didn't really care who to sacrifice now, as long as the finance minister was satisfied and the money exchange houses were back open.*

Ramon is watching us now with more interest. Perhaps he senses there is something passing between Culebra and me.

How do you want to do this? I ask Culebra.

He hesitates only a moment. *I think I would like to watch. See him suffer. Are you hungry?*

Yes. Please. Vampire purrs.

Culebra takes a step back. "Good-bye, Ramon."

I take a step closer.

Ramon looks puzzled. I have no weapon to threaten him, yet he feels threatened. His eyes are shadowed with fear. He looks past me to Culebra. "You don't have to do this. Let me go. I will make things right with Luis and Pablo. I will tell them the truth."

Culebra shakes his head. "It is too late. You killed my family. You were willing to sacrifice me for a lie to save your own skin."

"Not for me. For my family. For Maria and Gabriella."

I sidle closer. "And where is Maria? She did not try to warn you that I was free. Why do you think that is? Do you think she found out what you've been doing for Luis? About the girls whose lives you've ruined?"

"I had no choice." But there is no remorse in Ramon's voice. No trace of guilt.

"Do you know who Adelita is?" I ask, keeping my voice as low and human as possible.

His eyes snap to me. "That crazy bitch? I've never seen her before."

I'm right beside him now, so close my lips nuzzle his chin. "Are you sure?"

Ramon begins to see and feel and hear the changes taking place in me. The heat from my skin, the teeth at his neck, the timbre of my voice morphing from human to animal. "I don't know her. What are you doing?"

I take a nip, right at the jawline, let the blood trickle onto the collar of his shirt. "Sure you do," I manage to say. If I don't get this out quickly, I'll miss my chance. Vampire is clawing her way free. "You took her from her village with two other young girls. Promised them jobs. Promised to return them home. You did neither. Two are dead. You have to answer."

He looks into my eyes—vampire eyes, golden, slit like a cat's. "*¿Dios mio, lo que son?*" he whispers.

I glance at Culebra, give him one last chance to intercede on Ramon's behalf.

Culebra stands stiffly upright, his face rigid in its resolution. He gives a tiny shake of his head.

"What am I?" I whisper then. "Vengeance."

Anna is gone. Vampire rips into his throat, cutting his scream short. He struggles, but he's already weak from the snakebite and it takes only one hand to hold his head while steel jaws clamp down, seek the carotid artery, sever it with teeth that saw back and forth until the blood is freed.

Will his blood taste of the snake?

Vampire lets it flow into her mouth, sampling. It tastes like any other human blood—full of warmth, vibrancy, life. It flows like sweet, fresh water drawn from a well. There's no hint of evil beneath the skin. No hint of death and treachery. I put both arms around him as his body slumps into mine. Hold him up, shake him, make sure he's conscious. I draw my head away to look into his eyes. He sees. He's aware.

He's afraid.

I glance back at Culebra.

His face is stern. He meets my eyes and nods.

Vampire smiles at Ramon. In a dim corner of the human Anna's mind, a picture of a son driven to suicide and two dead girls lying in the back of a truck comes into sharp focus. It's all vampire needs.

She turns snapping jaws back to his throat to finish the job.

CHAPTER 49

RAMON SAGS AGAINST ME, DEADWEIGHT, THE LAST flutter of his heart going still. I step back and let his body drop.

Vampire is reluctant to relinquish control, but Culebra is close and his urgency comes through.

We have to go.

I let my head fall to my chest, shake it to clear away the animal and look up at Culebra with human eyes.

"Thank you," he says.

"It was for your family. And Adelita."

"I know."

Culebra hands me a rifle and we start after Max. There hasn't been a sound from the villagers, not a light has gone on in any of the shacks. It's full dark now, and as I glance back at Ramon's body, a shadow among shadows, I wonder if anyone will venture out to see if he's really dead.

Or maybe no one cares.

I stop to pick up the duffel, thinking it's beginning to feel like an extension of my arm.

But thanking Max for packing it.

Culebra and I move quickly and quietly through the brush. He doesn't seem to have any trouble seeing in the dark or keeping up with me. It's not long before I hear footfalls ahead and know we've almost caught up to Max.

From the direction of the road, the sound of an approaching vehicle moving toward the village. I tilt my head.

"I think Luis' men are returning. We'd better hurry."

We pick up the pace, trotting through the underbrush, oblivious to the growls and hisses that rumble around us as we disturb other night predators on the prowl. We are not challenged and in minutes, we see Max ahead.

He hears our approach and peers into the darkness. "Anna?"

"Right here. Luis' men are at the village. I don't know how long it will take them to learn what happened from the villagers. They don't know who we are, but they know we have Luis. They'll come looking for him."

Luis has been listening. He looks behind us. "Where's Ramon?"

"Dead," Culebra says.

Luis spits at the ground. "He was a traitor. He lied to you. He brought you here to die. Let me go and Pablo will reward you. You were a good soldier once, Tomás. You could be again."

I think Culebra is going to ignore Luis. He stares at him, no expression at all on his face. Then, with a single, quick thrust, he slams his rifle butt into Luis' gut.

Luis doubles over, unable to draw a breath as the air rushes from his body, gasping until his face is blue from lack of oxygen.

Culebra grasps a handful of Luis' hair and yanks him upright. "Your brother called me a traitor once, too. And had my family killed. Ramon told you lies about me and you believed him. When I left the cartel, I left this life behind. I took my vengeance in my own way. I never came after you or your brother. You and Ramon should have left it alone, Luis."

Luis struggles to breathe, his chest heaving. Culebra shoves him away and he collapses on the ground, rolling into a fetal position in an effort to force oxygen into his lungs.

Max takes Culebra aside. "We don't have time for this. When we get to Ramon's, you can beat the shit out of him. Hell, I'll help you. But we have to get there first."

Culebra's eyes are still on Luis, but he gives in with a grudging nod. He reaches down and hauls Luis to his feet. When he prods him with the barrel of his rifle, Luis moves. Unsteadily, at first, but faster as he catches his breath.

Adelita trots beside me as we resume our trek. "Is he really dead?" she asks.

"Yes."

"Did you kill him?"

"Yes."

"The way you killed the bastardo in the truck?"

I let my eyes find hers in the dark. Her expression is neutral. No fear. No unease. "Do you know what I am?"

She hesitates only a moment. "I think so. *¿Eres vampira, no?*"

"And that doesn't scare you?"

She raises her shoulders. "You have not hurt me. You have protected me. The evil in this place resides in the souls of men. Like Ramon and Luis."

"They can't hurt you anymore. Max will see to that. If you want, he can get you into a program across the border."

Adelita's expression sobers. "Then who will stay to protect other girls? To tell the world what is happening here?"

I remember the conversation we had when I convinced her to stay put while I went back to help Culebra in the village. "You can do both," I tell her. I think of Stephen. "I know just the person who will help you."

She lapses into silence, perhaps considering if such a thing could be possible. I'm silent, too. Wondering if introducing Adelita to Stephen is the last conversation Stephen and I will have.

CHAPTER 50

THE FARTHER WE GET FROM THE VILLAGE, THE SAFER we feel, and the mood of our little group lightens. Max and Culebra talk softly between themselves. Adelita strides with quiet confidence beside me, her eyes on Luis' back. I have a feeling if he tried to make a break for it, she would be on him before any of us.

I glance at my watch. It's almost three a.m. We've been walking for four hours. I don't recognize the terrain around us, but when I last came this way, I was following a scent, not noting the landscape.

"Max? How much farther?"

He stops and we gather together. "Should be close. Anna, you and I will go ahead. We saw the location of the security cameras so we know how to avoid them. Culebra, you stay with Luis and Adelita until we know it's safe. I don't want to walk into a trap. If Maria got out, no telling who might be waiting for us."

Culebra yanks Luis to a tree and secures the handcuffs around the trunk with a piece of rope. He pulls it so tight,

Luis' cheek rubs against the trunk. He yelps as his already bruised and battered face presses into the rough bark.

Adelita and Culebra smile at each other.

Max and I start out, Max scoping the tops of the trees with a flashlight, searching for the hidden cameras. I spot the first without needing a flashlight. I point it out to Max. From its location, it's easy for us to determine the location of the others. We quickly move forward, keeping low to the ground, until we get to the clearing.

But at that point we have to stop. There is no way to cross the clearing without being picked up by the cameras.

No way for Max, that is.

I take a look around.

The cameras are positioned to catch movement on the ground in the front of the cabin. Only one door, no windows. The place looks as if it's about to fall down, leaning precariously to one side. Designed to look unsafe, to discourage anyone from coming too close. There is a small gap up at the apex of the roof, caused by the uneven settling of the cabin's foundation.

I gauge the distance. If I can get up onto that roof without detection, I will be able to see if Maria or her daughter are inside keeping watch.

When I glance at Max, I see he's been following my roving eyes with his own. I point to the roof and he nods. Then I move into position so I'm out of the line of sight of the door.

I realize when faced with a challenge like this that I've yet to figure out all that I'm—that vampire—is capable of. It takes a situation like this to test the boundaries. I've scurried up walls and the sides of buildings and leapt *from* roofs. But I've yet to leap *onto* a building. I call forth vampire with a little thrill of anticipation. This will either be a spectacular success or a bone-jarring failure.

I gather myself to leap, muscles tense, tendons tight, feet flexed. When I launch myself into the air, there's a moment of exhilaration. A feeling of escaping gravity, of leaving the confines of the Earth. I hold my arms to my sides and look toward the spot I'm aiming for. When I'm above the roof, I straighten, head up, feet down, and float to a landing just above the gap.

It's magic. I feel like Superman. I'm so excited, I forget for a moment why I'm here. Even Max, when I look for him in the bushes, has a look of astonishment on his face. He smiles when he catches my eyes and gives me a thumbs-up. He mouths, *You can fucking fly.*

I have to force myself to push the excitement down and think about what I need to do next.

I lean over and peek into the cabin. The table has been levered down to expose the stairway. But no one is in sight. I listen carefully for noise from inside. I can't hear anything, but that may be due to the thickness of the cave walls, not the absence of humans. From this vantage point, I can't tell if the door at the bottom is open or not.

Only one thing to do. I gesture to Max to stay put and lower myself carefully into the cabin. There's not much room to maneuver and no way to escape being seen if anyone's standing at the bottom of the steps. I lay on my stomach and creep to the open trapdoor.

When I look over the side, the stairwell is empty.

The entrance to Ramon's secret hideaway stands open.

CHAPTER 51

FROM MY VANTAGE POINT AT THE TOP OF THE STAIR-way, I can't tell if the control is still broken and if the door was forced back or if it's been removed. I can see into the great room but can't hear the mechanical whir of the generator. I don't sense any human presence, either. There are no heartbeats, no familiar smells associated with fe-males, no deodorant, perfume, pheromones.

The place *feels* deserted.

Before I call Max and tell him to bring Culebra and Adelita here, I'd better make sure.

Once I make it to the bottom of the stairs, it's obvious how the door was opened. It's been removed, bolt by bolt, and lies on its side just inside the entryway.

Could Maria have done it? I heft one corner. I doubt it. The thing must weigh two hundred pounds.

I make my way quietly across the great room and check out the hallway and bedrooms. Empty. All Gabriella's things are gone as are Maria's. Only Ramon's clothes oc-cupy a half-empty closet.

So much for standing vigil.

With the generator turned off, the air in the cave is still, stuffy. The faint smell of pine that gave the place its open-meadow freshness is gone.

When I check out the kitchen and dining area, the pieces of towel I used to bind Maria lay in a heap next to the chair she was tied to. The broken cell phone is where I tossed it on the counter. Other than that, the only thing out of place is the slightly rancid smell of food from a refrigerator whose power has been turned off.

And the missing artwork that adorned the walls.

Maria took the valuables.

How long has she been gone? More importantly, who helped her with that door?

I run back up the stairs and call to Max. No need for caution now. He disappears for a few minutes and returns with Culebra, Adelita and Luis.

Luis is as dumbstruck by Ramon's elegant hideaway as Max, Culebra and I were when we first saw it. Adelita just stares. I'm sure she's never been inside a *home* like this, let alone a narco's secret safe house.

Max sniffs. "We need to get that generator turned back on."

"Any idea where the controls would be?" I ask.

Max heads for the kitchen and begins opening cupboards and cabinets. Culebra shoves Luis onto a chair and hands Adelita his rifle.

"If he moves, shoot him," he tells her.

Only she and I know she has no idea how to fire that rifle. Culebra doesn't. Luis certainly doesn't. The way she scowls at him, the rifle pointed at his chest, Luis hunches his shoulders and sits still. After what she's done to him, with what he knows she wants to do to him, he's not taking any chances.

Neither am I. I stand beside her and keep watch.

Culebra joins Max in his search. Finally, in a corner of a pantry, Max spies a metal panel. He pulls the latch and points to what looks like a computerized circuit board.

"Jesus, Max. Do you know how to work that thing?"

He grins. "How hard could it be?"

Culebra puts out a hand and grabs Max's before he comes in contact with the circuits. "Wait. Ramon may have booby-trapped the place."

Max jerks his hand back. "Like a self-destruct function?"

Culebra nods. "He was a clever bastard."

Max takes a step back. "Well, we're not going to be here that long, anyway. We're getting air from the open stairway. That will have to do."

Luis has not said a word since entering the cave. Now he straightens in the chair and says, "What happens now? Do you call your DEA buddies to come get us? Do you think I will tell the American police any more than I tell the *Federales*? I will tell them nothing. Pablo's lawyers will have me out in an hour if we cross the border. You have no authority. You are kidnapping a Mexican citizen. My government does not look favorably on such a thing."

Max smiles. "You are right, Luis. Which is why I have no plans to take you with us when we leave. It's your brother we want. It's your brother who has the bounty on his head in my country. You are going to tell us where he is."

Luis' battered lips curl in a sneer. "I will never tell you. Even if you threaten to kill me."

Max shrugs. "Okay. Adelita? Shoot him."

CHAPTER 52

A DELITA GRINS AS SHE RAISES THE RIFLE. I GET ready to jump in, but she sights along the barrel like a pro. Did Culebra give her shooting lessons on the walk here?

Luis cowers back in the chair. "No. Wait. What do you want? I can give you anything. Money. More money than you can spend in a lifetime."

"Don't need money," Max says. "What we need is your brother." He takes the rifle from Adelita and pushes the barrel against Ramon's forehead. He definitely knows how to fire the rifle. He moves the selector lever off safety and releases the firing handle. "One of the advantages of the AK-47 is that it can be fired at close range; did you know that, Luis? Of course you do. It's the weapon of choice for every fucking narco." He turns the rifle this way and that in his hands as though studying it. "It produces a relatively minor wound when the bullet exits the body, like it will your head, and doesn't have a chance to tumble and fragment. But it'll do the job. You'll be dead."

Luis bites on his lower lip, eyes locked on Max. But I can tell by the hatred in his eyes, he's not ready to talk.

I take the revolver I've been carrying around at my waist and step up to Max. "Wait a minute, Max. Let me show you a trick I learned from Luis himself. Remember this?"

I push the gun into the meaty part of his thigh, make sure I miss that pesky femoral artery by listening closely to the racing of his blood and fire.

Luis comes off the chair like—well, like he's been shot. He screams and falls over, blood seeping through his jeans in a crimson halo.

Vampire growls and licks her lips.

Luis is wide-eyed with pain and fear. "You are all crazy," he pants. "I'm going to bleed to death."

Vampire retreats. The human Anna feigns surprise. "You call us crazy? Really? Isn't this what you did to those villagers when they didn't give you the information you wanted? The difference is that they were ignorant about what happened to the girls and *couldn't* tell you. You do know. And I'll just keep shooting until you give it up."

Luis turns his head toward the floor and I hear what sounds suspiciously like a sob. "Pablo will kill me," he whispers.

No. We'll do that, I say. But to myself.

Max grabs Luis and hauls him back into the chair. With his bruised and bloody face now smeared with snot and tears I could almost feel sorry for him. Almost. Adelita's presence and two corpses in a burned-out truck chase sympathy away. He's more monstrous than any fanged, clawed or bloodsucking villain I've come up against.

Max has the rifle barrel against Luis' chest—more a prop to keep him upright than a threat. "Where is he?"

Luis raises his eyes. "Reynosa."

"That wasn't so hard, was it?" Max pulls his cell out of the pocket of his jeans and puts the phone to his ear. "Time to call in reinforcements."

Max speaks for a few minutes into his cell, then powers it off. "The task force will meet us at the hangar in four hours. We'll go after Pablo together." He looks at me. "A helicopter will pick us up at a military airstrip outside Reynosa in eight hours. Plenty of time to round up Pablo and get extradition papers just in case your government is not ready to cooperate."

Luis looks up. "My government will not allow you to take him. He has powerful friends."

"He has killed Americans, Luis." He crooks his finger toward Adelita, and she joins him. He puts an arm around her shoulder. "And when Adelita explains how she was kidnapped, raped repeatedly and almost murdered by you and your brother—"

I step up beside them, too. "How she witnessed the murder of two other girls, their throats slit because they resisted. How she was taken from her village by Ramon, a lieutenant in your cartel. How girls as young as twelve are gathered up and sold as whores and worse. All compelling facts, Luis. Facts your government can't ignore."

Max nods. "If your government wants to claim any kind of legitimacy, it will have to denounce Pablo. Then he will be ours."

Luis shakes his head. "Do you think that will stop what we do? There are a hundred ready to take Pablo's place. You fool yourself if you think you are making a difference."

"What I think"—Max leans his face close to Luis'—"is that I'm about to take two scumbags off the streets. Maybe more if we get Pablo to make a deal."

"Never." Luis spits the word. "Pablo will die before he talks."

Max looks over at Culebra and me, eyebrows raised. "Isn't that what Luis said?" he asks us, smiling. "That he'd die before he talked?" He turns back to Luis and presses the rifle butt against the wound on Luis' leg. "How'd that work out for you?"

CHAPTER 53

MAX GATHERS THE TROOPS—ADELITA, CULEBRA and me—and leads us to the bar.

Luis he leaves on the chair squirming in pain.

He pours us all a glass of tequila—full shot glasses for the three adults, a tiny taste for Adelita.

I take the bottle from him and top hers off. "For god's sake, Max, after all she's been through?" I cock a head toward the bottle. It's one of Ramon's most expensive. Then I wink at Adelita. "Fit for a warrior."

She smiles back at me.

Max says, "We deserve this." He raises his glass. "To a job well done."

We clink and drink, all emptying our glasses. Except for Adelita. One sip and she grimaces and carefully sets her glass back on the bar. "There isn't any soda, is there?"

Max grins and rummages beneath the bar, producing a bottle that he hands to her.

"When do you go after Pablo?" Culebra asks.

Max nods toward Luis. "As soon as we get the details of where he is and how he's guarded. Pablo won't be as easy to take as Luis. He'll be hiding in a fortress with soldiers, not among peasants."

"Was Luis really sent out as a decoy?" I ask. "Doesn't make sense."

Culebra shrugs. "Not a decoy exactly. Since the border trouble, the narco kingpins have had to go underground. Luis' operation wasn't big, but it was enough to keep the cartel's buyers supplied. Kept them from looking for other sources until normal operations could resume." He pours himself another drink and holds up the glass. "The Santiago brothers have a reputation for living large. No one would think to look for one of them in a place like that village. It was generally thought they were hiding in Central or South America. That he left Luis here does say something about their relationship."

"That he's expendable," Max says.

Culebra nods.

I roll my glass around in the palms of my hands, processing Culebra's words. "Then why would Ramon risk bringing you here? Why would Luis let him?"

"Ramon's deal. Pablo was suspicious. He knew Ramon's son committed suicide and he knew there had been bad blood between Antonio and Rójan. When Rójan turned up dead, and the minister demanded blood, Ramon was the logical suspect. Ramon and Luis must have worked it out that if he brought me back, dead of course, he'd be able to divert suspicion for Rójan's death and the minister's wrath to me. He'd already laid the groundwork. The gun deal. In return, Ramon would swear loyalty to Luis, who would speak on his behalf to Pablo. He and his family would be safe."

I pose the next question, mindful of Culebra's past association with Ramon, wondering if he has any regrets over killing him. "How did he know you were alive? Where to find you?"

Culebra pours himself another shot, downs it, before looking at me. "I thought I could trust him. When I settled in Beso de la Muerte I got word to him. I wanted him to know he had a place to come if things got bad. Wasn't very smart. But until now, he hadn't betrayed me." He casts his eyes downward. "Or so I thought."

Max lays his glass on the bar. "Let's see what we get from Luis." He refills the glass and takes it to Luis. He holds it under Luis' nose, waving it back and forth.

"Thirsty, Luis? Do you want a drink?"

Luis' head snaps back. He eyes the glass, his tongue darting from his mouth.

At that moment he reminds me of a snaked-out Culebra and I have to smile.

Max tilts the glass toward Luis' open mouth. When the alcohol touches his broken lips, Luis jerks his head back again.

Max keeps dribbling the alcohol, over his mouth, over his cheeks, saturating every inch of bruised and scraped skin until Luis is weeping from the pain. Blood-tinged tequila drips down his neck and onto his shirt.

When the glass is empty, Max lets it drop to the floor. It hits the tile and shatters.

Luis jumps.

Max leans close. "Where do we find Pablo?"

Luis nearly chokes in his effort to get the words out. "I'll tell you. I'll give you the address. Will you protect me?"

"Depends on what you give us. Has to be more than Pablo's address."

"I'll give you everything. Supply routes, operations, dealers in the States. Help me and I'll help you."

Culebra speaks from the bar, his voice hard. "The guns," he says. "They have not all been accounted for. I want to know where they are."

Luis doesn't ask, what guns? He nods. "Most are gone," he says. "But there are still several hundred in a hiding place. I can show you."

Culebra and Max lock eyes. Max pulls Luis to his feet. "Then we'll be on our way."

Adelita looks at me. "Luis will be protected? He will live?"

Max is the one who should answer her. But I think I better understand her—her rage, her wish for retribution. At the same time, I know Max is right. He is looking at the greater good. Information Luis will provide can mean one huge drug pipeline closed down.

Of course others will spring up, but . . .

Adelita has grabbed my arm. "He should die. He deserves to die. You promised me."

"I did. And I'm sorry. Max must take Luis and Pablo to stand trial. It doesn't seem fair to you, I know. But you can play a part in bringing them to justice by telling your story. Make people aware of what is going on in places like your village. Of what people like Luis and Pablo make you do."

Adelita frowns. Her fists are balled at her side and when I see her eyes go to the revolver at my waist, I deliberately slide it around until it is tucked into the small of my back.

"Don't be foolish, Adelita," I tell her, keeping my voice low. "You have good friends in Max and me. A chance for a better life. You are young. You don't want the memory of killing a man—even one like Luis—to follow you around for the rest of your life."

Max is moving Luis to the stairs. He's bound the leg wound with the same scraps of towel I used on Maria. He looks at Adelita and me and jerks his head toward the door.

I turn to Adelita. "Are you coming with us?"

She's fighting a battle, I can see it in her eyes. Culebra has already headed up the stairs after Max and Luis. That leaves just the two of us in the great room. I will only give her another minute to decide. Then I'll be off with my friends.

A long sigh escapes Adelita's lips. She looks around at the finely upholstered furniture, the mahogany bar, the plush rug under our feet. Her eyes stop at mine. *"Es un tonto el que dice que el crimen no paga."*

She says only a fool thinks crime doesn't pay.

I hook my arm in hers and we follow the men up the stairs.

Max details the plan as we go. It will take less than an hour to reach the place where he left his car, another two to three hours to reach the airstrip. It's almost dawn. Max's DEA friends will meet us at the airstrip at ten and when we get the information we need from Luis, we'll leave him in their custody. Adelita, too. I see her bristle when he says that but she remains quiet.

I also see the wheels turning in her head.

I'll make sure we check every vehicle for stowaways before we start out after Pablo.

The car is under the same camouflage net Ramon used for the Jeep. Max and Culebra strip it off, leaving it in a pile on the ground instead of hiding it the way Ramon had. We climb into the car, Max and me in front, Culebra and Adelita in the backseat. Luis is forced to sit with his back against the seat in the cargo area. Culebra bound his feet to a toolbox, just in case he gets the idea to open the hatch and jump out.

I can't believe how good it feels to sit on something other than the ground. And to be driven instead of walking or running. I know we won't go home until Pablo and Luis are behind bars, but at least now, we know who the enemy is. It wasn't always so clear.

I lean my head back. I wonder what Culebra is thinking, but when I reach out, nothing comes through but a feeling. Soft, cozy, like being held in cloud hands.

I sneak a peek into the backseat.

Culebra is asleep, his head propped against the window. Beside him, Adelita is asleep, too. She's slumped down in the seat and her head rests on Culebra's shoulders.

She looks like a little girl.

I catch Luis watching her over the backseat. His face no longer reflects pain, but his expression is licentious, shameless, as if he's remembering how it had been to take her. When he catches my eye, he smiles and turns away.

At that moment, I hope he tries something—anything—so that I can unleash vampire. I know what I told Adelita. I know what Max wants.

But if he looks at her like that again, I'll kill him.

CHAPTER 54

EVEN THOUGH IT HAD ONLY BEEN A FEW DAYS, I'D forgotten what a bone-jarring ride it was to the airstrip. The sun is up, the heat heavy. Max has the air conditioner on in the car, but with so many bodies packed together, the humidity makes everything feel damp and dirty.

No one has spoken in the last hour. Culebra and Adelita awoke from their naps, Adelita sliding away from him quickly, embarrassed that she fell asleep on his shoulder. It will be a long time before she trusts a man enough to want to touch him. Even accidentally.

Max drives with purpose. His expression is both serious and eager.

I understand. I have that quiver in my gut that comes with knowing we're about to wrap this up.

"Ten minutes," he announces after what seems an eternity.

I rest my head on the back of the seat. Ten minutes. A good thing and a bad thing because when we're finished here, it means going home to face Stephen.

Or going home to find him gone.

I'm not sure which is worse.

Or which I prefer.

I haven't thought of him in how long?

I'm an idiot.

Max's voice pulls me back. He's looking at his watch. "Anna, we have about thirty minutes before my guys arrive. I don't want to wait to question Luis. I may need your special talents if he suddenly grows a pair and decides he's not ratting on Pablo."

"You expect me to object?"

He laughs. "Hardly. I expect you to exercise restraint."

"You don't let me have any fun."

He clucks his tongue. "From what I saw you do to Ramon, you've had plenty of fun."

"You saw that?"

He drops his voice. "Adelita wouldn't go until she was sure you'd kept your promise."

"But I heard you leave."

"Well, we came back. Adelita insisted."

I think of our conversation. She knew what I'd done to Ramon. She watched. "Was she upset?" I ask quietly.

"No. And we didn't stay to see it all."

I glance back to Adelita. She's looking out the window, but I wouldn't be surprised to learn she'd been listening. She must feel my eyes on her because she turns her head toward me.

"Did you say something, Anna?" she asks.

My expression says no. I turn back to the front.

Max picks up the conversation. "Culebra, you take Luis into the hangar as soon as we get there. I'll speak with the pilot. It shouldn't take us too long to get the information we need. By that time, the task force should arrive. Then you, Adelita and Luis will be on your way to the border at Tijuana."

The hangar is in sight now. This time the doors are pulled closed. "Where's the plane?" I ask Max.

"Inside the hangar, I imagine," he replies with a touch of sarcasm. "Where else would it be?"

"I thought the plane was supposed to be ready to take off. I don't see the pilot, either."

Max pulls the Explorer to a stop and peers around. "Where *is* the pilot," he repeats as if to himself.

That quiver in my gut clenches like a closed fist. "Max, something is wrong."

The words still hang in the air when the hangar doors swing open and the pilot steps out. He motions to us to drive forward. He's smiling.

"See," Max says, putting the Explorer in gear. "There's nothing to worry about."

His optimism is short-lived. Three black Humvees roar out of the hangar, spitting gunfire in our direction. Bullets slam into the ground around us. Adelita, Culebra and Luis cower down.

Max slams the Explorer to a stop. He starts to put it in reverse, to turn around, but before he can, we are surrounded. Men spill out of the vehicles like circus clowns from a Volkswagen, guns trained on the Explorer. The passenger door of one of the vehicles opens and a man jumps to the ground. We hear Luis shout a greeting from the back.

"Pablo. *Hermano.* Thank god you are here."

CHAPTER 55

CULEBRA REACHES AROUND AND BACKHANDS LUIS. "Shut it."

But the sight of his brother has revived Luis. He spits at Culebra. "Now we will see who is the coward."

We watch Pablo approach. Unlike his brother, Pablo is lean, tall, dressed in a tan flight suit that emphasizes a runner's build—wide shoulders, narrow hips, long legs. His face is brutally handsome with dark eyes, a straight nose more Greek than Latin and thin lips so unnaturally red, I wonder if he's wearing lip gloss. He carries himself like a soldier though he has no weapon in his hands or at his waist.

The twenty or so goons with him make it unnecessary.

He approaches nonchalantly and motions for Max to roll down his window.

Max glances at me, then does.

"*Hola*, my friends," Pablo says. "How nice of you to bring my brother back to me." His eyes seek out Culebra's. "And my good friend Tomás, as well? An abundance of riches. Come, get out of the car. My men will take care of it." He glances at a big, gold watch on his left wrist. "I think we don't have much time before we are joined by our DEA colleagues."

A rush of air escapes Max's lips. Pablo has already opened his door and stepped back.

I send a frantic message to Culebra. *Should I make a run for it?*

Culebra is looking at the guards standing with pointed rifles at the car. *Too much firepower, Anna, even for you. Best wait for a better opportunity.*

Pablo has sent one of his men to the back of the car to open the hatch. He helps Luis out and uses his own hand-cuff key to release his hands. Luis rubs his wrists and joins his brother.

They embrace, then Pablo holds him at arms length and examines his face, the bandage around his thigh. *"¿Quién te hizo esto?"*

"El cerdo del DEA," he snarls. He jabs a thumb at Adel-ita. *"Y la muchacha."*

Pablo raises an eyebrow and looks into the back window at Adelita. *"¿La muchacha? Un qué gato salvaje."*

"Sí. Será un placer domesticarla."

Adelita listens to the words pass between Luis and his brother, but her face betrays nothing. She's stone-faced, like their words haven't touched her. But I know, too, what they said and I want to let her know that Luis will never get the chance to "tame the wildcat" that bruised and battered his face.

I'll kill him first.

Luis has opened Adelita's door and he pulls her from the car by her arm. I jump out. A guard puts out a hand to grab me, but I push him away. I hear him ready his rifle to fire, but I'm at Adelita's side before he can take aim.

Pablo holds up a hand to stay the guard. He examines me the way he examined his brother a moment before. "And who are you?"

"I am her friend. Your pig of a brother better take his hand off her or I'll break it off at the wrist."

Luis actually drops her arm. He's already had a taste of my strength—and my resolve. I'll bet he's not aware he's rubbing at the wound on his thigh. But that moment passes quickly. "Be careful of this one," he tells Pablo. "She is tougher than she looks."

"Ah. Another wildcat, huh? Maybe we both have our pussies to tame."

They chuckle like two frat boys.

Oh please. Take me somewhere alone. It's just the opportunity I need to—

I'm so busy glaring at Luis, I don't see the blow coming. Pablo's backhand sends me back against the car. Vampire is ready to retaliate, but I restrain her. Better to play the victim until the time is right.

I straighten slowly, swipe at the trickle of blood oozing from the corner of my mouth. Luis is grinning. Adelita gasps and takes my hand.

"It's okay, Adelita," I tell her, silently begging her not to say anything that will alert them to my true nature.

She doesn't. Perhaps she realizes that the odds are too great even for a *vampira*.

Pablo and Luis stride toward the hangar, leaving us to be brought along by their gunmen. They frisk us in a practiced, efficient manner. Not surprising since they've most likely been trained like Culebra, in a school for soldiers and assassins. They take our weapons and cell phones.

Max positions himself next to me while they herd us toward the hangar. "I know he can't really hurt you, but it looked painful just the same."

I touch the tip of my tongue to the cut on my lip. "It was. What are we going to do? Your guys are walking into a trap."

Max dips his head so his voice won't carry. "If they don't see the plane on the runway, they'll know something's wrong. They'll pull back and wait."

I shake my head. "You can be an asshole, but you're also a pretty smart cop."

That gets a small smile. "That's me. Half asshole, half good cop."

"Any idea how Pablo found out about us?"

One of the guards pokes Max with his rifle. *"Silencio. No hablan."*

We're almost at the door to the hangar. The Explorer passes us, a soldier at the wheel, and disappears inside.

"Wonder what other surprises the brothers Santiago have for us?" I whisper to Max, earning myself a sharp poke in the back from the same guard.

Didn't have to wait long to find out. She steps forward the moment the hangar doors swing shut.

Maria is all smiles. "Ah. Here you are. We have been waiting."

Luis is standing next to her, his arm around her shoulders. He grins at the disbelief on our faces. "I think you have already met my lover." His tone is smug. "It was a good plan, was it not? Rid ourselves of an old enemy and a troublesome husband."

She puts a hand on his chest. "You are very clever," she says. Her eyes shine with undisguised adulation.

Stupid bitch.

Luis plants a kiss on her cheek, then reaches to a table behind them and picks up a laptop. "Maria just told me. Those security cameras you were so careful to avoid? It did not occur to you that one could monitor the cabin from a distance, did it? As soon as we entered the clearing, we were spotted. Pablo had only to wait for you to return for the plane."

Pablo joins us. He takes Maria's hand and moves her away from his brother. The expression on his face makes my blood pump faster. It is no longer the look of one relieved to welcome his brother back, but the calculating look of a predator closing in for the kill.

He picks up the laptop. "It is true. We monitored your

arrival at the cabin. But we monitored something else, as well." He pushes another key on the computer.

Luis' voice fills the room.

"I'll give you everything. Supply routes, operations, dealers in the States. Help me and I'll help you."

CHAPTER 56

T HE COLOR DRAINS FROM LUIS' FACE. "YOU WERE listening?"

"Of course. Ramon was the one paranoid about listening devices. But then he was gone. It was Maria's idea to plant a bug in case Tomás and his friends escaped and returned to the cave. She has been a great help."

Maria now looks at Pablo with the same adoration she'd shown Luis a moment before and Ramon, days before that.

I amend my assessment. *Crafty* bitch.

Luis is backing away from both of them. "You know I lied, Pablo. I would never betray you. I said what was necessary to get them to bring me here."

"So you knew we had spotted you?"

"Of course."

Pablo steps after Luis, closing the difference between them. "So when you said Maria just told you about the cameras, you were lying."

Luis is caught in his own web. He backtracks. "Well, maybe I didn't *know*. But I knew you were too smart to let them get away. Tomás, the man who killed Rójan to get back at you? I knew you'd be keeping watch."

"So then you are aware I know the last shipment of *llello* is gone."

"I don't know what happened. I think Ramon—"

"Not Ramon." Pablo's tone is ice. "It was your perversion. *Su gusto para las chicas jóvenes.*" He takes a deep breath. "You sent six of your men away to find four little girls who escaped. You left the shipment unguarded."

"But the men ran away. It is them you should blame."

"They came to me. They told me what you had been doing. How business was taking a backseat to pleasure. I didn't want to believe them. Then I got the news about the shipment. I was on my way to see for myself when Maria contacted me. When she told me who Ramon had brought here and why."

Luis turns flashing eyes on Maria. "You told Pablo? Why?"

"Why do you think?" she snaps back. "You and Ramon are weak. You should have taken care of Ramon yourself when you knew he had murdered Rójan. Instead you let him talk you into this ridiculous plan. You left Gabriella and me rotting in that cave." She turns burning eyes to me. "And Ramon left us with that *puta*. I don't know how she did it, but she tied me up and destroyed the door. If Gabriella hadn't smuggled a cell phone in with us, we'd still be trapped in there."

I feel a smile tickle my mouth. I was right. Good for Gabriella! Bad for us.

Not so good for Luis, either.

Pablo says, "You are my brother. We have taken care of each other all our lives. It saddens me to see what you have become."

But there is no sadness in his face. Pablo's expression is harsh, cruel. His eyes have lost all traces of humanity. They are dead.

Luis sees the change. "I will go away, Pablo," he says, breathless with fear. "I will disappear. You will never hear from me again. I can't hurt you. You know that. Let me go."

Pablo half turns to one of his soldiers and holds out a hand. The man places a revolver in his palm.

"I give you a choice," he tells Luis. "Do the right thing. End it yourself. Or I will do it."

Luis looks at the gun in his brother's outstretched hand. He looks up at Pablo. There is no reprieve there.

I know what is going to happen before it does. Luis is not smart enough to realize that the choice his brother is offering him is no choice at all. He snatches the gun and turns it around on Pablo. The soldier who has come up quietly behind him fires before Luis can pull the trigger.

The bullet enters the back of Luis' shoulder, exits in front, sending bits of collarbone and a spray of blood onto the floor. It's a wound to injure, not kill. Luis topples forward, the gun falling from his hand. Pablo reaches down and picks up the revolver. Luis meets his eyes and he opens his mouth.

Pablo shakes his head. *"Vaya a dios, hermano."*

This time, it's a kill shot.

CHAPTER 57

PABLO STEPS BACK FROM THE BODY OF HIS BROTHER and snaps an order. Two guards come forward, haul Luis away by his arms and legs.

There is not a glimmer of sadness in Maria's eyes as she watches them. She doesn't even bother to turn to see how they dump him unceremoniously behind the plane.

Another adjustment. *Cold* bitch.

I glance up at Max. He said as long as the plane remains in the hangar, his troops will not approach. If they are watching, they saw what happened when we arrived. How long will they wait before the sounds of gunfire bring them in to save Max? I look around. Besides the twenty men they saw, there are at least twenty more inside.

Maria and Pablo are talking quietly. I feel Culebra's gentle intrusion into my head. *What do you think they're talking about?*

I smile—grimly. *Who to kill first, I imagine. Time for another snake act? How quickly do you think the guards would retreat if a giant rattlesnake suddenly appeared in their midst?*

Pretty quickly. Let's see, forty guards, a pilot, Pablo and Maria. I think we can take them. We need a distraction. Will Adelita help?

Are you kidding? It's too dangerous. I don't want her hurt.

Dangerous? As opposed to how secure her future is now? Shouldn't it be her choice?

And he's whispering in her ear before I can stop him.

She meets my eyes. "I know what to do."

"No." The guards closest to us turn our way. I lower my voice and they resume their stance, waiting for Pablo to give orders. "Adelita, it's too dangerous."

But she's already making her move. She runs toward Luis' body, screaming in Spanish—that he was a pig, that he deserved to die, that she hoped he was burning in hell. When she reaches him, she drops to her knees, pounding his corpse with her fists, dragging her fingernails across his flesh.

The startled guards near us move toward her. The others watch in idle interest, probably wondering who Pablo will order to kill her.

He doesn't. He goes to Adelita himself, picks her up and hands her off to the closest guard. *"Amarrala,"* he barks.

I feel relief wash over me. He's ordering the guard to tie her up—not kill her. I indulge the feeling the second it takes to realize Culebra is no longer standing beside me, but has slithered in snake form under the plane, shedding a pile of clothes like a second skin.

My cue. I nod to Max and let vampire free.

I'm on the back of the nearest guard, tearing at his throat, growling in his ear. He drops his rifle and I see Max move to snatch it up.

Vampire blazes into full control. There are so many necks to choose from. She takes a mouthful from the screaming guard in her grip, then snaps his neck, moves to the next. This one goes down without a fight, too shocked to do anything but stare as vampire feeds. Six go down in the time it takes vampire to jump from one to the next.

Commotion on the other side of the plane. Culebra has made his presence known. Shrieks of panic, screams of pain, sweet perfume of blood. It makes vampire's lust flare.

Sporadic gunfire erupts.

Then the hangar doors bang open and I hear footsteps racing for the outside.

Vampire is not yet satisfied. She follows the scent of frightened men. Her human consciousness tells her she should be looking for Pablo, but the chase is a challenge. She grabs two retreating soldiers, snaps their heads together gleefully, the spray of blood and brains a treat that she licks from her lips. She does it again and again until her hands are slick with gore and her own smell becomes an aphrodisiac ratcheting bloodlust to new levels.

More gunfire from the hangar. Human thought surfaces once again, questioning. Should she go back to protect her friends, or follow the blood bags running away like rats from a flood?

The decision is made for her. Vehicles with sides made of gray metal, a silver star emblazoned on the sides and front, thunder onto the airstrip after Pablo's fleeing troops. They shoot at the backs of the soldiers who fall one by one.

No need for vampire here.

She whirls around. She can see what is going on inside the hangar. A giant snake has cornered a man and a woman. The snake hisses with a tongue like a split rope, turning every few seconds to strike at a soldier venturing too close. One is too slow. Snake catches his arm in his jaws, shakes him until the arm comes free, spraying blood. He deposits the arm in front of the cowering man like a cat offering a mouse to his owner. Bullets whiz through the air around it, but snake is impervious. The woman shrieks and covers her eyes.

Vampire knows there is someone else in danger. She looks around, senses alert for a familiar scent. She catches it above the intermingled smells of blood and body waste. There. Under the plane.

Instinctively vampire knows that he is who she must protect. He has his arm around a girl, pushing her behind him, shielding her body with his. He is firing his rifle, aiming at soldiers who pass too close or stoop to shoot at him. His face is serious, intent. The girl, whose hands are tied at her back, cowers close.

Vampire fights her way to him. She feels the sting of bullets in her arms, in one shoulder, but the soldiers feel more than pain when she's on them and their blood flows in a molten stream into her eager mouth. One, two, three, four go down before her and then she's under the plane.

The man smiles at her. "Anna. Take care of Adelita."

The human inside responds to the name Anna.

The girl is smiling, too. Not afraid or preparing to flee. She holds out her hands. Vampire allows the human Anna to surface enough to tell her what to do. It is easy. It takes only a tug at the ropes at the girl's wrists and they come free.

The girl touches vampire's wounds. Her fingers are like a kiss.

The man is speaking. "Get Adelita out."

Vampire gathers the girl, as light as her touch, into her arms. She listens to the rhythm of the gunfire, determines where it has slowed or stopped and leaps forward.

There is one corner where all the soldiers lie dead or still. It's behind the giant snake and his captives. She makes for that corner.

Snake watches her come, but there is no challenge. Instead, he seems to bow his head at her in recognition. Vampire deposits the girl and leaves her in his care to go back to the man.

The sound of gunfire grows more sporadic. Most of it from the battle going on outside. But a group of soldiers are still firing at the figure under the plane. They are all around, knowing he is trapped, knowing he can only fire in one direction at a time. The plane reeks of spilled fuel as bullets pierce its metal skin. The stink curls vampire's nose. The man under the plane motions for her.

"Get away," he yells. "The plane may explode."

But vampire makes for the two soldiers closest to her, tackles them to the ground, snaps their arms and throws their rifles out of reach.

The remaining three see what has happened. Turn their rifles on her. But bullets are no match for vampire speed. She attacks them before they can take aim. The first two, she kills efficiently—snapping necks that pop like dried wood. The third she takes her time, pinning him to the ground, letting him see her eyes before she nuzzles his neck for the first nip. He is too scared to move, to fight her off. His heart thunders in his chest, which makes the taking of his blood all the easier. She doesn't have to pull with force or clamp tight lips against a squirming neck. His blood flows into her mouth with each beat.

His blood tastes the best of all.

In a minute his heart has stopped, his life force drained. Vampire rests her head against his chest.

Then her eyes drift to the man under the plane.

Blood. In a wide swath under him.

She doesn't have time to resist the human's pull. Anna is back.

CHAPTER 58

"MAX!"
    I scoot myself under the plane, ignoring the flashes of white-hot pain that shoot from my arms, my shoulder. I leave a crimson path as I crawl forward. I don't worry about the blood. The blood could be mine, it could be my victims'.

But I do worry about the blood around Max.

I look for the source. I have to raise him up to find it—center back. My breath catches at the severity of the wound. He coughs and I lower him again, gently.

But at least he's alive.

I cradle his head in my arms. His mouth is ringed with blood, dark, viscous. For once, the sight and smell of blood does not tempt vampire to reappear. I think she's sleeping it off.

I listen to what's going on around me. It's quiet inside the hangar and only an occasional stray bullet whizzes outside. I won't try to move Max until I know it's safe. I'm debating whether to leave Max and look around when a familiar voice calls out, "Anna. Where are you?"

Culebra.

"Here. Max is hurt."

In a moment, Culebra, back in human form and dressed, is kneeling to look under the belly of the plane. "Can we move him?"

"I don't know. He's been shot in the back. It looks pretty bad."

He scoots down to join me. After he's examined the wound, he sits back on his haunches.

I respond to his grim expression, heart racing. "Don't say it. Max is strong. His buddies are outside. They can call that helicopter, can't they?"

"Let's get him out from under here," is Culebra's curt reply.

We do our best to move Max as gently as we can. I keep expecting him to rouse and ask us what the fuck we're doing.

But he doesn't.

When he's out in the open, I look around.

Bodies. Everywhere. Some I know I'm responsible for, others dead from gunfire or the fangs of a huge rattlesnake.

Adelita is still in the corner where I left her. Only now she holds a revolver on a trussed-up Pablo and a weeping Maria. They are tied back to back. And Adelita is smiling.

Until she looks our way and sees Max. *"Dios mio. ¿Es él vivo?"*

From beyond the hangar door, a voice interrupts. "Agent Avillas! Max? Buddy? Where are you?"

"In here," I shout back. "He's been hurt."

Max still hasn't made a sound except that cough and even now, his eyes remain closed, his face relaxed. Like he's sleeping. It's not a good sign.

I watch for the man who called out. He's approaching with two armed men behind him, speaking into a radio on his collar. He looks Hispanic, dark skinned, dark eyed, built like a man who likes his beer. All three are dressed the same—khaki shirts and cargo pants, black DEA jackets. The one in front has a baseball cap and he's the one Culebra moves toward. He explains the situation. Baseball cap looks in our direction, but directs the two agents beside him to take Pablo and Maria outside. Then he hurries over to us.

He kneels down beside Max. "Did he stop breathing?" is the first question he asks me.

It only takes a heartbeat to know the reason. The blood around Max's mouth.

And around mine.

"No. But he's lost a lot of blood. He needs to get to a hospital."

The guy speaks into the radio. He uses the clipped, acronym-filled lingo of one agent to another. But when the answer comes back, it's something I can understand.

They will have the helicopter here in thirty minutes.

I look at Max. He doesn't look like Max anymore. He's gone from pale to ashen. I can see through his eyelids. The pool of blood under him is too big, too thick. His breath is so shallow, it hardly flutters his chest.

I touch his cheek. I hope he has thirty minutes.

FOR THE FIRST TIME, CULEBRA, ADELITA AND I ARE ABLE to sit together without a gun or the threat of violence hanging over our heads. We sit close to Max so we can watch one of the agents, a medic, attend to him. The medic packs the wound to staunch the flow of blood, runs an IV to replenish liquids. He won't give us a prognosis. And Max still hasn't regained consciousness.

The medic looks at me, bloodsoaked but apparently unhurt, and raises an eyebrow. "Are you sure you don't need medical attention, too?"

I shake my head. I can feel four bullets, one in each arm, one in my left shoulder and a fourth (which I didn't know about until it started moving) in my right thigh. I've been shot before, but it's always been through and through. I don't know what to expect with these wounds. Will the bullets work their way to the surface of my skin and have to be squeezed out like metal blackheads?

A charming visual.

I've had a healthy infusion of blood so I'm not worried about my body's ability to heal itself. Actually, I'm not even in much pain.

I dip my head in Culebra's direction. "What about you? Were you hit by any of those bullets zipping about?"

He shakes his head. Out loud, he says, "Lucky, I guess." Internally, he says, *Hard to hit anything when you're shaking so bad, you can barely hold a gun, let alone aim it. No human is prepared for the sight of a rattlesnake as long as two men.*

Adelita wrings her hands. "Max will be all right, won't he?"

She addresses the question to no one and everyone. I wish I could give her an unequivocal yes, but she's seen so much death today, unless Max opened his eyes and told her himself, I doubt she'd believe it.

Open your eyes, Max. I want to believe it, too.

Outside the hangar, the agents have rounded up the survivors of Pablo's gang and have them bound and gagged, awaiting the *Federales*. Only Pablo and Maria will be flown back to the border. I suspect most of the gang will be back on the streets in twenty-four hours. And with Luis and Pablo out of the picture, they'll be jockeying for leadership of the cartel.

So what exactly have we accomplished?

I look at Max, lying pale and still on the ground. What did he tell Luis? We might not have made a dent in the drug trade, but we've taken two predators off the street.

If he dies, was it worth it?

Adelita is leaning over Max, wiping his face with a damp cloth. She's alive.

There are four young girls in a safe house—unmolested and alive.

Max's body suddenly jerks. His back arches, his chest heaves as if his lungs can no longer draw air. The medic shoulders Adelita aside and listens to Max's chest with a stethoscope. "He has a collapsed lung."

He goes to work with items he pulls from his bag—a scalpel, a tube, something that looks like a manual suction pump. He makes an incision in the skin above Max's rib cage, inserts the tube and works the pump. Pale liquid flows into the tube and almost instantly, Max relaxes. The medic places an oxygen mask over his mouth and nose. He drops the suction pump and yells to his buddies by the hangar door, "How much longer 'til that chopper gets here?"

CHAPTER 59

I HAVE MY ARMS AROUND ADELITA'S SHOULDERS. WE watch the medivac helicopter rise into the air. I wanted to go along with Max, but they wouldn't allow it. Family maybe, but a civilian, no. They're taking him to a Texas trauma hospital in McAllen until he's stabilized. Then he'll be transferred to a hospital in San Diego, near his home.

He never regained consciousness. He doesn't know that Pablo is in custody. He doesn't know that Culebra, Adelita and I made it out alive.

We return to the hangar. A mop-up operation is in full swing. Body bags are laid out. Nineteen of Pablo's men were killed, several *Federales*, two DEA agents. The injured are on their way by ambulances to Reynosa—under heavy guard. Those forensic reports on Pablo's men should make for interesting reading. I don't know what kind of explanation will be offered for the number of broken necks and bloodless bodies or the suspicious fang marks of a huge snake on some of the bodies. Maybe no one will care how the narcos died.

Two rows of weapons are laid out, too, thirty AK-47s, ten Glocks and revolvers, a couple of knives big as machetes. Culebra can't seem to take his eyes off the rifles. His thoughts are cloaked, but I don't need the link to feel his despair.

Pablo and Maria are on their way by a second chopper to the San Diego border where both *Federales* and Federal agents are waiting to take them into custody. And to make sure they stay in custody. The U.S. government made it clear that this time, there will be no loopholes for Pablo to wiggle through. There was another incident of American tourists killed in narco cross fire just this morning. If Mexico is unwilling or unable to hold him, Pablo will be extradited to the U.S. to assure he is tried for his crimes. Baseball cap accompanied them along with a half dozen armed guards. They are taking no chances.

That leaves ten DEA agents, some *Federales*, Culebra, Adelita and me. The pilot and remaining uninjured narcos have been taken into custody by the *Federales*. The hangar is heavy with the smell of blood and death.

One of the agents sees us standing by Max's car and walks over. For the first time, someone asks for identification. Culebra fishes his from the pocket of his jeans. It takes me a minute to remember where mine is—the glove compartment of the Explorer. I retrieve it with my wallet and hand it over.

He examines them. "You are free to go," he says, handing our passports back. His eyes go to Adelita. "Are you a Mexican citizen?" he asks.

Culebra answers for her. "Yes. I'd like Adelita to come with me. She may be called as a witness against Pablo Santiago. I'm sure you've heard how he allowed his brother to kidnap and rape her. Then they destroyed her identification and left her for dead. I would like to assume responsibility for her safety. Agent Avillas made arrangements for her a day or two ago. If you check—"

The agent waves a hand. "I'll take your word for it. But she is going to need papers. I'll check with our field office and see what we can do."

Once he's walked far enough away, Culebra whispers to Adelita. "Do you want to come with me?"

"Think maybe you should have asked her first?" I ask.

Adelita looks from Culebra to me, her face sad and serious.

Culebra draws a breath. "I'm sorry. You have family here. I should have thought. We can explain to the agent when he comes back. I'm sure he'll make arrangements to get you home safely."

Adelita shakes her head. "I do have family here," she says slowly. "Family that did not raise a hand to protect me when Ramon came for me. No one held them at gunpoint or threatened them. They must have known there were no jobs waiting for us. Other girls have been taken. None returned. Yet they let me go." She stops abruptly, takes a breath. "You and Anna and Max have done more for me in three days than they had done all the years of my life. I would be proud to go with you."

I frown at Culebra. "You can't expect her to live with you in the cave."

Adelita's eyes grow big. "A cave? Like Ramon's?"

"Uh—no." Culebra's shoulders hunch a little. "But it will only be temporary. I'll get you enrolled in a good boarding school in Tijuana. I'll come visit you every weekend."

Adelita hooks her hand in Culebra's arm and turns my way. "Do you live in Culebra's cave, too?"

I laugh. "No. More like the bar. Actually, I live in San Diego. My home is right on the ocean." I give Culebra a glance, realizing he's never been to the cottage. "We'll get Culebra to bring you to visit soon."

Culebra raises his eyebrows, but Adelita has already chimed in with, "I'd like that," so he can't argue.

The agent who checked our IDs is coming back. He has a paper in his hand. "This is a temporary ID," he says, handing it to Adelita. "You were right. Max had already set it up. But this is only temporary. You need to get official papers as soon as possible."

"I'll see that she does," Culebra replies.

"How do you plan to get back?"

I glance at Max's Explorer. "Can we take Max's car? I'll see it gets back to his apartment."

"I don't see why not." The agent grins at me. "Max used to talk about you all the time. Then he stopped. If what broke you up can be fixed, I bet Max would make the effort. I'd never seen a man more crazy in love."

I feel color flood up my neck. What broke us up is Max seeing something like what happened here—and running away from it as quickly as he could. Some damage can't be repaired.

Even if Max survives.

The agent sees my discomfort. "Sorry. I shouldn't have said anything." He makes a self-conscious noise in his throat and changes the subject. "Do you have the keys?"

I cross to the driver's side of the Explorer and look in. "Keys are in the ignition."

"Then we have all the information we need. You are probably anxious to be on your way." He gives us a two-fingered salute to the bill of his cap and turns on his heels. I think he's the one anxious to get away, embarrassed he said anything about Max and me.

I gesture for Culebra and Adelita to join me. Hand the keys to Culebra.

"You want me to drive the first shift?" he asks.

"I want you to drive home. With Adelita."

He raises an eyebrow. "You're not coming?"

I glance toward the helicopter still visible in the distance. "I'm going to the hospital. Stay in McAllen until I know Max is all right."

Culebra tilts his head and peers into my face. "Don't you have someone waiting for you at home?"

"Probably not," I answer. "I'll call Stephen as soon as I can."

"Where are you going to stay? Do you have money for a hotel?"

I wave my wallet. "I'll be fine.

Adelita steps up to me and hugs me so fiercely, I gasp. Then I laugh and hug her back. "Call me as soon as you get to Beso de la Muerte."

Culebra watches as she crosses to the passenger side of the car. "You should be proud of what we've done today," he says.

I blow out a breath. "You, too, my friend. Only one regret. Luis didn't tell us the location of the guns. I saw you looking at the rifles. I should have made him talk before we left Ramon's hideout."

Culebra shrugs. "We thought we'd have time. Maybe with Luis dead and Pablo in jail, the cartel will be more involved with fighting each other for control then drug dealing. At least for a while they'll use the guns on each other. Might give the DEA and *Federales* a chance to turn up the heat again. Close down some of the growers. Get to the source."

His words make me think of Esmeralda and her sister. Stolen from their schoolyard while teachers looked on. The cancer runs deep.

Culebra looks around. "I guess it's time to go."

Still, he makes no move to get into the car. His thoughts are cloaked, but his feelings once again come through.

"You aren't responsible for Max being shot," I say quietly.

He looks reflexively toward the guns, watches a DEA agent as he goes from one to another, noting serial numbers. "You can't know that."

"Max wouldn't hold you responsible. You fought with him. You have been a better friend to him than I have been to you. I am sorry for that."

He opens the car door and slips inside. The emotion coming through now is mingled relief and sadness, both too deep to be put into words.

"Max has a GPS system," I tell him, grasping for a way to breach the awkwardness. "Do you want me to show you how to use it?"

He scoffs, grinning at Adelita. "I know how to get home. *Yo no necesito ningún apestoso GPS.*"

Adelita looks puzzled. "Why don't we need a *stinking GPS*?"

I laugh. "It's Culebra's idea of joke. A line from a movie, *The Treasure of Sierra Madre*."

"Greatest movie ever made," he says.

"Probably the last movie you ever saw, right?" I say.

"That, too." He turns to Adelita. "Buckle up. We've got a long ride ahead of us."

Adelita pulls on the seat belt. Culebra puts the Explorer in gear and they back out of the hangar. Culebra is smiling and for the moment at least, his mind is at peace. Something it shocks me to realize I've never felt from him before.

I wave until the car disappears.

CHAPTER 60

I'M SITTING BY MAX'S BEDSIDE. IT'S BEEN TWO DAYS and his condition has not changed. Loss of blood and the damage done by a jacketed bullet to his internal organs make his prognosis iffy at best.

I can't leave him. As far as I know, he has no family. No one has showed up to visit except fellow DEA agents. They come to check on him and pay their respects. Capturing Pablo made him a hero.

But at what cost?

I've had lots of time to sort through the events of the last few days. Vampire has never been so virulent and aggressive as in that hangar. I don't regret anything that happened, but I wonder if I'll always be able to exert control over her. We are two sides of a single coin but one seems to turn up slightly more often. Right now, it's the human side. But I can't forget the thrill I felt as vampire, making Ramon pay, chasing and killing Pablo's men.

I, the human me, was there inside, but I didn't try to surface. Didn't try to temper or restrain vampire. It felt too good to let go. Adrenaline and blood make a heady vampire cocktail.

Then there was Luis. I was strictly human when I shot him to make him talk. I was human when I dropped that grenade on the drug truck, knowing there were men inside.

Do I regret doing any of those things?

No.

Should I feel guilty?

I look at Max, as pale as the white hospital sheets. Tubes in each arm.

If I'm honest, no. I don't regret one drop of blood I spilled—or drank.

My thoughts turn to Culebra. The way he telegraphed an inner peace when he left with Adelita. It strikes me that he may see her as a chance to make up for losing his own daughter. For being responsible for the death of his family.

My cell phone vibrates, telling me I have a message. I turned off the ringer when I came into the hospital. Now I check the display and when I see who the call is from, my shoulders bunch.

Stephen.

We've been playing telephone tag since I got to Mc-Allen. I checked into a motel near the hospital and tried to call him right away. The call went directly to voice mail. Then I called his sister in San Diego. I got a very chilly reception from her. "Stephen is in Washington," she said abruptly. The "as if you care" part left hanging in the air like an icicle.

Since then, Stephen and I keep missing each other.

I sigh and get to my feet. If I call back right now, I should reach him.

It's time.

I step out into a sunny Texas afternoon and walk to an outside patio area off the hospital cafeteria. There are a few occupied tables but most are empty so I choose one in a far corner and press Send.

Stephen picks up right away. There is a long silence before he finally breaks it. "Anna."

I let another long moment pass before I get the courage to say, "Hi."

Hi. Really great.

Stephen's sigh resonates so much emotion through the phone line that I cringe. Disappointment, sadness, anger, disillusionment. All in one exhalation of breath. All directed at me.

I say the only thing I can. "I'm sorry."

No reply.

"Are you in Washington?"

"Didn't you speak with my sister? You know I am."

Crap. "Well. I just called to tell you I'm sorry. I never intended for this happen."

"For what to happen, Anna? For you to disappear out of my life with no explanation? For you to go days without letting me know what you were doing or if you were living or dead? You know, it's been in all the newspapers. How you and your DEA buddy were involved in taking down Luis and Pablo Santiago and dismantling their cartel. Quite a story. I wish I could have covered it."

"Stephen, I didn't know it was in the papers. I was never interviewed by anyone except DEA agents. I never spoke to the press. We didn't *dismantle* the cartel. You know how impossible that would be. It's all hype."

Another loud sigh. This one of impatience and fury. "It doesn't matter. I'm glad you are safe. I'm sorry about your friend, Max. I hope he recovers and I hope things work out for you."

"Work out? You hope what works out?"

"You and Max. That was an interesting human-interest element of the story. Two former lovers reunite to battle against the forces of evil. Nice touch."

Now it's my turn to breathe fire into the phone. "There is no Max and I. Goddamn it, I don't know where the papers got this shit. But that's what it is. Shit."

"Yeah. Well, whatever. Nice knowing you, Anna. Maybe our paths will cross again someday. I just hope it's here, on Earth, in a restaurant maybe and not in a fight to the death battle against some otherworldly creature you've pissed off. One of those in a lifetime is enough."

"Stephen, you are not giving me a chance to explain—"

But he's gone. The click of his disconnect is final. As final a sound as I've ever heard. Fucking final. Fucking final. Fucking final.

I'm left staring at the phone, emotions running the gamut from rage to immense sadness to . . .

Relief.

CHAPTER 61

RELIEF?
       Stephen broke up with me. I didn't have to break up with him. I didn't have to come up with the thousand reasons I couldn't make the move with him to Washington.

I don't have to feel guilt. I don't have to feel remorse.

When I realize what I *am* feeling, that I'm off the hook, another emotion wells up.

Alarm. Because I must be crazy. Certifiable. I just lost one of the most wonderful men I've ever known and all I want to do is breathe a huge sigh of relief.

And celebrate.

I am seriously deranged. Or am I in shock?

I push myself up from the table and start back to Max's room. On the way through the hospital lobby, I stop at the gift shop to check out the newspaper headlines. There it is on the front page of the *Monitor*. Two days and the battle against Pablo's men and his subsequent arrest is still front-page news.

Along with a photo of me sitting at Max's bedside in the hospital.

I stomp to the elevator. Fucking cell phone cameras. Anyone could have taken that picture of me with Max and I'd never have known it. I *didn't* know it. It could have been someone on the staff, one of Max's DEA buddies, a reporter.

Anyone.

No wonder Stephen was so pissed. The expression on my face, the way I'm bending toward Max. It would be easy to misinterpret concern for something else.

And yet . . . Why am I getting angry?

I'm halfway down the hall when my phone rings. I'd forgotten to turn it back off. I duck into a waiting room and check the caller ID. It's David with a text message.

It's simple. *Sorry to hear about Max. Take as much time as you need. Call if you need anything.*

Good old David. At least he's one man I don't have to worry about disappointing.

We're way past disappointment.

IT'S BEEN THREE MORE DAYS AND MAX STILL HAS NOT regained consciousness. I'm going crazy from the anxiety, the boredom, the hopelessness.

My own wounds have healed, the bullets working their way to the surface of my skin as I expected and pushing their way out. It hurt like hell when they erupted like pieces of shrapnel. I have them in a little glass jar. Macabre, but I figure Max will get a kick out of seeing them when he recovers.

Once he gets over being pissed because my wounds healed so much easier than his.

If his wounds heal . . .

An annoying, worrisome thought has worked its way into my head the last few days. *I* could save Max. I could turn him.

But at what cost? If I could be sure he would not condemn me for turning him into a creature he once ran away from, I would do it.

When I try to ask him, to whisper the question in his ear, I get no response.

I have never turned another human. I realize I am not ready to take the responsibility without his consent. I am too much of a coward.

And so I sit and watch and hope I've made the right decision.

On the sixth day, Max's doctor tells me to go home. That Max's condition is not likely to change soon—if at all. The damage to his internal organs is severe. The loss of blood, the trauma, has led to pneumonia. The fact that he is unconscious is really a blessing. At such time as they deem it safe to move him, he will be transported to a hospital in San Diego. I can check in every day by telephone and if his condition does change, they will notify me.

I hate to leave. I don't want Max to wake up and be alone. His DEA buddies assure me that someone will visit every day. The same agent who embarrassed himself by telling me how crazy in love Max had been with me promises to keep in close touch with the hospital and with me.

I'm bone weary and homesick so I agree to leave. I call my pilot from the hotel, but as luck would have it, my plane is in for its annual inspection. There is an "international" airport in McAllen where I book a flight to San Diego. It's going to take five hours and one plane change. I'm spoiled. I'd forgotten how much trouble it is to fly commercial.

I pack the few things I've acquired since coming to McAllen, stop one last time at the hospital, board the commuter jet for the first part of the trip and settle in for the flight.

I have a window seat so I buckle in, sit back and close my eyes. The same themes that plagued me for the last five days slide into my consciousness.

Max. Stephen. Vampire.

Nothing I can do about Max now, or Stephen. Vampire

is content and quiet for the time being so any control issue is moot.

Another person worms his way into my consciousness.

Two people, actually.

Daniel Frey and his son.

I realize I want to see them. I realize I *need* to see them.

And I'm suddenly flooded with warmth.

CHAPTER 62

WHEN I UNLOCK THE FRONT DOOR TO MY COT-
tage, I find I have to push at it to get inside. Something's jamming it. At first, vampire instincts kick in and I
think, shit, someone broke in. I drop my carry-on and brace
myself to face an intruder.

But I detect no strange smells nor do I hear anything
except the ticking of a clock and the chirping of my telephone alerting me that I have voice mail.

Allowing my shoulders to relax, I shove the door inward. As soon as I'm inside, I see what's wedged against it.

My things from Stephen's apartment. The clothes I'd left
there, some toiletries, a toothbrush. All deposited neatly
inside a paper bag. At some point, the bag had fallen over,
which explained the jam.

There's a note, too. From his sister, Susan.

*Stephen didn't have time to return these things before
packing his apartment and leaving for Washington. I*

told him I'd do it. You'll find your key under the door-
mat. Not very original, but then, neither are you.

Susan

Whoa. She's really pissed at me. The only thing missing is "bitch" at the end of the last line. I suppose it never occurred to her how difficult it would have been for me to leave San Diego.

Then again, Stephen is her brother. She may have seen those pictures of me with Max at the hospital, too. She was here to experience Stephen's hurt and anger and sense of betrayal firsthand.

It doesn't matter that there was no betrayal.

No *intentional* betrayal anyway.

I crumple the note and toss it into a wastebasket on my way upstairs, drop the bag and carry-on on the floor in my bedroom and throw myself across the bed. My bed.

Feels good.

SUDDENLY, MAX IS STANDING AT THE FOOT OF MY BED.

I sit up, rubbing my eyes. Did I fall asleep?

He smiles. "Hey."

He's wearing jeans and a T-shirt. He looks good. "Hey, yourself. When did they let you out of the hospital?"

"An hour ago. I was afraid you weren't going to wake up in time."

My head is fuzzy with sleep. I give it a shake and focus on Max. "You really look good. I just left Texas a few hours ago. You made a miraculous recovery."

"In a way." He takes a seat on the end of my bed. "I have something to tell you. And I don't think I have much time."

I smile. "Why not?"

"Oh, you know, places to go, people to see."

"You realize Pablo is in custody."

"Yes. But that's not why I'm here."

I prop myself up straighter against the headboard and try to concentrate. My brain isn't cooperating. It seems to be trying to cut into my thoughts, to tell me something. I tell it to shut up, that I only want to listen to Max. I lean toward him. "Go on."

He sighs. "First, I owe you an apology. I didn't treat you very well when I found out you are a vampire. I was afraid of what it meant—to me. Stupid because it meant nothing. Not really. Above all, you are a good *woman*, Anna, and my biggest regret is that I realized it too late."

I shrug. "You can make it up to me."

He shakes his head. "No. Believe me, it's too late. But there is something else. Learn from me. You have a real chance at happiness now. Take it."

My turn to shake my head. "If you mean Stephen—"

"No. Not Stephen. There is another. You know who it is." He stops, tilts his head as if listening. He nods. "I only have a few more minutes. Don't regret what happened in that hangar. I know you've been wondering whether you will always be stronger than vampire. You only need to want it. All the strength you need is within yourself. You are right about Culebra. He has found new meaning for his life with Adelita. He has found a way to make up for past mistakes. He has finally found peace. Make sure he understands he is not to blame for what happened to me. He fought as hard as I did to stop Pablo and Luis. He needs to concentrate now on the future. Let the past die."

I tilt my head. "But how did you know what I was thinking at the hospital? You were unconscious the entire time."

"All the same, I heard your thoughts. Loud and clear. In fact, it was those thoughts that kept pulling me back when I was ready to let go." He laughs. "Your will is too strong. I was relieved when they sent you home."

"I don't understand," I say while my gut is saying, of course you do. *You know.*"

"It was my time, Anna."

Anger wells up and with it fear. Fear of losing a friend. Fear of losing Max. "No. I don't want you to go."

"It's too late. It's a tribute to your power that I was allowed to hang around this long. To say a proper good-bye. I'll miss you, Anna."

"No." I lunge forward on the bed, reaching for his hand. It slips through mine as though made of fog.

He smiles a slow, sweet smile and raises his hand in farewell.

And then before I can reach out again, he is gone.

It isn't until I'm awakened by the ring of the telephone on my bedside table that I realize the truth. That I realize Max had come to me in a dream. I know what Max's doctor is going to say before his somber voice officially informs me.

Max has died.

I hold my head in my hands and let the tears fall.

CHAPTER 63

I'D BEEN TO THE FUNERAL OF ONE OTHER LAW EN-
forcement agent—Warren Williams' "son," Ortiz. Max's
funeral is full of the same militaristic pomp and circum-
stance. Over a hundred agents are in attendance as well as
high-ranking officials of the DEA and its Mexican counter-
part. I'd forgotten that Max had been a marine until a
twenty-one-gun salute echoes like ancient thunder over the
hills of Fort Rosecrans National Cemetery. As Max had no
family, the flag that draped his casket is taken to be flown
on the cemetery's Avenue of Flags.

David came with me to the funeral. He and Max were
never friends, but he respected him. He also knew that Max
and I had been lovers once. He was the first one on my
doorstep when he heard of Max's death. He holds my hand
and lets me lean on him as the proceedings come to a close.
One by one the guests leave.

Now we're the only ones left. I insisted on staying out of
sight during the service. I hate funerals. I've never been
comfortable sharing my feelings, especially with strangers.

David didn't question it. He's never been big on public displays of emotion, either, and he knows my history—I lost a brother when I was seventeen. There were enough public displays of emotion at that funeral to last an eternity.

I touch David's arm. "You can go now, David. I appreciate your coming with me, but I'd like a few minutes alone."

He looks around at the deserted gravesite. "How will you get home?"

"I'll go back to the caretaker's office and call a taxi," is what I say. In my head, I'm thinking a little physical exercise, like an eight-mile run home along the Pacific, is just what I need to clear my head. I dressed in jeans, a T-shirt and athletic shoes this morning for just that reason. And as another excuse to stay out of sight of the more traditionally clad mourners.

I knew Max would understand.

David nods and leans over to kiss my cheek. He doesn't ask why. He doesn't try to talk me out of it. He simply leaves.

I wait until he's gone before approaching Max's grave.

I kneel down and touch the side of the casket. "Culebra sends his love. He couldn't come, Max. He didn't want to leave Adelita and she doesn't have her formal papers yet. He was afraid they'd have trouble getting back across the border. I think it was more than that, though. He knows you were shot with one of those ATF rifles. He's sick about it. I told him you didn't hold him responsible, that it's more the fault of the ATF genius who thought up the gun sting, but he doesn't believe it. Maybe *you* could tell him, pay him a visit the way you did me?"

I stand up and pull a rose out of one of the floral arrangements and drop it onto the casket.

"Thanks for saying good-bye, Max," I whisper. "Sorry if I held you up. Safe journey."

CHAPTER 64

THE RUN ALONG THE COAST RENEWS MY SPIRIT. THE air is crisp and the sky clear. A low winter sun sends shards of light bouncing off a calm ocean. A perfect January afternoon.

A hell of a start to the new year.

Max gone.

Stephen gone.

My family gone.

At least with my family, it's only "gone" in the sense they no longer have a home here.

No. Not true. They'll always have a home with me.

I'm back at the cottage, seated on the deck off my bedroom, watching the ocean. I spoke with Culebra after I got home from the service. He will not be easy to console; his guilt over Max runs deep. But Adelita is there, and his voice when he speaks of her is hopeful and full of wonder. He's already enrolled her as "his niece" in a Catholic school in Tijuana. She starts at the beginning of next week. In the meantime, she is adjusting to his unconventional lifestyle and even finds the rather special clientele his bar caters to fascinating. I think the fact that she revels in feeling safe and secure for the first time in her young life has much to do with the ease of her acceptance.

And spending a week with a vampire.

The parallels between Adelita and Trish are remarkable. Both have found real family in bonds of love rather than biology.

A car honking in the alley draws me back. I look down to see a taxi pulling into the driveway. I wave that I see him, shut and lock the slider, grab up my bag and run downstairs.

I have one more journey of my own to make.

To a Navajo reservation.

I wonder how my parents will feel about a new grandson.

**From National Bestselling Author
Jeanne C. Stein**

CROSSROADS

AN ANNA STRONG, VAMPIRE NOVEL

*As a bounty hunter, Anna Strong knew how to find trouble.
But now that she's vampire, trouble seems to have a knack
for finding her . . .*

The death of Anna's old vampire mentor is causing ripples
in the mortal world. His forensic report has brought up some
anomalies, and people are asking questions—questions that
no vampire wants to answer.

Anna needs to lie low, but with the sudden discovery of a
slew of drained bodies near the Mexican border, and some
stunning news from an unexpected source, she soon finds
herself on a journey that may threaten her existence—and
that of all vampires.

"[Anna is] a heroine with the charm, savvy and intelligence
that fans of Laurell K. Hamilton and Kim Harrison will be
happy to root for."   —*Publishers Weekly*

"I cannot wait to see where Anna's adventures take her
next . . . an excellent book."   —*Bitten by Books*

penguin.com

M891T0511